WHEN PRIDE FALLS

T0348796

OLIVIA ANNE

WHEN PRIDE FALLS

Copyright © 2024 Olivia Anne

Print ISBN: 979-8-35098-035-6
eBook ISBN: 979-8-35098-036-3

Formatting and cover: BookBaby
7905 N. Crescent Blvd
Pennsauken, NJ 08110

Editors: Jill Applegate; Brooke Farrell; Joyce Applegate.
Contributors: Lydia Veazey; Tina Poulias; Audrey Voth.

olivia.anne.wpr@gmail.com

ACKNOWLEDGEMENTS

I would like to start by thanking my God for giving me the ability to write and create stories. This story. I am only using the abilities that He has given me. I am so thankful for his patience with me as I have worked through so many things. Thank you Lord, for never changing and loving me unconditionally no matter what. I don't deserve all the chances you have given me, but I am eternally grateful for them. I love you.

Aunt Jill, you worked so hard to edit and structure this book. It has been an honor getting to work with you and see your expertise on the wording of things. As I read your edits and suggestions I would say out loud, "Oh, Aunt Jill, that was good"! I was a little nervous at first to give you the power to suggest changes, but as time went on I realized how thankful I was that it was you who I had given that power to. I loved going online and seeing your initials signaling that you were editing. Watching you work was mesmerizing. Thank you for your encouragement and your honesty when it came to things that needed to change or didn't make sense. You 100% made my book better. I love you so much. Thank you.

Mom! You are such a blessing to me. You have always believed in me through all of my life, but through writing this book you have been my cheerleader and my biggest fan from day one! You are such a role model for me and I am so blessed to be your daughter. Truly. Thank you for always being a listening ear when I rambled on and on about the changes I needed to make or the things I was going to add in. You never complained once. As you say "I'm here for the people"! And you really are. Thank you also for being such an amazing role model for me. I hope that someday I will get to show my kids the patience, love, and devotion that you have shown me my entire life.

Mom and Dad, thank you for helping make this dream come true! Love you to the moon and back!

Grandma Applegate, thank you so much for taking the time to go through and find all of my unnecessary commas and adding in different punctuation that I had missed. It is tedious work, and I greatly appreciate you for being willing to do that for me! Thank you for being willing to learn how to edit on a computer, too! You did wonderfully! I love you so much and am so thankful for your (and Grandpa's) love and support you have given me through my whole life. I am so blessed to call you my grandparents!

Lydia… You have truly been my biggest fan since day one. (Well, since the day I sent you my partial rough draft!) Thank you for your enthusiasm and love for my writing. Thank you for reading, and re-reading, my book as I changed things time and time again. Thank you for being a listening ear and for making some of the hard decisions for me (unknowingly) as the book came together. Thank you for your dedication to these characters and for fighting for them and what they deserve, even if we didn't agree on everything. Thank you for being an amazing roommate and an even better friend. You are so caring and generous and I am extremely glad that God put you in my life.

DEDICATION

This may seem silly, but I am dedicating
When Pride Falls to my cat who passed away around
the time I was finishing up writing this book.

Talia,

you were my pride and joy for so many years.
Thank you for being the best cat a girl could ask for.
You will be forever missed. I love you.

PRONUNCIATIONS

NAMES

Naia - Nye-uh

Javil - Juh-vill

Picel - Pie-sill

Zaxton - How it sounds

Quinlan - Quin-lynn

Luria - Lur-ee-uh

Gibor - Gih-boar

Rhyson - Rye-son

Ahiam - A-hi-m (H from back of throat)

Ishvi - Ish-vee

PLACES

Arilos - Air-ih-lous

Rowynala - Roh-win-all-uh

Flykra - Fly-Kruh

Joris - Jor-iss

NAIA

As I opened my eyes, I immediately smelled smoke and looked out my window. Flames were reaching the trees just before our little cottage, and cries of villagers rang out as they were struck down by enemy swords as they tried to escape.

"Sweetie, grab some clothes and run for the river," my mother said calmly, but with fear in her eyes, too. My mother was never afraid. She always handled situations with ease and grace. She was pretty fierce. I wanted to be more like her. Mom always seemed out of place, but she was exceptional at her occupation of being a mother, wife, and occasional seamstress.

"Mom, what's happening?" I asked, throwing some dresses and underskirts into a burlap sack.

"Honey, our village is under attack. We need to get to safety! Please, I will explain everything, but right now we have to go! I'll get your brother. Meet at the river. Your father is already there getting the boat ready!"

My brother, Rhyson, was fourteen- six years younger than me. He must have been scared out of his mind because, as Mom was about to fetch him, he came bursting through the door to my room; his eyes flooded with tears. He never let anything get to him. He was the one who would stand up for the kids who were getting picked on- the one who would fight. He was tough, but not tonight. I held out my arms and he ran into them for comfort. I brushed some strands of his sandy blonde hair from his eyes and then wiped away his falling tears.

"Come on, Rhy. Let's go. Mom will follow." I said, a little too cheerfully, and glanced at Mom. I could tell she was waiting for us to go so she could get some things situated before following us. She looked conflicted, knowing she needed to take care of her kids, but also needing to focus on whatever secret she had been keeping from me. She nodded in approval and with that I dragged Rhyson out of the room.

Running after us as we left the house, I heard Mom yell at me to stop. I turned around to see her standing at the front door with a sword in hand and a bow and arrow strapped over her shoulders. My eyes widened. *Where had those come from? I have never seen her with weapons before. Does she even know how to use them?*

"Naia, take this," She said, shoving the sword into my hands. "Swing it at anyone who comes close to you. Even if you think you might know them- you might not. Be careful. Please." With that she raced back inside, slamming the door behind her.

I strapped the sword's sheath and belt around my waist, re-grabbed Rhy's hand, and we raced into the night.

Bodies were everywhere- fires were catching on homes, trees, and people. I shuddered at the sight. As we ran, I shielded Rhyson's eyes so he wouldn't have to be scarred by the images I knew I would be haunted by for the rest of my life. People were wailing and crying out, begging for help, but we had to keep moving. We had to get to the river. Dad would be there, and he would take care of us- how he would do that I had no idea.

"Naia, help, please!" A voice called from the night, the river was right in front of me. I couldn't risk it, but I knew that voice. It cried out again.

"Naia, please!"

It was a boy from my study group. We had been learning how to make herbs into medicines together. I paused and looked over my shoulder. There was no one there. I groaned, not wanting to make the choice I knew I had to make, but I knew the right thing to do. I surged ahead pulling Rhyson along, remembering what Mom had said about not trusting anyone. Could he be bad? *No.* I shoved the thought from my mind.

Twenty-five yards later we reached the riverbed. I scanned the length of it searching for my father. *There!* He was dragging a boat out from a shed which had been hidden by leaves and moss. He spotted me and subtly waived for us to hurry.

He started waving his hands higher in the air. I waved back, too late, realizing the panic that had appeared in his eyes, even from a distance. He was trying to warn me of something. *Thud.* I hit the ground hard and cried out in pain, my face in the dirt. I heard a scream. *Rhyson.*

Someone had tackled me from behind. I landed on some rocks and pain surged through me. *That's gonna leave a mark.* I looked up and, standing there, was a warrior. He didn't look very old, but still. *Why are there warriors here?* He was holding a long weapon and his dark, angry eyes were staring at me. He moved towards me swiftly, extending the weapon above his head, ready to strike me down.

"I got her!" He yelled to no one, but everyone at the same time.

"No, you want me!" I heard another familiar voice call from behind him. *Mom. Mom help!* I couldn't move. I had no way to defend myself. *Wait! She gave me a sword! How could I forget? Did she know I would need it? How?*

My attacker stood, momentarily distracted by the yell from my mother. *He wanted her? What does that mean?*

While he faced her, I silently withdrew and raised the sword while jumping into a fighting position. I had no idea what I was doing, but then he turned back to me, and I knew I needed to figure it out… immediately. He lifted his weapon, and I brought my sword up just in time to avoid being maimed, but I knew my strength wouldn't hold out for long. I had no training in battle at all and would tire easily. After about three blocks against his sword my arms started to give way. *This sword is heavy!*

Out of the corner of my eye, I saw my mother rushing Rhyson the rest of the way to Dad at the boat. Good. At least He would be safe.

As I was distracted, the warrior came down on me hard, knocking the sword from my hands, sending it flying just out of reach. I groaned. He was going to kill me. I was going to die. He kicked me to the ground and I saw him lift his weapon. I closed my eyes, ready for the blow, but it never came. Instead, I heard impact from swords colliding together, a grunt, and then silence. I forced myself to peek through my fingers and was relieved when I saw my mom standing in front of me, triumphant. The warrior was on the ground. Dead.

I looked at her in awe as she stood there. Sweat dripping from her brow, a small trickle of blood running down her left temple.

"Naia, are you alright?" She asked, clearly knowing I wasn't. I gave her a small nod and she reached out her hand to help me up.

"Pick up your sword. Come on, let's go," she said as she started jogging toward the boat. Her voice was tight but steady.

My dad had it in the water already. It was a large rowboat and could probably hold eight. Thankfully we only had four to get to safety.

I had so many questions. Where had the boat come from? Did my parents know that we would need it eventually? Why did Mom know how to use weapons? What else were they hiding from me and Rhyson? I knew that it wasn't the best time to ask them all, but I would demand answers eventually. Mom said she would tell me… I would hold her to that.

Dad and Rhyson were already in the boat and seated. Dad had the ores in hand and was ready to steer the boat down the river. Mom had untied the ropes and was waiting for me to hurl myself over the edge. I jumped in and landed on the bottom with a thud. I scrambled to a sitting position as Mom pushed the boat from the edge of the water out into the deep. *Who is she?*

As she jumped in, I saw her glance at my dad and they locked eyes- sharing a thought. She looked guilty, afraid even, but he looked back at her with understanding in his eyes. I looked from Mom to Dad and then dared to speak. I couldn't wait anymore. I needed to know what was going on.

"Mom?" was all I got out before she held up her hand for me to be quiet.

"Not here," she replied. "Later."

I looked at her, raising my eyebrows in question, but she just put her hand on my knee and sighed.

"Naia," Mom whispered softly. "Just trust me, please. It isn't safe, and your brother…" She looked at me with pleading eyes, begging me to let it go. I didn't want to, but gave in and sat back down on the bottom of the boat and rested my head against the wooden bench behind me.

I was jolted awake as I was thrown into the side of the boat, landing on my injured shoulder. I winced as I sat up to face my parents who had sprung into action.

"Mom?" I questioned. "Dad? What is going on?"

"Rapids," my mom replied tensely.

"Luria, we waited too long!" My father cried as we were pulled to the other side of the river. He tried to steer us back, but it was no use; we were in the hands of the river and in the hands of God.

"I'm so sorry, I was trying to get us further away," My mom cried. My dad took a moment and took my mother into his arms and gave her a passionate, deep, kiss. A sob escaped my mom's lips as he pulled away. They looked at each other like it might be the last time they would be able to embrace each other like that. They looked at each other like they would be saying goodbye.

"Naia, Rhyson," she turned to us. "I love you both so much, I am so sorry," she looked at us directly in the eyes as she said our names. There were tears starting to stream down her face. This *was* goodbye.

From there chaos ensued. Mom and Dad were scrambling to tell Rhyson and me what to do if we fell out of the boat. Rhy was scared out of his mind. I tried to comfort him, but was jerked away from him by a sharp turn in the riverbend.

Water started crashing over the sides and we were thrown from one end of the boat to the other. Mom and Dad had lost control. Anything that happened was now out of our hands. *God, help us.*

I gripped the edge of the boat so tightly, my knuckles turned as white as snow. Water was spraying into my face, and my soaked hair was blocking most of my vision. I didn't dare to let go to fix it. I heard Rhyson scream and saw a small figure fall over the edge through the torrent of the water. *No! Rhyson!* Right after, I saw another figure dive in after him. I didn't know who it was until I felt my father's strong hand on my shoulder.

"Naia," he yelled over the roar of the rapids. "Brace yourself!" The next thing I knew I was flying, and then falling. We had gone over the waterfall.

NAIA

I couldn't breathe. I swam upwards, but I wasn't moving anywhere. I cried out, too late, remembering I was underwater. I needed to get to the surface and fast. I dove down, trying to find the object that was holding me under. My dress was caught on something. *Agh, Mom just fixed this one.* I pulled and tugged, but it was no use. I was stuck, and I was almost out of air. *I can't give up, I won't, I…* a strong arm circled my waist, as another pulled hard on my snagged dress. It came loose! We were moving up towards the surface, and that was it. I blacked out.

"Hey, Miss? Are you alright?" A gruff voice said as I came to, spitting and coughing up water all over the place. The man turned me over so I wouldn't choke. After a few minutes I calmed down and was able to look around. I was at the edge of the river below the waterfall, about a hundred yards from the base of it.

"You were under there for a while, Miss. I wasn't sure if you were going to make it. I had to rip your dress to free you. I do apologize."

My eyes fluttered open and I struggled to sit up. The man who had spoken put his firm hands on my back and neck, and guided my body to a sitting position. He was holding me with his left arm, his hand just below my shoulder, like a father would, while he reached for something with his right hand. A blanket. I hadn't realize how cold I was.

"You are trembling miss. Can I wrap you up in this and my cloak?" The man said softly.

I nodded.

He took off his wool cloak and wrapped it around my shoulders, looking into my eyes with his own kind gentle eyes then tightly wrapped the blanket over that.

He looked around my father's age maybe a couple years older. He had a salt and peppered beard and mustache and short silver hair. He was quite muscular, which I don't know why, but that surprised me. Under the cloak he had been wearing was a ragged tunic and leggings. He wore torn up boots that he had most likely owned for many years and had a rope belt to keep everything together.

I had stopped coughing and sputtering up water, so the man offered me a cup of warm broth he had been making over the fire for himself, before my arrival.

"Maybe in a little while, but thank you." I said, still recovering from the water, but I leaned in towards the fire.

"Where am I?" I asked as he poured himself a bowl.

"You are in the lower forest of Rowynala, Miss. Ahem, I don't believe I know your name," he chuckled.

"Oh! My name is…" I paused, taking my mother's warning from earlier into consideration. We were so far from home; this man couldn't have known anything. *Right?*

"My name is Edwin," he said before I could share mine. He must have sensed my hesitation to tell him who I was. I smiled politely and then finally responded. There was no reason not to tell him the truth. He had saved my life.

"I am Naia," I said quietly, wrapping myself up tighter in the blanket. I felt an uneasy sense of vulnerability. I didn't like it. Mother's warning had scared me.

"Naia, such a beautiful name," he said, offering me the broth again which I gratefully accepted.

"Thank you."

"How did you get out here all alone?" Edwin questioned.

It was that moment when it all hit me. I had lost my home, my life, everything I knew, my brother, my mom, and my dad… oh, what had happened to Dad when we had gone over the waterfall? I started to tear up. Setting down the broth I put my head in between my legs and sobbed.

"Ok, Miss, Naia, let's get you inside to the fireplace where you can dry up. My wife has some clothes you can wear. You can tell us what happened once we get you warm and dry," he said as he started gathering his things. It looked as if he had been fishing or was about to.

"Can you walk, Miss?" He gently inquired as I thought about how I would escape in a time of trouble.

"I think so," I said, starting to rise.

Pain flooded my ankle, and blood rushed up to my head making me dizzy and lightheaded. I cried out in pain and plopped back onto the ground.

"That's a no," he said. "May I carry you? It is only a ten minute walk."

I thought for a moment, debating my options, realizing this was really the only one I had. My mom and brother were who knew where, and my father, if he had survived the fall, could be anywhere as well.

"Yes, please," I told him. I was hesitant, but it wasn't like I could walk myself even if I wanted to.

He effortlessly lifted me into his arms and trodded down the path leading to his little home.

Upon arriving, he hollered to his wife through an open window, asking her to open the door. I heard him use her name, *Ingrid*, as he called into the house.

She burst through the door, almost tripping on the wooden beam at the entrance in her hurry, grabbed a small tree to steady herself, and rushed over to me, her arms stretched out as she ran. She started fussing over my injured leg and wet clothes, while pulling at Edwin's arm, nagging at him to bring me inside and lay me down as quickly as possible.

"Good to see you too, dear," he chuckled lightly, and obediently did as she asked.

Ingrid was a bit shorter and wore a light pink apron over her gray dress-it only went to her calf's. For shoes she wore black laced boots that extended up to her ankle.

She quickly shooed her husband out of the house and shut the drapes so she could help me get changed in private. Ingrid helped me strip off my wet dress and left me in my white undergarments which were now muddy. She gave me a onceover and proceeded to dig through a trunk to find a dress suitable for me. She ended up finding a beautiful forest green dress with a cream colored apron. She turned around as I took off my underclothes to change into her fresh dry ones, and then helped me tie the corset for the beautiful dress she selected. It had long sleeves that flared out a little at the wrist, and was simply elegant. I looked at her wide-eyed. This was clearly the most expensive piece of clothing she owned, and she had selflessly passed it on to a stranger.

"Oh don't look at me like that, girl," she said, noting my shock. "I haven't fit into this dress in years, and I have not a daughter of my own to give it to, so now it is yours. And I must say, you look marvelous! Edwin, you can come in now!" she hollered out to her husband, who came through the door with a new rip in his tunic, grumbling and covered in dirt.

"Darling, what did you do to yourself?" She asked with a laugh. Clearly she had experienced this with him before.

"Oh, Ingrid, I was trying to get the goat out from being stuck and I fell and caught my tunic on the post," he replied. "I hate farm life," he added.

"I know, dear," Ingrid said compassionately and rubbed his shoulders. "I wish I could…" he looked at me and his voice trailed off.

As Ingrid finished preparing dinner, I asked how they met and the two of them took turns telling me. Edwin used to be a guard of the king and Ingrid was a servant and nurse in the castle. They met while they were working there and ended up moving to the forest after Edwin had a bad injury at the castle.

The evening was so carefree, it almost made me forget about the tragedy I had just experienced. It had to have happened at least a day ago if not a little longer.

The three of us talked and told stories until finally I excused myself to the room Ingrid had made up for me. She said it used to be their son's, but he had gone to Castle Arilos to train to be a warrior. They wondered if he would try to follow in Edwin's footsteps, but hadn't heard any word if he was trying for the King's Guard position or not. He had a lot of work cut out for him since he had grown up on a farm in lower Rowynala. Edwin had taught him a lot, but he would need to gain a lot more skill and knowledge at the castle to become King Zaxton's guard.

I had grown up on top of the waterfall, the upper forest of Rowynala. It had been named Rowynala years ago after the red oak trees that surrounded the forest. It was also filled with pine and other trees that bloomed beautiful flowers in the spring– pink, purple, yellow. But the oak trees were the most prominent. It was filled with small villages like my own that band together to survive. We helped each other, tending to each others' animals if one of us needed to go to the big market or visit the castle because of a summoning.

The market wasn't behind the castle all the time like it used to be, Mom had told me once. It now traveled between the different villages and the castle itself. Arilos was the name of the Kingdom, but within it there were three villages. Joris, the Farmlands, Flykra, the snowy mountains, and Rowynala- the forest, herbs and some livestock.

I had never been allowed to go to the marketplace. Only Dad and Rhyson went, which I always found strange, but it was just how things were. All of my friends were allowed to go, but I wasn't. So when Edwin said he had needed to go to sell or trade his goat, and asked if I wanted to come along, I immediately agreed! It was the chance of a lifetime.

Unfortunately, because of my excitement, sleep was not my friend. I tossed and turned for hours. When I finally did fall asleep, I was overcome with nightmares and woke up with a start a few times throughout the night. I threw the pillow across the room and let out a groan. I might as well stay awake.

As I laid there my mind flooded with memories of my family, wondering what had happened to them, where they were now, if they were even alive. The thought of their possible death sent me into a crying frenzy, followed by brief periods of restless sleep and more crying. My dreams filled with the fire and going over that wretched waterfall.

The next morning, after finally falling into a deep sleep, I was gently shaken awake.

"Naia, good morning, sweetheart," I heard, my eyes still closed. I jumped a little, hoping that the last couple days had been a dream.

"Mom?" I mumbled groggily.

"No, dear, just me, Ingrid," She must have noticed the look of disappointment on my face as her words registered to me… *it wasn't a dream. I am living a nightmare.*

"I'm sorry, dear," she said tenderly. "I made you breakfast, though, for the road. Edwin will be ready to leave within the hour. It is a four hour journey to the market at a walk. Since you can't walk well, you will ride on the mule and Edwin will walk."

"Oh, are you sure? I can try to walk if I nee-" I was cut off by Ingrid insisting I ride the four legged creature.

I reluctantly agreed and we set off for the Castle.

I could hardly contain my excitement. I was jumping for joy on top of the mule, so much so that Edwin had to gently tell me to stop.

At the last minute Ingrid decided she would come with us to get some fabric to make me a new dress. I begged her not to spend her earnings on me, but she insisted that she wanted to help.

This time around, the market was located at Castle Arilos. I stopped in awe as we came into view of Castle Arilos. It was magnificent! It was three stories tall; the gold and royal blue flags flew at the four corners, and it had a drawbridge providing easy access to the Market located behind the Castle's oasis. I had always pictured the market as an organized gathering place for people to sell their goods. As we came to the top of the dune that overlooked the market, I saw it was the complete opposite. There were people running everywhere waving their arms like they were giving directions. I asked Edwin about it, and he said the place was so big people were paid to know where everything was so they could show people around at each location. It was more amazing than I had ever imagined!

As we got closer to the far edge, I could smell the livestock. People were selling live pigs, sheep, and cattle. They must have come from Joris. Its people are responsible for a lot of the animal trade with the other lands. I loved the smell of cattle and sheep. It reminded me of home. Rowynala's main form of trade is herbs– mint, basil, parsley, rosemary, and so many others, but we did tend to a few different flocks and herds.

I noticed that there were a large number of warriors that walked through the paths of the marketplace. I wondered if that was normal, or if it was because of the attack on my village. I had heard whispering from different people around us, talking about how awful it was. It took everything in me to not break into tears thinking about my lost family.

Edwin eased me off the mule and made sure I was okay to walk a little bit and then Ingrid directed me towards the fabric section of the market. My ankle was tender but with help I could put a little weight down.

While Ingrid and I were shopping, Edwin went to try to trade his goat for some weapons. He wanted to be extra cautious after hearing of the attack on the upper village. Trading for weapons wasn't usually allowed, but he was going to try.

As we passed the food area, I could smell the meat sizzling, hear the popping of the grease and oils used to cook it. I smelled freshly baked bread and could feel the heat from the stone ovens. I saw fruits of all different shapes and colors. We had some fruit, but this was more elaborate. Some were shaped like a human heart, others shaped like spiky balls, and others like mushrooms with no stem. Weird.

"I wonder if we will see Quinlan here today!" Ingrid said suddenly. "We don't get to see him very often as he is really busy with his job," She said, but I was no longer paying attention; my eyes were fixed on what was before me. The fabric section of the market.

I stopped, my mouth agape. I had never in my life seen so many different types of fabric. We used wool or cotton usually, but Ingrid told me that here they had silk- silk was so smooth. There was also velvet, and lace… the options were endless.

I ended up choosing a wool fabric, as winter was fast approaching. It was olive green. It reminded me of my things back in Rowynala, and the color suited my skin tone. I told Ingrid I would just use her cream apron if she was ok with that. I didn't want her spending more earnings on me than she had to. While we were there, she let me pick out a pair of flats to wear too. I chose some simple brown ones.

We walked back through the market and saw the herb tents, which smelled like mint and rosemary- like home. After that we came to the jewelry tents. The merchants there were selling different jewels that had been twisted into metal necklaces, bracelets, and rings. My favorite piece was a light purple stone on a rose gold band. It could have been an engagement ring! Something I could never afford in my life, so I walked away quickly, not wanting to make myself want it even more–the ring or the wedding.

We made our way to the edge of the weapons area and met up with Edwin, who was finishing up bargaining with the weapons merchant. After a while, he finally convinced him to take the goat and give him a sword and a dagger in its place. He had been hoping for a quiver of arrows too, but was ultimately satisfied with what he had traded.

We went to a tent to rest for a few minutes before starting our trek back, and were munching on some different fruits and cheeses when there was a voice outside that made Edwin and Ingrid leap up.

"Quinlan," they said together, smiles on their faces.

"Naia, come, if you can! Maybe he has a moment to speak to us!" Ingrid said hopefully.

We walked through the flap of the tent, and the two searched the crowd for a moment before hearing their son and then, after seeing him, raced towards him, arms outstretched.

"Quinlan? Quinlan!" Ingrid cried as she got closer.

I hobbled after them, struggling to keep up with my hurt ankle. I watched the ground making sure I wouldn't trip on anything and injure myself further. When I caught up with them, I was shocked at the scene playing out before my eyes.

Two men standing with someone, whom I assumed to be Quinlan, turned, swords drawn and they charged at Ingrid and Edwin.

"Stay back!" The one on the left yelled.

"State your names!" The other bellowed

"Oh um, I am…" Ingrid started, but was cut off by Quinlan, who stepped in the way of the guards sharp swords as they neared his parents' throats. He was fearless.

"Mom? Dad? Warriors, lower your weapons. These are my parents," he said, extending his hands out in front of him.

"But, Sir," the left one said… "Our orders…"

"Do you argue with me? Your Captain? Lower your weapons," he said again, his voice and body unwavering. He was not afraid to take charge.

The men hesitated but, after a moment, lowered their swords and sheathed them back in place at their waists.

"Oh, my boy, it has been too long!" Edwin said, tears flowing. I blinked and scrunched my eyebrows in confusion. I had never experienced such raw emotion from a grown man.

"I missed you so much," Quinlan said, taking his mother into his arms. "Why are you here? Did you not have enough from what I sent you this month?"

"Oh, no, my boy, we had plenty. We came to get fabric for this young lady. She appeared at the bottom of the waterfall a few days back," Edwin said, gesturing to me.

I froze as Quinlan looked into my eyes. He was so handsome. He had light brown waves that came to just above his shoulders and the most stunning chocolate brown eyes. He had a little stubble for a beard and a pronounced square jaw.

"M'lady," he said, bowing slightly.

I hesitated.

"Sir, I am just a village girl," I replied. I was so embarrassed.

"Just a village girl?" He asked, his brows furrowing.

"Quinlan, we have work to do," a voice called from out of sight. Quinlan's attention immediately focused on the voice and he sighed.

"I am sorry, Mother, Father, but I must return to my duties. "The prince is calling me. I love you, and am glad to have run into you today."

"So soon?" Ingrid said, tearing up.

"Mother, there was a Flykryn attack upon Rowynala. We are going to ride out to see the damage, and see what we can do to help."

I looked at him, distressed. I had been having such a good day and then the attack just had to be brought up. I know he didn't have any idea what had happened, but it was hard.

The attack, flames, death. Mom, Dad, Rhyson. Where are you? Oh, how I missed them.

I shoved the memory aside as Ingrid and Edwin said goodbye. I hope they never have to experience what I did.

"Be safe, Son," Edwin said, clasping Quinlan's arm. There was fear lining Edwin's eyes. *Did he know something from when he was the King's Guard?*

"I will, Father," Quinlan said, returning the motion.

He turned to me and gave a slight nod then walked off to the voice that had commanded his presence. *He seemed more than a knight in training.*

NAIA

A couple weeks had gone by living with Ingrid and Edwin. I missed my family every day, but I had grown to love it there with them. But I knew I couldn't stay forever. They shouldn't have to take care of me. I was an adult, and I needed to find my way on my own.

One night outside my room I heard a crash and a quiet yelp. I crept to the door of my room, slightly creaking it open, and saw Edwin in the torchlight heading to the front door.

"We are looking for a woman named Luria." I stifled a gasp as they said her name. They were looking for my mother. Why were these men looking for her?

"What do you want with her?" I heard Edwin whisper, trying not to wake me or Ingrid.

"She is a wanted woman," a voice said. The other man muttered something I couldn't quite make out.

I heard Ingrid get up and go stand by her husband, who started speaking again.

"What has she done?" Edwin asked.

"That is not your concern," a second voice grumbled.

"Have you seen her?" The first voice asked again, more harshly.

"Sirs' with all due respect, we don't know who that is," Ingrid said quickly.

I struggled to breathe. I needed to get out. Fast.

I felt bad leaving Ingrid and Edwin in such a rush after all of their hospitality towards me, but I had to get somewhere safe. Where that was I had no idea. Maybe the Castle. Maybe they would take me in as a refuge. *I could work for the King.*

I threw on the cloak Ingrid had loaned me, found an old pair of boots in the trunk, and put them on too. They were a little big, but if I cinched the laces really tight and shoved a cloth into the toes, they would be okay. Opening the drapes, I shoved my body through the small window that was on the far side of the room as fast as I could without drawing attention to myself. I hit the grass with a soft grunt as I was still recovering from my fall from the waterfall. The pain wasn't super bad, but I wasn't sure how I would do on a four hour journey to the castle on foot, and I didn't want to hurt it again before I even started. As I dropped to the ground I froze, listening to see if anyone had heard my commotion. They hadn't. I was safe for the time being.

A few hours later I was at the edge of the forest and desert, the sun peaking over the horizon. It was one of the most beautiful things I had ever seen in my life. The pinks and oranges spanning the sky, letting the world know it was a new day. Spectacular.

Having decided definitively to go to Castle Arilos, the next couple hours of the day I would be walking out in the open, exposed, but

I couldn't turn back now. I had gone too far, and I needed to figure out why these people were after my mom, and that meant going directly to the King. I took a step, and headed into the open desert ahead.

I thought I could get to the Castle, but I was wrong. I must have swerved in my tiredness and lost my way. Hours had gone by and it was so cold. Winter had arrived in the desert overnight, and I was not dressed for the occasion. It was 30 degrees during the day, and I only had the cloak for warmth. I trudged on hoping not to cross paths with anyone dangerous, or preferably anyone at all.

I let my mind wander again to what could have happened to my family. There was a good chance Rhyson had drowned before Mom could get to him, and another chance Mom had drowned before she got to him too. If she hadn't, she could have hit her head on a rock or the bank. I shuddered at the thought of her lifeless body falling over the waterfall.

Dad had made it over the edge alive, but there was no knowing if he had survived the fall. I still had no idea how I had. I wept as I trudged on- the bitter wind blowing across my face. My tears started to freeze as they fell, making me even colder. I swayed left and right as I walked, not being able to keep a straight line. Hunger overwhelmed me, as well as fatigue, but I couldn't stop.

My feet were numb and I stumbled with each step. I couldn't make it much further. I knew that much. I was going to die out here in the desert. How ironic was that? I had grown up thinking the desert was always hot and making people sweat, but apparently there were deserts that snowed. Of course this would happen to me– stumbling on the cold desert instead of the always hot one. I knew it was just a part of nature, and I had nothing to do with it, but I felt the need to complain. I had every right to.

As I reached the edge of a dune, about to descend, I saw it. The castle. I was so close. I stepped forward, but as I did, I heard a noise from behind me. It was a group of men. *How long have they been following me?*

They came up from behind and, before I could put up a fight, started shoving me around. One ripped my cloak from off me, choking me before the cloak button finally gave way. That sent me rolling head over heels down the dune. They came running after me, kicking my back and abdomen. Once they had their fun, they walked away, continuing their journey as if I had never existed. Defeated, and in excruciating pain, I couldn't stand or even crawl, so I resorted to curling into a ball, lifeless, waiting for a cold death to release me from any more struggles.

4

JAVIL

"You think you can beat me, Javil? Truly? Ha! We shall see about that!" My older brother, Picel, grinned while throwing another punch.

Picel had always been the better fighter even as boys, but I was right behind him. I had to be. It was my job to protect him. I moved to advance at him in our game, but he quickly threw me to the ground.

"Come on, Picel, let me up! At least give me a chance!"

"A chance! You had one! You missed it!" He said pinning me to the cold sand. It trickled down the collar of my tunic and I cringed. That would be maddening to get out. With as much as I was sweating it would stick everywhere. I struggled to get him off me, but it was no use; he had me beat again.

"Do you yield?" He asked, smirking.

"Yes, yes, I yield," I said, rolling my eyes. "Come on, brother, let me up," I groaned.

He didn't. He shoved my head further into the sand. It was almost in my ears. I squinted at him, trying to figure out his next move. I was about to wrangle free, when he released me and helped me stand. I swatted my hand back at him, refusing his gesture of peace, and started walking away when I felt a boot on my back. I hit the sand hard, pain shooting up my wrist as I reached out my hands to catch myself. *That was foolish. I knew better than to fall like that.*

It's on. I flipped over onto my back and kicked up to stand. I threw a punch, connecting solidly with his jaw. He winced, and staggered backward. *Take that brother.* I smirked before seeing a trickle of blood coming from the side of his lip. *Oops.*

He glared at me and swung. I ducked and swept his legs out from under him. As he hit the sand, I lunged for his chest, drew my sword from its sheath, and drove the hilt into his ribcage. He curled and then threw his head back into the sand, putting his hands out in surrender. I won.

A slow applause rang out from behind us. *Quinlan.*

Quinlan, was our father, King Zaxton's, guard. Originally hailing from Rowynala, he had proved himself as a warrior, like his father before him, and my father had promoted him to his personal guard fairly quickly.

"Surprise, surprise," he said laughing. "Looks like you had it in you after all, Javil," he said, making his way over to us. Quinlan was also Picel's and my best friend, so he was allowed to call us by our first names when things were unofficial. The other warriors were not granted that permission.

"Shut up, Quin," Picel muttered, now sitting up, his wavy brown hair a mess, though not as bad as mine.

"There's a first time for everything, Picel," I joked, tying my hair back with a leather strap. Strands of black wrapped around my hands as I tightened the leather against my scalp. My hair was getting too long.

"And a last," Picel muttered. I laughed at his bitterness.

Picel was next in line to be the King of Arilos which was currently ruled by our father, King Zaxton. He took his Father's place when he had died only weeks after he became King. No one knew why. There were whispers that he killed his father, but I wouldn't believe it until he told me himself.

The first thing Father did after taking over as King was create an army to protect the castle and the surrounding villages. What once was twenty-five to fifty men was now close to one hundred; always ready for an attack, but the attacks never came.

Picel sat up after sulking for a moment and I held out my hand. He reluctantly grabbed it and I pulled him up.

"Weren't expecting that, were you, brother?" I laughed.

"Definitely not, Javil, but I'm impressed. Well done."

As we joked around a bit the horn blew, reminding us that it was time for our daily ride to scout the perimeter of the castle's land. We threw our cloaks over our tunics and button ups and made our way to the stables to gather the other warriors.

As the Crown Prince, Picel was over the whole army, while I was in charge of the offensive maneuvers. Quinlan was not only the King's Guard, but also captain of defensive tactics and charged with protecting The King or Picel if there ever were a battle. King Zaxton had retired from battle a few years ago. He knew Quinlan, Picel, and I could handle anything that came our way and that we would protect him with our lives if anything arose.

Even though I had never experienced an actual conflict of war, I knew protecting the kingdom is where I excelled and what I wanted to be doing. I would be good on the battlefield if I ever had a chance. I wasn't a killer, but I was a protector. I would do *anything* to keep those I cared about out of harm's way. Anything.

After going over the route for the day with the warriors, Picel led the way out of the gates and across the drawbridge. Quinlan and I followed in sync behind him. We raced out and turned right, circling the castle, looking at the marketplace that was being dismantled to travel to the next location. We broke off into two groups. Picel and Quinlan took one, and I took the other. Usually we stuck together, but we had a meeting with Father later in the morning and needed to be back sooner. I was always the one to veer off. My brother always had extra protection as the Crown Prince, whether there was a threat or not. It was frustrating sometimes that we trained so hard and had nothing to show for it, but at least our people were safe.

My group went straight ahead and took a right, while Picel's went left. As we rode, it started to snow a little. I loved winter. It was peaceful- quiet. There were no storms, and the market wouldn't be back till spring, so we could relax a little more.

We had just crested the last dune before turning back, when I saw a pile of clothes at the bottom of the dune going away from the Castle. I held up my hand to my men silently ordering them to stay put as I descended to check it out. *Finally something interesting.* As I got closer, I saw blonde hair peeking out from a cloak. I jumped off my horse and rushed towards the figure. Something was wrong. I knelt down next to the figure and moved the hair so I could see a face. It was a girl. I leaned down to see if she was breathing. Her breath was barely there.

I yelled at the men to bring my horse down. I didn't know if she was a friend or foe, and normally I would be hesitant to bring her inside the castle, but I couldn't leave her out in the desert. I wasn't heartless. The temperatures were dropping quickly and, depending on how long she had been out there, getting her to warmth was critical. I wouldn't have an innocent life on my hands. No way.

I scooped her into my arms and handed her off to a warrior while I mounted my horse and then took her back, laying her across my lap, cradling her as we rode back. Upon arrival at the castle, I told my men to report to Picel when he returned, and I took the girl to the infirmary. A servant offered to take her, but I kindly refused her offer. I needed to find out who she was.

The infirmary was stationed in the corner room in the back right of the castle, so it took me a minute to get there. I walked through the door and called for Zahir, the castle medic. He had met my father on a journey, before he became king. Father had promised that he would always take care of Zahir and his family, so when the medic job opened up, Zahir was sent a letter immediately offering him the position.

Zahir was a half head shorter than myself and had a muscular build. He had trained with the guards and warriors throughout the years and could protect himself, and his patients, in the event of an attack.

I laid the girl on the bed, and a servant quickly came over to undress her and put her into a garment which would allow Zahir to examine her. Wanting to be respectful of the girl's privacy, I turned away. Once she was modest again, I turned back and watched as Zahir inspected her. Her ankle was bruised and Zahir determined that the injury had happened a few weeks prior. I had no idea how she had traveled as far as she did walking on it. Her shoulder was also bruised, but it wasn't fresh either. Zahir estimated it was about a three to four week old injury. He also said there were some new bruises forming on her torso, bad ones. She had been attacked recently.

The whole time he was examining her, she was unconscious. It wasn't until he had walked away to go get some ointment for a guard who had come in with a bleeding toe that she started to stir. She started to sit up and, without thinking, I reached out to keep her still, so as to not cause her further injury. That was a bad idea. She started screaming and thrashing about. I gently placed both my hands on her shoulders and sat down next to her on the bed. I was careful with her wounded side, knowing she was in pain, and not wanting to inflict more. I looked deep into her eyes, begging her to calm down, to take a breath, but she wouldn't. Finally, the servant came to my aid. She gently pushed me aside with a stern look on her face as if I should have known better than to hold down an abused girl. I should have though.

The servant calmed her down, probably because she had a matronly presence, instead of a man; a prince, still dressed in his battle gear- even though the cloak did cover a lot of it.

The girl eyed me carefully as she started to drink some medicine the servant had given her. I don't think she expected the taste because she choked and started to cough it back up all over her fresh gown. The servant talked to her softly, assuring her that it was ok, and she would get it cleaned up, and get her a new dress. Giving me one last look of *don't touch this girl, Sire,* she left to get some clean clothes for the girl.

I moved so I was sitting on the edge of the bed, getting closer to her. She flinched backwards, and I paused. Rethinking my movements, I scooted back and rested my left leg on the table next to her bed with the other on the floor. I leaned onto the elevated leg and looked at her, not threateningly, but curious. She looked down and gave a shuddered breath. She was terrified.

"What is your name?" I asked as softly as I could.

She didn't say anything, but started fidgeting with the sheets under her.

"Please, tell me. I did carry you all the way back from the desert and, if you are going to be staying in my castle, I would like to know who you are." At this, her eyes widened and she looked up at me slowly.

"Are you the King?" She asked, with fear lacing every syllable.

"No, but I am a prince. Not The Prince, that's my brother, Picel. I am Javil," I added.

"Sire," she spoke cautiously. "I don't think it is wise for me to tell you who I am."

I paused, considering my next words carefully. The way she was talking, she was making it seem like she was an enemy, but how could she be? She was half beaten to death. She could just be afraid because I was one of the princes, but the switch had been made in my mind and I was leaning towards her being an enemy.

"And why is that?" I decided on saying.

"People are looking for my mother, and I don't want them to find me too."

"Your mother's name then." I demanded this time, not willing to accept anything but the answer.

"Luria," she whispered. I inhaled too quickly. *It was her.* She flinched back, anticipating a strike. I wasn't going to hit her, but I wanted to. In her mother's place.

Her mother's name had come up when I was a boy... I blamed her for an experience I'd had regarding my dying mother.

I took a breath. I had gotten myself into this mess; I had to get myself out of it. *Why hadn't I left her out there to die?*

"Come with me," I commanded. I didn't care that she was in a tremendous amount of pain anymore.

"Sire?" She replied, panic flooding her eyes.

"Please, don't make a scene," I grunted, lifting her up from under her arm, half dragging her out of the infirmary. She started to struggle, but I was stronger and easily held her. I decided the best option was to take her to my father and demand answers. I half dragged, half carried her into the throne room where my father would be taking requests from the villagers.

I threw open the doors and walked down the center aisle that separated the seats in half, where the villagers waited. King Zaxton, Father, gave me a scolding look when I approached his throne without asking for permission, but then noticed the girl I was dragging and raised his eyebrows in question. Picel looked on in curiosity. He was learning how to handle the villagers and their requests; soon he would be responsible for them himself.

I threw her on the ground in front of Father's throne and she winced, curling into a ball for a second, then rose to her knees, still hunched over, her hands covering her face.

My father looked at me and stood.

"What is this?" He asked, taking a step forward towards the girl. *The enemy.* I thought.

"Javil, what is going on? Who is this?" He demanded now.

"Father," I said quieter this time, pressing my face close to his ear to avoid others' hearing. "This girl is… I don't know her name, but her mother's name is…" I paused again, moving to face my father eye to eye. I leaned in and whispered the name of the girl's mother in his ear, not wanting to cause alarm if it wasn't necessary.

My father stared into my eyes for a moment, then glanced at the girl, who was still crying on the ground.

"You are sure?" He asked, unmoving.

"I am sure," I replied.

He moved until he was kneeling before her. Gently, he lifted her hands from her eyes and placed one of his hands under her chin. Tears were streaming from her face which was red and puffy from crying so much. After a moment he let out a soft exhale, as if blown away by her presence. I was livid. How dare he treat her with such... Kindness.

"Everyone leave but my sons," he commanded, looking only at her. No one moved. He looked up slightly.

"Now," he demanded. "Quinlan, wait. Stay," Father instructed. Quinlan paused for a moment and then took his place behind my father's throne again; watching.

The guards and servants started to file out the villagers and then scrambled out themselves as I took my place on my throne, to the left of my father's. I looked over at Picel and he gave me a questioning look, like I knew more than he did. He wasn't wrong, I did know more. I shrugged my shoulders and turned to watch how my father would punish this girl.

5

NAIA

"What is your name, child," The King said, brushing the tears away from my eyes.

"Naia," I whimpered, he was the King, I *had* to tell him my name. I did not know what he wanted from me, but if he was anything like his son, I wanted no part of it.

His response surprised me. He kneeled down on the floor next to me and put his hands on my shoulders.

"Naia," he said softly. "Such a beautiful name."

Prince Javil was furious. He scoffed and threw up his hands as he walked toward his brother's throne to probably talk about my presence here. I didn't like him, and he clearly didn't like me either, but I had no idea why.

I turned my attention back to King Zaxton. His kind eyes; his welcoming smile.

"What happened to you? Who did this?" He asked, clearly concerned for my safety as he noticed the visible injuries on my body.

I looked up at him, shocked at how he was treating me, a stranger. I was expecting to be punished, not loved. Clearly that was what Prince Javil thought would happen too. I closed my eyes and shuddered, starting to sob even harder as I remembered the beating I had endured.

King Zaxton then pulled me even tighter into his arms and just held me there. What was this? What kind of King consoles someone his son claims to be an alleged enemy in his arms? *A good one.*

"How did you come here?" He asked softly. So I told him. I told him everything I had been through– the attack on my village, the fall over the waterfall, Ingrid and Edwin, meeting Quinlan in the marketplace, having to run from the men who came to their door. He waited until I finished speaking and only then pulled back, his hands still on my shoulders as he whispered something in my ear, looked into my eyes, and gently let go of me. He stood to face Quinlan.

"Quinlan, I am entrusting her to your care for the time being until we can get her situated and find her a position in the castle." At the King's words Prince Javil blew up.

"What? You are joking? You want him, *your* Personal Guard, to take care of the enemy? And you want her to remain here? Absolutely not. No way," he said as he rose from his chair and walked towards us. *So Quinlan was more than a Knight. He was the King's Personal Guard. Why didn't his parents know?*

The King then reacted, standing up and moving towards his son. He grabbed Javil's tunic and drove him hard into the nearest wall. "She is not the enemy," he snarled, spit flying into Javil's eyes as he enunciated each syllable.

Javil clenched his jaw and scowled at him, curling his lips and growling back in objection. As Javil reacted, something switched in King Zaxton's eyes. They hardened for a moment and his face started to form a scowl, but just as quickly, his eyes went back to normal and his face softened again. He released Javil and took a step back. *What was that?*

"I am sorry, Javil. I don't know what came over me," he apologized and started to walk out of the Throne Room.

"You will watch after her, Quinlan," King Zaxton repeated at the doors. Do not let any harm come to her," he said, looking directly at me. Quinlan looked at the King and slightly nodded his head in understanding. He was my personal guard now.

JAVIL

Father forced me to give up my seat, *my throne*, for the girl as punishment for arguing with him, and then took his place on the center throne. I took position behind Picel, and Quinlan stood behind the girl. I would not call her by name.

Father had called the rest of the guards and the Councilmen back in and they started taking their seats. The villagers had been sent away with a sincere apology for cutting into their time, and were told there was other business the King needed to attend to.

Quinlan glanced over at me, clearly sensing and seeing I was upset. I shook my head slightly and looked straight ahead. I would not speak at all during the whole meeting. *My opinion doesn't matter anyway.*

Once everyone was seated again, Father raised his hands to get our attention even though he already had it. He always had everyone's attention.

He looked more tired than I had ever seen him. And his face was white like he had seen a ghost. There were bags under his eyes and his skin was pale. Meeting this girl had tired him, well, maybe that was me. I'd made him exert a lot of energy. I caught Picel's eye, glanced at Father, and then back at Picel. He looked over at Father and, when he looked back at me he had concern written all over his face too.

"Attention, everyone," Father said tiredly. "Today we are going to be talking about the Coronation of Picel to become King. I have been intently thinking and I have decided to step down early."

I glanced at Picel who was frozen in his seat. No one had seen that coming. Father was supposed to rule for another year. Until Picel was thirty. To step down so soon meant something was seriously wrong. *What wasn't he telling us?* The people in the room started to murmur.

Father looked to his right and spoke directly to Picel.

"Picel, my son, I know I have sprung this on you sooner than anticipated and for that I am sorry, but I have been sitting on this for a year now and think it would be best for the Kingdom if you took over sooner rather than later.

All eyes went to Picel. We all waited for him to say something, but he was still in shock. So I stood.

"Father, Your Majesty, are you sure this is what you want? Is this really the best thing to do? With the recent attack on Rowynala and a *certain company*," I forced myself not to look at the girl, "is it really best for him to rule?"

That was a mistake. I had already defied my father once. My father wasn't violent, he had made a vow not to be, but I could tell now that he was trying to hold back his anger. He glared at me and rose. Drawing his sword he held it out aimed at my throat.

"Do you dare question the King in front of his people? Do you *dare* insert your opinion again, once I have made my decision?" the second "dare" being more enunciated, yet quieter, than the first.

Picel interjected quickly. He always had my back and was always saving my rear end, "Father, Your Majesty, I think Javil is only asking for my sake. Not that he doubts your ruling, but he wants to make sure I am okay. Is that correct, Javil?" He said, turning to look at me, pleading with me to agree.

"Yes, of course. I was only meaning--"

"Silence!"

"Yes, Your Majesty." I said, hanging my head, defeated. I didn't even try to call him "Father" Right then all that was acceptable was 'King' or 'Majesty'. I was dumb sometimes, but I wasn't stupid.

Picel looked back at Father and continued, "Your Majesty, I would be honored to take the Throne, but I do ask the same as Javil. Are you sure it is the right time? After the attack and everything... Your Majesty."

No one knew how King Zaxton was going to respond. He took a deep breath and stood. Walking over to Picel he knelt down. The room was silent. The King wasn't supposed to kneel before another- ever. He took Picel's hands in his and spoke.

"Yes, Son, it is time."

Picel rose and kneeled next to our father, bowing his head to his chest. "As you wish, Your Majesty.

NAIA

"Naia, a word please," King Zaxton said, as everyone filed out of the Throne Room- even Javil and Picel.

"Your Majesty," I said, curtsying as I stood from my chair and approached his throne.

He sat in silence for a moment, waiting for the last man to clear. The only one who remained was Quinlan, as instructed.

"I knew your mother," he repeated the words he had whispered in my ear earlier. "We were friends when she was about your age." He said sorrowfully. He actually meant his words. I was shocked.

"The Flykryns, do you know why they attacked?" He asked and I shook my head. "Has your mother told you anything?"

"No, Sir, I have no idea… and no she hasn't. She was going to, but we were separated and…. I don't know if she…."

"Ah. I am so sorry," was all he replied.

"Do you?" I asked bravely. It wasn't an accusation. I was just genuinely curious if anyone had an explanation for what had happened to my village, my family. If anyone had the answers, King Zaxton seemed like the person to have them.

"That is not for me to say," he said carefully. "I also do not think you are ready for the information that comes with your question," he admitted. "My son's aren't even aware of what happened. It is too dangerous."

"Oh," I said. I was sad he wouldn't tell me, but also kind of relieved. Since he had known my mother, maybe I could trust him. *Maybe.*

"Sir… umm… your Majesty," I corrected quickly, "May I ask… were you close with my mother? Or just acquaintances?"

"You ask an impossible question for me to answer, my dear," he said softly. *There is a story behind his eyes.*

"I am sorry, I didn't mean… I just thought…"

What? What had I thought? That I could be a Princess? That he could have sent her away not knowing she was carrying his child? That they had some crazy romance story years ago my mother hadn't told me about? Wait, I loved my family, I loved my father! I was thinking like a girl, not a woman. Not an adult. I shoved those thoughts aside as he spoke, reading my mind

"You are not my daughter, Naia."

I tensed, and looked up at him. A part of me was sad, but I was also relieved that Javil was not my brother, well, half-brother. That would have been a horrible nightmare.

"Are you sure?" I dared to ask.

The King chuckled sadly, as if wishing that I *were* his daughter. "Yes, I am sure. Your mother and I, we never…" his voice trailed off, either embarrassed to finish the sentence or too sad to. "You look so much like her," he said, breaking his own silence. "So beautiful."

"Thank you, your Majesty," I curtsied, and he took my hands in his for a while. We stayed there in silence for what seemed like ages. And then he sent me away so he could think.

"Naia, come with me, I will show you to your room," Quinlan said as we exited the King's presence. He hadn't acknowledged yet that we had met in the marketplace. Maybe I was too beat up for him to tell.

"Now there are some rules," he started as we ascended the stairs. "You are a guest and will be up on the second floor in the right wing. And only the right wing. You are not to enter the left wing. Do you understand? That is where the King, the Princes' and I sleep. I think Javil might kill you if he sees you over there, and there will be nothing I could do to stop him. Naia, do you understand?"

"Hmm? Oh, yes. No going to the right wing on the second floor," I repeated.

"The left!"Quinlan exclaimed and grabbed my arm.

"Oh, the left," I said, a little embarrassed.

I had been admiring the artwork on the walls, the paintings of the royal family, some with pastel colors, some of the oasis out back. They were all beautiful. There were woven tapestries of the symbol of Arilos, a lion. A Pride; it felt like a castle.

"Naia, I am serious, I don't want to see you killed! And selfishly I would be stripped of my title if anything were to happen to you and I have worked too hard…"

"Okay, okay, I understand. I promise I won't go to the left side," I interrupted. I didn't want him to panic anymore.

"Good," he said as we made it to my room.

It was stunning. It was a corner room that had a circular build to it like the rooms you dream about being in a castle.

There was a bed with a metal frame, not wood, and clean cream sheets that were so fluffy! There were chairs in a lounge area that were upholstered in beautiful purple fabric along with the sofa and a rocking chair. The curtains were cream colored as well and fell all the way to the floor, not just covering the windows. I gasped as I took in the view and Quinlan chuckled.

"You really aren't a royal lady," he said, grinning, finally acknowledging that we had met. Maybe he didn't want to say anything in front of his leaders. That would make sense, especially with Prince Javil's reaction to me.

"I told you," I smiled softly and jumped onto the enormous bed.

"Well, miss," he said with a slight bow. "I will leave you to get settled. You should be fine; just remember not to go to the other side of this floor." And he left. And I slept. And I didn't dream. *Finally.*

QUINLAN

After I had seen Naia to her room I went to speak with Picel about her. I knew he would be more level-headed about the whole situation, unlike Javil, who was completely blowing it out of proportion. Picel had decided that since King Zaxton seemed to like Naia, we should be kind to her and assist her as she needed.

"She seems okay," I told Picel based on the five minutes I had spent with her. *Like that could prove anything about her character.*

"Maybe she could be helpful around here," he replied. "She is from Rowynala. They are good with herbs and medical things. She could prove useful if the castle were ever attacked."

"So true," I said, nodding my head in agreement.

"What are we talking about?" Javil said, entering the study, arms crossed.

"Nothing that should cause you any concern, brother," Picel replied smoothly. He was right. Javil would want nothing to do with the conversation that we were having. Best to try and leave him out of it.

"The girl?" Javil growled, quickly picking up on the code. *Or not.*

"Would that trouble you?" Picel questioned, glancing at Javil in jest. He was trying to get his brother riled up. *Imbecile.*

"What do you think?" Javil spat back.

Smart or not, it was working.

"Brother, relax," Picel said at last, realizing he had taken it too far. "The girl will be no trouble. I think Zahir could use her in the infirmary or Pepper, in the kitchen. What do you think?" He voiced.

"I think she needs to be sent away or killed, but why would my opinion matter? I am not Crown Prince or King," Javil grumbled.

"Ah, but you don't want to be the Crown Prince nor the King, brother, so therefore, this discussion shouldn't matter to you," Picel bounced back.

"Forget it," Javil said, and he stormed out of the room.

"You think he will forgive me for that?" Picel asked me with a glimmer in his eyes.

"Oh, Picel. You are a moron," I replied, smacking him on the side of the head.

"What!" He laughed, balling p up a wadded up piece of parchment and then throwing it at me.

"Just… nevermind." I said, swatting the parchment away, and opened a book to forget about the idiocy of my master and best friend.

JAVIL

A few days after the girl showed up, while she was resigned to her chambers, Father called Picel and me up to his study to discuss a private matter.

"Boys, there is something I need to inform you of... I..." he sighed and hung his head. "Your mother would do this better." I froze. Father didn't talk about mother often. Adira. Our beautiful selfless, loving mother. I missed her dreadfully.

She had started slowly declining in health a year or so after I had been born and had gradually gotten worse until she passed. It was hard to believe that it had been almost ten years since her death.

I'd held her in my arms a few nights prior to her leaving us. Father was gone and Picel, at only nineteen, had to run the castle, so that left me taking care of our mom. The memory of feeling my mother tremble against me as she struggled to breathe would haunt me forever.

Lightning filled the room and thunder crashed shortly after, jolting me back into reality. We hadn't seen a storm like that in years. I had just positioned my knight to check Picel's king piece, when there was a knock at the door. Our father had returned. He had tear stains on his cheek and was trying not to break into tears again.

He came over, sat on the edge of the bed, tugging at the sheets below him like he was trying to gain strength or find the right words to say. He looked at me and then at Picel and spoke the words we had dreaded for months.

"Picel, Javil, as you know your mother has been gravely sick for a while… she," he stopped, trying to gather his emotions. "She has fought long and hard in her suffering but, just moments ago, her heart gave out and she passed. Please, now would be the time to go say your goodbyes, before Zahir comes for her body. I am so sorry. I know this will not be easy for either of you. I know how much you both loved her."

Picel and Mom had been close, but not as close as she and I. I had been the one to get her to smile or laugh as she battled her sickness. No one else was able to do that. Not even Father. He was there for her, he was her strength, but I was her escape.

I changed that day. I stopped joking around as much and became very serious; stoic, like my father also became. If he wouldn't show emotion, neither would I.

Upon hearing the news of our mother's passing Picel looked to father, slowly stood, and left the room without another word. Picel was about to start taking over things one at a time. He would start with taking over the daily tasks warriors and guards, then as time went on would start training the recruits. He'd wanted Mom there to support him during the long, hard process of learning to become King. He was about to endure a lot of trials and it would be very difficult to do without her constant and unconditional support.

Picel and I had always been pretty close, but it was as he walked out of his room, to say his goodbyes to our mom, that I promised myself Picel would never have to be alone. He would always have my support and encouragement. I was younger, but I could still be there for him. I didn't care what happened to me. As long as he was okay. I was only fifteen when I made that vow.

I shook myself out of my thoughts when a scout came bursting through the doors to the briefing room- I had missed half of my father's lecture while I had been reminiscing on the past. The scout was out of breath and was flinging his arms everywhere, but managed to get out a sentence or two before collapsing from loss of breath.

"Your Majesty, your Highnesses, there's an army in sight. Enemies. Swords... Armor... Sound the Alarm!"

Picel and I raced down the stairs and into the guard and warrior quarters. Picel started yelling directions at the warriors who were off duty to get dressed and meet us in the armory as fast as they could. Once the majority of the men were assembled and dressed, Picel started talking in a quieter, yet assertive voice. He *will* make a good King.

"Men, enemies are almost upon us. I have just been given word by a scout that they are a mile out. They are coming from Rowynala, but are dressed like Flykryn. They should reach us within a quarter hour. We move to protect our castle, our people, and our King. Under no circumstances will you let anything happen to His Majesty."

A shout of yesses echoed in the room.

"Good. I want defensive warriors to split between the upper walls and the courtyard, and I want my offensive to split being in front of the drawbridge and being ready to repel down the walls if needed."

"Yes, your Highness," they echoed again.

"The rest of the offense, you will set out immediately and meet them in front of the castle. Understood?" More murmurs of understanding came from the men.

"Good. Javil," he said, turning to me. "Godspeed. Quinlan, do not leave my side." Picel said as Quinlan walked through the door.

"Of course not," Quinlan replied, immediately at attention.

"Javil, are you sure you are okay to fight with your injured wrist?" Picel asked. "I don't want to put you at risk."

I had forgotten about my wrist injury from earlier due to all the activities of the day. I nodded. Hurt or not I was going into battle.

My men and I exited the armory and made our way to the castle entry. We drew our swords and waited. Picel, caught my eye and we looked at each other like this was normal and we had done this before. He clenched his hands around his sword and drew it out, his arms ready to swing. Following his lead, I did the same. We were ready to face the enemy.

10

NAIA

There was shouting and men running in all directions. I ran and hid back in my room where I would be safe. It was one thing to attack Rowynala, but Arilos itself? These people must be crazy.

I crawled under my bed and stayed there for a while until the thought crossed my mind that Zahir could probably use my help with fallen warriors. I didn't doubt the strength of the warriors at Arilos. I just knew with every battle came casualties.

I took the back way to get to the infirmary since the main route was flooded with men preparing for battle. It was utterly terrifying. It was something I never thought I would see and something I never wanted to see again.

When I got down to the main level, I saw servants coming and going to prepare different triage areas for injuries. I could hear Zahir, the medic who had helped me earlier, instructing some servants on how to stitch wounds. "It is similar to sewing clothes," he said. "There's just more resistance with the skin." Some of the girls winced while others nodded.

"The servants' quarters will be used as a resting place too, just in case the infirmary runs out of beds to hold injured men." Do you understand?" He asked the group. There were murmurs and some more nods.

As I watched Zahir, a servant came through the door about to drop a whole bucket of water. Water sloshed everywhere and I knew she was wasting precious resources. I leapt up and steadied the other side, only getting a little wet in the process. She looked at me with grateful eyes and I asked where she would like it to go. She motioned with her head behind her, so I followed her to a room in the back. It was filled with grain and hay. It must be where they kept the food for the horses. We dumped the water into a bigger tub that looked like it could be used for a bath, but I was pretty sure it was normally a water trough.

I felt the sudden urge to help more. I wasn't able to do anything for anyone when my village was under attack. It wasn't my place at all, but King Zaxton had been so kind to me. I knew I owed it to him to help however I could.

"What can I do?" I hollered to the servant I had helped before who was now rushing towards me with bedsheets in her arms.

She looked me over, scanning me from head to toe, and laughed. Clearly not convinced I was strong enough to do anything in my state. She might be right, but I had to try.

"Please, I want to help." I pleaded.

She sighed and then started talking, telling me what to do. I was relieved she was willing to use me. I really didn't want to go back up to my room and be alone during all of this.

"Go down three doors and grab as many bed sheets as you can and line the empty cots with them. Then go two doors down and do the same with the pillows."

Easy, there was no problem doing that. I was extremely grateful she hadn't tasked me with something harder, but I would have done my best if she had.

I found the closet and grabbed as many sheets as I could manage, then lugged them back to the cots that were being set up. I dropped everything on a made bed and started to make the others. It didn't have to be perfect, seeing as the sheets would probably be all bloody by the end of the day, but I still wanted to do a good job. Mother and Father had always taught me to do my best no matter what. If they were really gone, I wanted to honor their name. It is also what I was taught that God would do and that was an even more important reason for me to do my best.

I finished my tasks and was about to go ask what else I could do, when the first warrior stumbled through the door.

He crashed onto the first available cot. I staggered backward half a step. I had never seen a real warrior this close before, dressed in a full battle uniform. In stumbling back, I ran into the nurse who was rushing over to help the fallen warrior. As she approached him, I realized what had happened. He had an arrow lodged into his shin.

Then the floodgates opened. Soldiers started coming in one after another, some dragging others in, others walking on their own. There were mostly lacerations and cuts, but there were a few with broken bones sticking out or fractured ankles or deep stab wounds. It was the most horrifying thing I had seen up so close. I started to back into a corner to assess where I could be the best help when a nurse grabbed my wrist and dragged me over to a boy, no older than myself, who had a deep cut on his bicep. She handed me a needle and thread, showed me how to tie the knot to keep it from coming loose, showed me three stitches, and left me to fend for myself.

I had stitched up people in Rowynala before. I had a job assisting the medic in our village for a while, but had never seen anything as brutal as this. My experience was cuts and scrapes from kids falling out of trees or men falling off ladders.

I looked at the boy and grimaced. Not wanting to inflict any more pain on him than necessary, I splashed some more liquor on his wound to sterilize it better, and then made the first stitch. He tensed, but didn't cry out. I finished up and he was left with eight crooked stitches on his arm that would scar badly, but he would live. I was out of practice for sure.

From there I stitched up five more men and, when I had finished the sixth one, with perfectly straight stitches, I heard a huge commotion going on outside. I walked towards the door, not prepared for what I was going to see.

JAVIL

The screaming started. Wailing filled the walls of the castle. Men from both sides were dropping left and right, but Picel and I fought strong. We took down one enemy warrior after another, slowly pushing them away from the doors. Looking back, we should have met them further out, but it was too late for that. After half an hour we had ended up about a quarter mile from the castle gate. At least the people of the castle were safe.

I had no idea how there was an army this big that we were not aware of, but there was. They kept coming over the dunes endlessly. I was getting tired. Quinlan was pinned on the ground by an enemy warrior, and Picel and I were both fighting one on two. I had no way to defend him since I was defending myself. And I had a sprained wrist to factor into every swing. I glanced over at my brother. I would never forgive myself if something happened to him.

Out of the corner of my eye I saw Quinlan gain leverage against his opponent and take him out. I breathed a sigh of relief as he placed himself back at Picel's side, slicing one of the attacker's arms and sending him, in pain, to the desert floor.

It is going to end quickly now.

Just as quickly as I had the thought, I heard a grunt behind me and I whipped around. Picel had fallen and he was crying out in pain. Quinlan was fending off two new attackers. I knew Picel must have been injured badly for him to be making a noise about it. He was usually the last to show pain, at least in a fight. I looked harder and saw there was blood streaming down from a wound on his temple. I searched for the trumpeter and upon finding him signaled at him to make everyone aware the battle was over. The Heir had been injured... The battle was over. And we had lost... badly.

Nothing happened.

I motioned for the trumpet to be sounded again, but the battle did not stop. I was pushed away from Picel by three more warriors and they advanced upon me quickly. I was going to lose this fight and potentially my life and my brothers.

My wrist gave out and my sword fell to the ground. *This is it.* I threw my arms up to protect my face and heart as one of the men raised his sword to end me. I closed my eyes and prepared for darkness, but the hit never came. I heard a clash above my head and opened my eyes. Quinlan had blocked the blow and had taken over fighting. He quickly took out the man who had tried to kill me. I scrambled for my sword and jumped back to my feet. It was one on one now.

"What are you doing?" I yelled. He knew full well he had left my brother's side to come fight with me.

"Picel commanded it, Javil. I protested, but he wouldn't have you fighting alone."

Unbelievable. I was grateful for my brother sending help, but I needed to be the one to die if anything happened. He was the future King, not me. I would have words with him later, reprimanding and then thanking him for his decision. Like it or not he saved my life.

I heard a yell from behind me. *Picel.* I whipped around in time to see one of the men Picel had been fighting standing over him with a dagger, ready to strike. I lunged at the warrior, hoping Quinlan could fend for himself.

Without hesitation, with one hand on his throat, I pried the dagger from his grasp. Mistakenly, I threw a punch with my injured wrist and let out a scream of anguish, but continued to press on, determined to take down the man who went after my brother. I threw punch after punch, not letting up until the warrior was lying dead on the sand beneath me.

As I turned back, I saw Quinlan had reappeared by Picel's side and was tearing a piece of his own tunic to wrap around Picel's head. Good.

I propped Picel up over my arm, and Quinlan took his other side. He needed to get to Zahir as soon as possible. The blood was already seeping through the makeshift bandage. I called a warrior over who had a horse and the three of us managed to get Picel up onto the horse with me behind him, without him falling off. That itself was a miracle.

12

NAIA

Looking outside the infirmary, I could see the two Princes and Quinlan, stumbling through the hall, coming my direction. The eldest Prince, Picel, was basically being dragged through the courtyard, blood dripping from a bandage wrapped around his head, sweat soaking every inch of his body, despite it being the middle of winter. They came barreling in and put him on an empty cot.

Zahir dropped what he was doing and instantly went over to the Prince to assess the damage. He looked up and saw me watching so motioned for me to come assist him. He didn't know me, we had only met officially once, but he'd seen me work on other warriors and must have been pleased enough with my work to trust me with the Future King.

Together we managed to get Picel's tunic and undershirt off, leaving his chest bare. I gasped when I saw it. There were bruises lining his entire abdomen and rib cage. Zahir looked at Javil and motioned him to follow him to the room behind.

"Naia, do you know what to do?" Zahir asked sternly. I nodded.

As they left, I quickly grabbed a cool, wet cloth and started dabbing his forehead, trying not to wake him as he had either fallen asleep or gone unconscious from the pain. The latter being more likely.

The bruising was darkening by the second and, upon bending over his body, I could see it was wrapped around to his back. I lightly pressed on his stomach and cringed. It was completely rigid. Not a good sign. He was probably bleeding inside.

I ordered, well, I asked Quinlan to assist me with the cooling of Picel's body. He rushed outside to fill a burlap sack with sand. It wasn't as cold as ice, but could still be used as a cooling help. I placed one on each side of Picel and then sat down and went to work on stitching, then rebandaging, his blood-soaked head wound.

Quinlan watched in awe as I worked flawlessly on the Prince's wounds, never missing a beat, never hesitating at what I needed to do. I would not let this man die.

He moaned a little, but remained mostly unconscious, thankfully. I had just finished rewrapping his head when his eyes shot open and he attempted to sit up.

"Sire, Picel!" I said sternly, but softly. "You need to lie back down! Please!" I cried as he tried again.

Quinlan rushed over to assist me, placing his hand lightly on Picel's upper chest. Something registered in his brain at Quinlan's touch and he stopped struggling and stared at me, searching my eyes for- well I didn't know what.

"Who are you?" He grunted.

"I am Naia, the servant from the Throne Room. Your father spoke to me?"

"Ah, yes. Naia." He responded weakly. "Are you settling in alright?"

"Sire, that should be the least of your concerns. You have sustained terrible wounds in battle and need to be kept under a watchful eye at all times until you are cleared by Zahir."

"Is that so?" He asked.

"Yes! If I am found here and you're dead, then I will be most terribly punished!"

"So this is really about your safety, not mine then?" He joked, laughed a bit, and then started wincing and coughing in pain.

"Sire!"

"Picel, please, I beg you, be still," Quinlan pleaded.

I looked over at Quinlan, confused. Calling the Crown Prince by his first name was not something I had ever expected someone to be allowed to do, but maybe they were friends outside of their roles. We finally got him to sleep as Zahir returned.

13

JAVIL

We didn't know how badly he was injured until we got him to the infirmary when Zahir took a look at him.

"Javil, Your Highness, I need to speak with you in private about a delicate situation," Zahir said to me after we entered his chambers.

I sat down on a chair in the corner with my elbow resting on his knee and my fist on my forehead. This was not going to be a pleasant conversation.

"Javil, your brother has been gravely injured," Zahir said, putting both of his hands on my shoulders. I tensed, as I didn't like to be touched.

"It is more than Picel's head that is an issue–it is his ribcage and his heart I am worried about. He suffered a ghastly blow to his chest and there is much swelling and he could be bleeding inside I am afraid."

I almost gasped, but caught myself before I did. I was the prince and I needed to stay calm—even upon hearing this devastating news.

I looked at Zahir and took a deep breath, then exhaled slowly, processing the information he had just given me. Then I stood up and started pacing across the room.

"I can't lose my brother, Zahir. I need him. If he doesn't make it— please do everything you can." I pleaded. *So much for staying calm. Breathe Javil.*

"Sire, I know this is a lot to take in, I know what you are thinking, but hope is not completely lost. He is still alive, but he needs you. Be strong for him."

I nodded my head slightly and took a shaky breath. I tried to muster up the courage to go out to see my wounded brother.

Zahir, sensing this said, "I will give you a moment, Sire, but then I strongly encourage you to sit with your brother. Know that Naia and I will be doing everything we can to keep him alive for you and your father."

I looked at him, skeptical about Naia watching over him, but nodded, knowing Zahir wouldn't put my brother in danger.

And with that he left me alone.

NAIA

As I was almost done tending to Picel, an old servant with a limp came in to tell me the King wanted to see me. I was very confused, but quickly curtsied, making sure Zahir was okay if I left. I rushed upstairs to see King Zaxton.

I was nervous to go up there, as Quinlan had told me it was basically forbidden, even though the King had summoned me himself, but I was also a little excited. I liked the King.

I knocked on his door, but there was no answer.

"Hello? Your Majesty? You wanted to see me?" I called.

I peeked in and gasped.

There was blood. Lots of blood. It covered the white satin sheets of his bed. I rushed in and saw a dagger lying there. Rowynalyn. No. I needed to get out of there. If I were to be caught, they would think it was me! I would be executed for murder! *The King's murder.*

I was about to sprint out again when the King gasped for air and grabbed my hand, covering it in his blood.

"Your Majesty!" I exclaimed.

"Naia, please, I need to tell you something," he wheezed each breath, each syllable a struggle to get out.

"Majesty?" I repeated weekly.

"There is something you need to know," he struggled as he tried to get out another sentence. "You... are...."

15

JAVIL

When I finally went back out Picel's breathing was staggered–every breath was difficult. I truly didn't know how much time he had left. His face was bandaged, as well as his chest and hands, thanks to Naia. There were cooling towels laid across his body to keep fever and infection away. I had to give her some credit. She really had done a good job taking care of him. I softly told Picel that everything would be okay, that he would make it through.

I was about to change the towels on his chest, as they had heated up with his body, when an old guard came bursting into the room, locked eyes with me and motioned for me to follow him. I hesitated, not wanting to leave my brother, but got up and followed him out, as he started talking to me a mile a minute.

"What is going on?" I hissed. "Can't you see I am tending to my brother? He is gravely injured!"

"Sire, Have you not heard?" He looked at me wide eyed awaiting a response. *He looks familiar.*

"Spit it out man, heard what?" I asked impatiently.

"Sire, your father, The King, has been attacked in his chambers. He is close to death. The servant girl, the one who just appeared, Naia, is with him as we speak."

My head started spinning. I was going to lose it. I had three seconds to decide how I was going to respond. One... Anger set in. *Naia? Of course, she had something to do with this. How dare my father trust her! He should have listened to me!* Two... Fear swept over me– my heart started to race. *What if I were left alone and had no one to turn to. How was I going to make it?* Three... times up... pushing all my fears and doubts aside... unwavering determination...the mindset of a King.

"Take me to him."

Upon entering my father's chambers, I was jolted back to reality. Naia was kneeling by my father's bed, holding his hand, begging him to tell her something.

"What happened?" I roared. "What did you do?"

"Sire," she yelped, jumping up, but still holding onto my father's hand. "I... the King called me up here, a servant told me that... I found him like this, I swear. He was just about to tell me something important when you burst in here. I was just with Zahir and your brother; I must have just missed you. Please! You have to believe me. I am innocent." She cried.

WHEN PRIDE FALLS

I threw her to the side, away from my father, just as Quinlan came bursting through the door.

"Captain! Where have you been?" I yelled, turning my attention to him as he approached.

"Sire, I…" he faltered.

"Where?" I roared. I was not going to play games.

"I was with Naia down in the infirmary. After she was summoned by the King, I went to change," he said slowly, calculated. "What happened?"

"I am about to accuse this *murderer* of murdering my father!" I shouted.

"Sire, with all due respect, it can't have been her… she was with Picel until ten minutes ago."

"Ten minutes is enough time…"

"Javil, look at her. She isn't strong enough to drive a dagger through someone's chest. It had to have been someone else," Quinlan explained. He was right. Naia didn't *look* strong.

"Someone else? You don't think it was the girl?" I asked.

"No, I don't. Your father trusts her."

"Yeah, well, he shouldn't," I spat back. "Look where that got him."

"Javil, I…"

"Enough!" I shouted, shoving him away.

Father had always taught us to give people a chance, innocent until proven guilty, but that was very hard for me to do. The girl was in the room covered in blood and even standing next to my father with a dagger laying on the floor next to her! I didn't see a reason to think it was someone else. Apparently my father's own personal guard did. Ridiculous.

Father had also taught us not to let anyone see our emotions. At least the raging ones. I tried to live up to that, but it was nearly impossible with what was going on. I quickly wiped away an angry tear before anyone could see, besides Quinlan. I took a breath, wanting to live up to my father's expectations of me in his final breaths. Be strong, no tears, no pain. I walked towards him and then stopped, glaring at Naia.

"Father," my voice cracked despite my efforts. "Father," I repeated, stronger the second time.

He didn't respond, but I could still see his chest rising and falling. His body was covered in blood and bandages that Naia must have placed to either prevent excessive bleeding or to cover up what she had done. I clung to my father's shallow breaths. It meant he wasn't gone yet.

I turned as Zahir entered. His eyes were wide as he looked at me with great fear and sorrow.

"Picel?" I asked, not prepared for what he would say.

"He's okay for now. What happened here?"

I breathed a sigh of relief at my brother's condition and repeated to Zahir what I had been told happened to my father, still not believing half of it. There was no way she was telling the truth. None.

"I don't know. A guard told me Naia was up here with him and he was close to death. She claims she was summoned up here by the King, but I don't buy it. Quin is covering for-" A voice interrupted mine and I fought to keep my anger controlled.

"He was attacked with a dagger. No one saw who came or went. They must have had the timing down perfectly. He was stabbed multiple times, one just missing his heart," Naia whispered from the corner where she struggled to stand after I had thrown her to the ground.

Quinlan approached me and told me he had sent men to check the surrounding area for any possible suspects, but there was no one around. Naia was looking more and more like the attacker.

I turned to my father again. Our last direct conversation hadn't been pleasant. I had disrespected him in front of his most trusted people which was unacceptable. Granted, I hadn't been trying to, at least in asking about Picel becoming King, but that is how he took it. I felt awful. That moment could be the last interaction he and I ever had. I really didn't hate him. I just wanted to keep my family safe.

"I really do love you, Father," I whispered in his ear. Maybe he could hear me, hopefully, but I didn't know.

What I did know was that if he woke up, he would be worried about Picel's not being in the room. I didn't want stressing about Picel's well-being to be the last thing he did before he died. *Is that where things are?*

I shook the thought from my mind and was about to put my head on his shoulder when he started to struggle. Naia, without my permission, walked over and gently put her hand on his shoulder to keep him down. He gave in easily and rested his head back on his blood stained pillow. He mumbled something about a lost love and pride, and then quieted. *What is he mumbling about? The woman?*

I wasn't sure if I would be able to have a solid conversation with him but, at that moment, he opened his eyes and looked at me. "Will you forgive me?" He choked. "I shouldn't have thrown you into the wall. Please, forgive me."

"Yes, Father, of course. Of course I forgive you."

"Please forgive me for defying your orders, I know that you know what is best for Arilos."

"You are forgiven," he gasped.

He then motioned for Quinlan to come to his side. Quinlan leaned down so my father could whisper something into his ear. *I wonder what that's about.* Quinlan looked at him hard and then gave a solemn nod and backed away.

Naia, seeing her opening, made her way back to Father, and started adjusting pillows, dabbing up blood and sweat, trying to make him as comfortable as she could. It infuriated me. I was about to go tell her off, when there was a commotion at the door. People were scrambling to get out of the way as someone made their way through the crowd.

Picel. How?

He came wobbling into the room as fast as he could with the injuries he had sustained. I was surprised Zahir let him out of the infirmary, but then remembered Zahir was in the room taking care of the King. *Who dared leave Picel alone at a time like this? Someone was going to pay.*

I surged over to Picel and threw my arm under his. Quinlan did the same and between the two of us, we managed to get him into a chair next to father's bed, which Naia had pulled up for him. I looked at her furrowing my brow, but then gave my attention back to my family.

Picel, with difficulty, reached over and took my father's hand in his, and spoke, tears streaming down his face.

I knew that there was nothing else that could be done for my father so I commanded everyone to leave, but grabbed Quinlan's arm for him to stay. He should be with us when Father passes on. Naia looked back with pain in her eyes, but she left as she was commanded. Zahir gave me a questioning look, but did as he was asked and exited the room with the others.

"Father, I am not ready." Picel croaked out, partly from emotion and partly because he was so weak. "I can't do this without you," he said with the slightest waiver in his voice.

I don't know what I expected him to say, but it most definitely wasn't what came out of his mouth. That was only the second time in my life I had heard Picel not be confident. The first being when Father told him he was going to step down as King and Picel would take his place. He was more qualified and ready to be King than anyone, obviously because he had trained for it, but Picel just radiated "King." If anyone could do it, he could.

Our father didn't respond– he just stared at Picel, then me. After a few moments he began to speak but, before he could get anything audible out, he started coughing… my eyes widened… blood. I panicked. Somehow Picel stayed calm; he was probably too weak to react.

"Zahir! Get back in here!" I shouted, rushing to the side of the bed opposite Picel. My whole body started to tremble.

Blood seeped from the cloth pieces that were packed in his chest and side from the coughing that wracked his body. He was going quickly, and there was nothing I nor anyone else could do. Picel would be the new King in a matter of minutes, or less, and if he didn't make it, the role would fall on me whether I wanted it or not.

Before Zahir reached us, the King's hand went limp and he breathed his last. His pain was no more. He was gone.

I wept silently over his body and felt a hand on my shoulder. Quin. I put my hand on top of his, allowing the touch, and we wept.

After a few moments, I wiped my tears. Picel attempted to stand but collapsed immediately. I rushed to his side and looked at Naia who had entered the room with Zahir. I didn't like her, but at the moment she was the best option to tend to my father. I needed Zahir with Picel.

"Naia, take care of the King, and prepare him for the burning. I will send for some guards to move his body so he won't be laying in this mess."

"I can see to that, your Highness," she offered softly.

"Fine," I said, turning to Picel who was starting to fade.

"Brother, hey, Picel, Stay with me. Please stay with me." I whispered, cradling him in my arms. It wasn't looking good. He looked up at me and his eyes rolled back in his head, his head lulling back as well. "No!" I grunted. "You don't get to leave me too, not today. Picel!"

His breathing was slow, and he didn't have much energy and there was a slight crackle every time he breathed in and out.

"Zahir, we need to get him back to the infirmary," I said, a slight panic lining my voice.

"No, his room is closer; take him there," Naia interjected, looking to Zahir for support.

"She is right. Sire, his room is the best option," Zahir replied.

I rolled my eyes, but nodded and turned to Quinlan to instruct him to keep people quiet until the official announcement was made. He nodded and started speaking to each person who had been in the King's room in the last hour.

Together, Zahir and I half dragged, half carried Picel to his room. Only Quinlan's room separated Picel's and Father's.

Naia, after begging to help with Picel, pulled back the sheets on his bed. Zahir and I laid Picel down as gently as possible. Father could wait. He was already gone. Right now we needed to save my brother.

I began unwrapping his head bandage to change it again while Zahir raced downstairs to get more supplies and medicine. I had tended to injuries before from practice fights among our men with accidental injuries, but I hadn't seen Picel's wound without the bandage until now - an intentional head wound.

When I removed the last layer, I winced. It was bad. I thought he had been sliced with a dagger, but it was deep. The weapon had to have been more like an ax. It penetrated through half of the bone and was a good four inches long. I grabbed the water pitcher from the table and poured it into a bowl. Taking some cloth, I dipped it in and started dabbing the wound, trying to keep it clean. I yelled for a servant to bring some strong liquor to sterilize everything again. I knew Zahir and Naia had both washed the wound earlier, and Naia had stitched it shut, but it was always better to be safe than sorry. Picel moaned as the cloth touched his gash and tried to pull away.

"I know it hurts, Pi," I said as I gently held the other side of his head so he couldn't move. "I know."

We sat in silence then, his breathing getting slower and slower. *What was today? So much death and destruction had taken place in such a little amount of time. Picel I can't lose you too.*

16

NAIA

When I walked back into the room after tending to the King, I saw Javil sitting there, his hands on his brother's face, studying him as he cleaned Picel's head wound again. *So there is a soft side to him. I guess I had seen it before he found out who my mom was. Why had that changed his heart? Maybe I would never know.*

He tensed up as I re-entered, and Zahir whispered in his ear, "We need her, Sire. She is good at her job."

"She doesn't technically work here," Prince Javil mumbled under his breath, but didn't push for me to leave again.

I was glad Zahir and Quinlan trusted me so much. I'd be in the dungeons for sure if they didn't keep standing up for me. *Or dead.*

Zahir got out a medium sized black bottle that was sealed with a cork. It had a white label that said Flax and Honey. He handed me a small wooden spoon and told me to spread it over the wound before rewrapping his head. I was about done securing the bandage when Picel started to struggle. His breathing was too fast, but short, like he couldn't take a full breath. I glanced at Zahir with pleading eyes, begging him to do something. He gravely shook his head.

Javil went into a frenzy, but Zahir grabbed him and sat him down. I sat down next to Picel and gently stroked his hairline, whispering softly that he needed to remain still. Thankfully he listened.

"Sire, upon further inspection, I believe the King has a bruised lung from a blow to his chest in battle. Unfortunately, there is nothing I can do to assist with that." He paused and looked at Javil carefully. "Sire, I need to make you aware. Your brother might not make it through the hour."

My heart sank. I knew he was right that there could be a very good chance Javil would be King by morning, and I would most likely be killed or imprisoned.

Javil stood up slowly and walked over to me as I was ringing out a towel getting ready to wipe Picel's face.

"You did this," he said in a hushed growl.

My eyes dropped to the floor and my heart tightened. "Sire, I-"

"You did this!" He yelled, flipping over the water filled basin on the table next to him. I leaped back, colliding with the wall behind me. His strong hand was on my throat in half a second.

"What were you thinking?" He snarled, leaning in closer. I could feel his breath on my face. I wanted to throw up. *I can't breathe.*

"Javil, let her go," Quinlan demanded, storming into the room. "You have to stop hurting her! This isn't her fault! Let her go. Now," he demanded and started to approach us, but stopped as Javil held up his free hand.

Javil paused, keeping his hand on my throat, but not pressing in harder. *Help! God, please! I can't breathe. Someone do something. Get him off me!*

"Sire, Quinlan is right," Zahir said carefully. "The girl is not at fault here; release your grasp on her. Please. You could damage her vocal chords and her airway. She is too young for this and, on top of that, she's innocent."

Javil stared into my eyes, his nostrils flaring, his jaw fluttering, his breathing heavy. He let go.

I gasped for air, and Quinlan rushed over, grabbing onto me as I fell to the rocky floor below.

"Breathe," he whispered in my ear. "I've got you– it's okay," he said as he shielded my body, not allowing anyone to get close to me. Not allowing Javil to get close to me.

I shuddered as I looked past Quinlan and saw Javil's face. It was filled with pure hatred, pure loathing, complete abhorrence. He looked like he wanted me dead. I wished I *were* dead.

JAVIL

Quinlan glared at me as he held Naia. Anger raged in his eyes. *Why does he protect her? She is the enemy.*

He stated that I should change before going out to the public, and that I needed to "calm down". *The nerve.* I took a shaky breath, furious that he was telling me what to do, but knew he was right. I removed my bloodstained shirt and tossed it on the floor of Picel's room. Quinlan raised his eyebrows, questioning my decision, and I shrugged. Who was he to make sure I acted like a prince? He was only a guard, not my mother.

A servant girl walked in then, and saw the blood soaked shirt crumpled up on the ground. She looked at me, mortified, and sprinted right back out.

I looked down at my bare torso. There were scratches and bruises covering my chest as well and, twisting my head over my shoulder, I could see my back was in similar condition. Zahir got my attention and asked if I wanted assistance or medicine, but I shook my head at him. I could see to it myself.

I wasn't usually this heated, but the stress that had been put on me was almost unbearable, so I let it out the only way I knew how. Anger, blame, and violence.

The night that followed was the longest night of my life. I didn't sleep a wink. I watched Picel constantly. I only took my eyes off him for moments to closely watch Naia as she tended to him throughout the night.

Zahir had left, insisting Naia was more than qualified to care for Picel, who slept through most of the night, but when he was awake, he was in constant and almost unbearable pain, tossing and turning in his bed. In those moments, I gently tried to get him to drink some water or a little of the flax and honey mixture. He would get about half the spoonful down and then would start coughing it back up. It was no use.

"Sire, let me try," Naia would say, fear in her voice, but knew she was tasked with taking care of my brother. Quinlan was at her side the entire time to make sure I didn't come near her again.

Picel took it for her. Why her and not me?

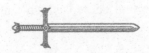

WHEN PRIDE FALLS

He stopped breathing.

Naia had left to get fresh water, and Quin was asleep in a chair by the door. I jumped up and was about to thwack Picel's chest with my fist, when Zahir came through the door, sliding around Quinlan, to bring more ointment. Seeing what I was about to do, he cried out!

"No!" He shrieked. "You mustn't put weight on his chest! It will make him worse!"

"Then what do you expect me to do?" I snarled. "Let my brother, your King, die? Do something!"

The world started spinning. I don't remember the next few minutes. I saw Naia run into the room and Zahir quickly whispered something in her ear. Her eyes widened, but she did what she was asked. I zoned out then and woke up in bed an unknown amount of time later with her infuriating presence at my bedside.

NAIA

Zahir asked me to breathe life into Picel's lungs by physically putting my lips on his and plugging his nose to keep the breath in. I looked at him completely confused, but did what I was told. How I would explain this to Javil and the King himself, I had no idea. Hopefully, they wouldn't take it as anything inappropriate since it was Zahir who instructed me to do it in the first place.

After about five minutes of having my lips on and off the King's, my breathing in and his being forced to exhale, he took a weak breath by himself, then another, slowly getting stronger. I took a shaky breath, as I was light-headed from giving him my breath. Zahir noticed my slight distress and escorted me to a chair, then offered me a cup of water. I took it gratefully and closed my eyes. I was so tired, and hadn't seen sleep in what seemed like a week, but it was probably closer to two days.

Quinlan came back in after getting Javil to bed, pulled a chair up next to me, faced it backwards and sat down resting his chin on the back support.

"Are you okay?" he asked tenderly, as he reached for my neck. *Where Javil choked me.* I jerked backwards.

"I'm sorry, sorry," he said quickly, pulling his hand back. "I just... you didn't deserve that. He normally isn't like this. He just..." he paused, trying to find the right words.

"I get it, he is stressed. I would be too in his situation," I replied, trying to put myself in his shoes.

"Yes, but it's more than that. He has taken it upon himself to be the protector of this place."

"I thought that was your job," I said.

"My job is... was... to protect the King..." Quin's voice trailed off. "Naia, what I am trying to say is Javil's circumstances, while unfortunate, don't justify the way he is treating you," he said plainly. "He needs to be punished."

"I thought you were best friends," I said softly.

"We are."

We shared a small smile, but then Picel started to stir. I hastened to the side of the bed where Zahir was not and talked to him gently, asking him to lie back. He stilled and slipped back into a deep slumber.

I went back to my chair and put my head in my hands. I was so tired. Quinlan read my mind.

"Naia, when was the last time you slept?" He asked, kneeling down next to me.

"Ummm," I said tiredly, "when I was at your parents cottage, before the strange men showed up at their door in the middle of the night."

"You are joking. That's not okay," he said softly. "My room is right next door. Please, go to sleep. I will come get you if Picel wakes up."

"Are you sure?" I asked, wanting to be polite, but also longing for a mattress under my body to hold the weight of my entirety. I truthfully didn't know how I was still standing.

"Yes, I am sure," he said as he carefully helped me to stand and take a few steps.

I took his offered arm, and he led me to the door and pointed to the left. *When had he become my friend and not just my guard?*

"It's the first room there. Rest well, Naia," he said, and then positioned himself back where he could see Picel's sleeping body as I softly closed the door.

I dreamed of home, my family, my friends, before the fire when everything in life was easy, almost perfect.

It seemed like minutes later when I was gently awakened to see Quinlan standing there. I squinted at him.

"Hey… is something wrong?"

"The King would like to see you," he said casually.

I started panicking. My breathing quickened and my heartrate spiked. "Am I in trouble? Did I do something wrong? Why did you let me go to sleep?" I screeched, jumping up as quickly as I could, and then collapsing back onto the bed just as fast as I had stood up. *I really am weak.*

"No, no, no!" he exclaimed. "He wants to thank you," Quinlan said, sitting down next to me on the bed.

"Really?" I asked, not convinced at all. The Prince hated me. *Why would the King want to talk to me other than to scold me for making his brother so upset?*

"Yes," was all he said, extending his hand.

Quinlan escorted me back into the king's chambers and bowed to Picel before leaving me alone with the new King.

"You are Naia? The woman from the Throne Room my father was so taken with?" Wow, what a way to start.

Picel was looking much better. There was more color on his face and there wasn't blood seeping through his bandages anymore. He was sitting up, leaning against the headboard of the bed that was carved into the shape of a lion.

"Yes, your Majesty," I said meekly, still not convinced that I was not in trouble.

"I was told you saved my life more than once," he added. "Is that correct?" He questioned.

"Well, I don't know about that," I said, trying to sound as humble as I could.

"Thank you," he said, with the most sincerity, and took my hand. "Truly, thank you, Naia."

"It was my pleasure, your Majesty," I said, my face reddening in embarrassment when I realized how that could have sounded. My lips *had* been on his for five minutes. He chuckled, noting my accidental choice in wording.

"Sire, I didn't mean, I just," I stumbled over my words.

"Naia, you are okay. Really. I didn't take it that way."

"Oh, good," I breathed, relieved. What a story to tell... *who would I even tell?* I shook the thought away. "Your Majesty, how long have I been asleep?"

Picel looked at me strangely, like that wasn't a normal question to ask the leader of the Kingdom, but graciously replied.

"I am not sure, but my brother has outlasted you. As of twenty minutes ago, he was still deep in slumber," he responded.

He then asked me something that was the last thing I wanted to do but, because he was King, had every right to ask.

"Naia, you have helped me greatly. Might I ask a favor?"

"Of course, your Majesty," I said, eager to help.

"Would you go tend to my brother as well? He needs someone to look after him. I am worried about his mental state." *He doesn't know.*

"Might I *tend* to him?" I repeated hesitantly.

"Yes, would that be alright with you?"

No, no it is not alright. He is abusing me, hitting me, choking me, I can't, I won't. I am sorry, Your Majesty, no. I took a breath, hating my response, but knew it was the right thing to do. Serve, even when inconvenient. Submit to authority. Maybe I could get him to like me… tolerate me. No, it wasn't okay that he was abusing me, but I knew I owed the late king my life, so I was willing to put myself in that situation. *For now.*

"Of course your Majesty. I will ready the supplies right away," I said, dread and fear already building inside me. After giving a small curtsey, I left to get what I would need to tend to the man who hated me more than anything in the world.

19

JAVIL

When I woke up, Naia was holding a cold, damp towel to my face. Quinlan was in the corner tapping his foot, and three guards were standing in my room holding swords at the door. *Quinlan's doing no doubt.*

"Naia," I scowled, looking over at Quinlan.

"What is she doing here?" I shouted.

Quinlan started to speak, but I screamed over him, demanding for everyone to get out. I didn't care what she was doing in my room– I just knew I wanted her gone.

"But, Sire, she was only doing what…" Quinlan said tentatively.

I shoved her away from me and screamed again to get her away. Why couldn't these people respect such a small request?

Quinlan rushed at me, socking me in the jaw. Rage surged through me. I started to rise, but was pinned down by Quin's strong grip. There was a reason he was the King's Guard.

"Enough," He growled in my face.

I scowled, but loosened my body. He released his grip and walked to the door where Naia was waiting.

"Let's go," he instructed her. She followed without protest. She wanted to be away from me as much as I wanted to be away from her.

I was sore, my father was dead, and my brother was dying. He might be dead–I didn't actually know. I didn't want to see anyone, let alone Naia, and she would be with my brother.

I slowly sat up and grimaced. *Ahhh.* I was worse off than I had let on. My wrist was throbbing and the cuts on my skin were on fire. I had just taken off the covers completely to inspect the lacerations on my chest and back. *She* walked back through the door and stood there, consternation lining her face. *Of course.*

"I am here to serve you, Sire," she said, her voice wavering slightly.

"Really?" I scoffed.

"Yes," She replied. "The King-"

"Come here," I commanded. She did. Hesitantly.

"Will you serve me after I do this?" I said, backhanding her across the face. She collapsed to the floor letting out a yelp as she fell. She looked up at me, tears welling in her eyes, and spoke words which surprised me, even more than hearing that my father was dying. "What can I assist you with this morning, your highness?"

"Really?" I gaped. "I choked you and pinned you against a wall, and now have just backhanded your face, and you ask how you can serve me? Who are you?" I sneered.

"I am a servant of your Father, who treated me with kindness, and now, at your brother's request, I am here to tend to you. Whatever you need, I will do it to the best of my ability," she said, standing back up and giving a low, trembling curtsy.

I was taken aback and waved my hand for her to leave.

"Go be useful to someone else. I don't care what my brother said, I am relieving you of your duty to me," I said, turning my back to her. "I have nothing for you to do here."

She stood there, silent, contemplating her options.

"I said get out," I repeated, getting angrier.

"You said you didn't have anything for me to do and that isn't true. You are just too prideful to ask for help," she retorted, motioning to my injured body. *She was asking for it now.*

"Please, let me get you cleaned up. You shouldn't go out and see your people looking how… well, looking how you do. It is not king-like.

I glared at her, and she realized her mistake.

"Sire, that isn't what I meant. The King, your brother, is fine. I saw him through his spell and then he called me in later to have a talk. He… asked me to tend to you." she said.

"Picel is okay?" I asked, momentarily relieved.

"Yes. I saw to him myself last night."

"Did you." I stated.

"Yes, and he lives. Now, at the request of the king, your older brother, I am going to get some clean rags and some fresh water, and I will be back to clean you up," she said kindly, but there was a firm tone.

I looked at her, my mouth wide open, as she turned and left. How dare she think she can boss me around like that. I knew she was terrified of me, but she was also abiding by my brother's wishes. And that gave her a new found strength. That made her a problem.

Not listening to her plans or really caring about them in the slightest, I got up slowly and made my way to my brother's chambers to see for myself if he was as well off as Naia had claimed. If he wasn't, she would pay.

20

NAIA

He was impossible! Why in the world did I think I would be able to do this? Quinlan had made it quite clear that I didn't have to be this man's servant. I could tell the King what his brother had done to me and he wouldn't in a million years make me tend to him, but I wanted to respect Picel's wishes. He had been so kind to me. I also wanted Javil to see that I was not his enemy. I still didn't completely understand why he hated me.

I had always been taught growing up, *Love your enemies,* but this was hard! This guy was so angry! Granted he had just watched his father die before his eyes and had almost witnessed the same with his brother, but so had I with my family, and I wasn't screaming at people.

I grabbed the strips of cloth and the water and, after telling Zahir the situation, I headed back up to the second floor where the Royals' rooms were. On my way, I ran into Quinlan who raised his eyebrows as I walked towards Javil's room. He was so protective over me. Tingles crept over my body and I gave a small, scared smile, and shut the door behind me.

"Sire, I have returned with your…" I sighed. He wasn't there.

I set the things down and walked down the hall to his brother's room and softly cracked open the door.

"Should I trust her, Pi?" Javil was asking. "Father seemed pretty sure she was not a threat, but you are the King now, so I am asking what you think."

Picel coughed and stirred a little. As he did he happened to glance up to see me peeking through the door.

"Ahem," he said, with a small smile and beckoned me inward. I liked him.

"Can we help you, Naia?"

"Oh, um, Your Majesty, I was just looking for Javil to tend to his injuries. When he wasn't in his room, I figured he had come to visit you, Your Majesty." I said with a slight curtsy and bow of my head.

"Ah, impossible this one, isn't he?" he said, nudging his brother and giving me another small smile. Javil rolled his eyes. *Was the King flirting with me?*

I had always thought kings were supposed to be professional and always serious. It was nice to see a king who was willing to have some fun. I wasn't expecting that from what I had heard about how seriously King Picel had taken his role of learning to rule. He spent just under ten intense years preparing. It was a big deal for him. Looking over at his brother, he was having the same thoughts. Confusion was spreading on Javil's face. And he spoke, confirming my thoughts.

"Picel, what are you doing? Why are you smiling? You almost died, Father is dead, and we have an enemy in the room. How are you joking around with her?! Who are you and what have you done with my brother?"

"Javil, relax," he said, as relaxed as can be. Maybe almost dying had changed his thought process– how he looked at life. "No, I don't Naia had anything to do with our father's death. She took care of me last night. There is not an evil bone in her body. Be at peace, brother."

Javil looked at his brother, questioning every word, but ended up nodding his head in submission.

"Fine, but you will tend to me here, so I can remain at my brother's side. I will not leave him again."

"As you wish, Sire." I said, exiting to go get the cloth pieces and water bowl from his room.

Upon returning, I convinced Javil with great difficulty to take his shirt off that he had put back on in my absence so I could tend to his wounds. I felt so much safer with Picel in the room. There was no way that Javil would lay his hands on me with his brother present.

He laid down on the bed opposite his brother and looked up at me smirking. He really was enjoying seeing me uncomfortable.

"Your Majesty," I said, turning to the king. "Do you have any liquor in here by chance? I need to clean some of these deeper cuts to make sure they don't get infected."

"Sure, it's in the cabinet over on the far wall," he replied.

"Thank you."

I wetted a cloth in water and another in the liquor and then turned to Javil, holding up the cloth.

"Sire, this is going to sting a little. Would you like a strap of leather to bite down on?"

"You can't hurt me," he snarled. "I am a warrior. A Prince!"

That's a no on the leather.

Moments later the liquor made contact with the broken skin. He tensed and let out a mangled moan.

"Can't hurt you, huh?" Picel said, laughing. I'm glad he found this funny, because I was scared for my life.

"Shut up, Picel," Javil said, swatting at him lightly, taking into consideration his brother's lingering injuries.

I smiled slightly, enjoying the brothers playful banter, even in my fear, and continued dabbing Javil's cuts with the cloth. Javil stopped moaning and grunting after the first two, but was still tense. You could see his muscles flexing as he was trying to show that he could feel no pain, but his hands were clenched in the sheets, and his breathing ragged, proving otherwise. *So prideful and stubborn.* I sighed.

How did I even end up doing this? I guess I was stubborn too. *At least I got to make him miserable in the process,* I started to think, but corrected my thoughts. *Love your enemies.*

As I tended to Javil, I remembered the days when I was running through the forest with my friends without a care in the world except having to do my studies and be home in time for dinner. Those were the days. I missed mom's cooking. She would bake the best chicken and dumplings. She would send dad to trade clothes she had made for flour and yeast to make bread. It was my favorite thing to come home to. We would all sit around the table and tell each other about our day and laugh and mess around. Before dinner, mother would be sewing, creating, fixing clothes. She had been a seamstress, which was not normal in Rowynala, but I guess every village needed one or two.

It was such a simple life. I wished I could go back to living that way, but it will probably never happen again. I was here now, a servant to an impossible prince, and I had to accept my new life. At least I wasn't still wandering in the desert.

"Naia, Naia, goodness woman, answer me when I am speaking to you!" I heard suddenly, Javil, shoving my hand away and sitting up on the edge of the bed.

I saw Picel tense. *He didn't like his brother's actions. Would he intervene?*

"You have been dabbing the same wound for ten minutes, and it *hurts!* What the heck are you daydreaming about?" He spat.

"Sire, I am so sorry. I was thinking about home, my parents, my brother. They all died two weeks ago. I just…" *Don't cry. Don't do it, Naia…* "I miss them." I went to wipe a falling tear, but Javil grabbed my wrist and pulled me towards him, forgetting where we were.

"I don't like this any more than you do, so I suggest that you hurry this up so we can be done with it. Do you understand?" He gritted.

"Javil, calm yourself," Picel said, trying to relax his brother. But that only aggravated Javil even more.

"Calm myself? Calm myself? Father is dead, you almost died, and this… this girl," He shouted as he flung me back, "is going to ruin everything that father ever worked for! Don't tell me to be calm!"

At that moment Quinlan walked through the door. Feeling the tension in the room he spoke quickly. "Javil," he said, nodding to the prince. "The people are awaiting the news. The castle is in eager anticipation. Are you ready to tell them?" He noticed me and gave a small smile, then a worried glance after seeing what I had been tasked with, or rather *who* I had been tasked with. "Does it look like I am ready, Quin?" he growled. I had noticed that he did that a lot. Growled.

"I'm sorry, Sire. I will leave you to… whatever it is you are doing." He started walking towards the door.

"Javil, brother," Picel said, struggling to sit up against the head-board. He was still so weak.

Quinlan rushed over as Javil turned around. They managed to get the King into a sitting position, but the effort left him drenched in sweat and drained of energy. I felt so badly for him. He was the new King, taking over after the death of his father, but he wasn't even able to get out of bed without assistance. I couldn't imagine what that must be like. At least he was in good spirits. He was handling the whole situation fairly well, unlike his younger brother.

Then I thought of Javil and the agony he was in after losing his father and having his brother be in such a horrible state. I had heard that Javil had never wanted to be King. Now he was being forced to take responsibility because his brother was unable to. It humbled me a little. *Love those who hurt you. Pray for those who put you down. Breathe.*

As a kid my parents had taught me to put myself in other people's shoes, to try to understand why they were acting the way they were. It was supposed to make me less selfish. I had my moments, but usually I was pretty good about taking a breath to think about what they might be going through. And in this case I already knew. And I couldn't begin to fathom the pain coursing through both Javil and Picel, and what they were having to deal with both emotionally and physically.

"... change your attitude, do you understand me?"

I caught the end of the king lecturing his younger brother on how to behave.

Javil nodded, clearly annoyed, but he had received an order from the King and would comply. For now.

"Now," King Picel continued, "would you please go address the castle and update them on the circumstances or at least help me get out of bed so I can?" He said, eyebrows raised. *Don't question me,* I was sure was what he was thinking.

"I don't think you should leave your room yet, brother," Javil said quickly as he stood. "I will go."

"Thank you," the King said, his face relaxing a little.

He then turned to me, giving me a pained smile.

"Naia, would you be so kind as to help my brother dress appropriately for his address to the castle? And when you have completed that, return to me please." *How could he be so ignorant of what was happening?*

"Yes, your Majesty. Right away." I glanced at Javil who had stopped dead in his tracks, thinking the same thing, and then I walked out the door. Javil would follow; his brother would see to that.

JAVIL

When I got to the room, after some convincing from Picel, she had already laid out, on my bed, a few options of clothing to wear. I had never had a servant do that before. There were never options. I looked at her quizzically as she stood there in silence, waiting for further instruction. She was different. I would give her that. Kind, even when I had hit her, and compassionate, even after my yelling. I didn't get it, but I noticed.

I decided to try being nice. My brother had told me that if I wasn't there would be consequences. *What harm can it do?*

There were three outfits. One was navy and silver themed, another green and gold, and the third red and black. I looked over at Naia and motioned for her to join me. She distrustfully walked over and stood a few feet away from me.

"What one do you like?" I asked, waving my arm carelessly towards the clothing.

"Me, Sire?" she replied, timidly.

"Yes, you," I spat. "Who else?"

"Well, I would lean towards the navy and silver."

"Why?" I inquired.

"The gold, I think, should be reserved for the king, at least from stories, but I wasn't certain how things worked here, so I set it out just in case. The red and black make you look like a villain; I think the navy and silver would best suit the occasion. I could put some others together if you prefer," she added.

"No, I will go with the navy and silver. Thank you. Would you kindly grab a fresh white shirt from my drawer?" *Kindly?* I shuddered. *Who am I?*

"Of course, Sire," she said with a quick curtsy.

While she turned around to grab the shirt, I quickly changed my pants from black to white and stood before her as she held out the shirt for me to put my arms through. It was hard to move because of my injuries, but she was so gentle and careful with her movements I almost didn't notice. I stood there as she buttoned me up, leaving the last few undone, then reconsidering, buttoned the last two except the top. From there, she grabbed the navy vest and buttoned that and then the overcoat. Lastly, she draped the matching cloak over my shoulders, as winter was in full swing, curtsied again, and stepped away.

I looked in the broken mirror I had in my chambers. I had gotten mad one day a few years back and had smashed it. I didn't want my father to know, so I covered it and hadn't requested a new one.

I looked at myself and realized how messy my curls were. I looked at Naia and sighed while pointing to my head. She nodded, and went to get a brush and some water.

"Why are you being so kind to me?" I asked suddenly. I caught myself off guard asking her that, but not her. She turned around and walked back towards me, a kind look of sympathy on her face. All she said in response, "Why not?"

Why not? Why not? I was deeply moved by her response. So much so, that I felt... feelings. She had to go.

"I can tend to my hair; you are free to go tend to the king. Thank you for your help. Goodbye." I said, quickly escorting her out of my door and into the hall.

"But, Sire! You still need-" I cut her off, slamming the door in her face. I couldn't do it. Be kind to her. She was so aggravating with her kindness and selfless heart.

I punched the wall- barely keeping myself from screaming when I did so. Instead I let out a growl.

She heard the commotion. She hadn't left the doorway.

"Sire, are you alright?" She asked gently from the hall.

"Leave me alone, Naia!" I snarled.

Silence.

I opened the door.

She was there.

I raised my hand.

I swung.

22

NAIA

N o one was in the hall when it happened.

It wasn't a backhanded swing this time. He lifted his arm and stepped towards me. Before I could react, he hit me so quickly and powerfully. With every ounce of strength that he had. He was letting every ounce of pain, anger, sadness, and fear go, all onto me. Pain radiated all across my face; my cheek felt like it was on fire. The scathing sting as the blood flowed through my face, let me know something was not how it was supposed to be. He smacked me so hard that I flew into the wall and collapsed onto the floor. Blood trickled down the side of my head where I had made contact with the rock wall. I wouldn't cry. No way. I would not give him the satisfaction.

I moved to my knees and looked up at him.

So many emotions were going across his face as he realized what he had just done. It almost looked like regret. Almost.

"Naia, I…" he stopped. He walked away, rubbing his hands through his hair as he did. It was only when he rounded the corner to go upstairs that I let the tears fall.

I don't know how long I had been in the cold, rocky, corner, but because it wasn't a public walkway, and everyone was gathered in the courtyard waiting for Javil to arrive, it could have been hours. I woke up, curled in the corner, to a familiar and safe voice. "Naia, hey, Naia. Are you okay?"

I opened my eyes and saw Quinlan crouching next to me, one hand on his knee, the other on my face. I recoiled, hitting the back of my head on the wall behind me and cringed.

"Woah, hey, it's okay. It's just me," he looked at me, fear in his eyes. His mouth was twisted into a perplexed scowl as he tried to figure out what had happened to me.

He traced the back of my neck, brushing my hair away to reveal my neck and saw the bruise that had formed from Javil's choking me before. He gasped and pulled back, looking into my eyes. Devastation. Anger. Pain. *He hurts for me. Why?* He leaned in closer and grazed just under my eye with the tip of his thumb and I whimpered. He exhaled with his jaw clenched and his eyes searched mine.

I brought my hand to my face, biting my thumb as a tear escaped. He slowly wiped it away. I let him, though, still not speaking.

"Naia," he whispered. "Did Javil do this?" I said nothing, and the tears came again. I couldn't speak. I couldn't breathe.

"Can I carry you?" Quin asked, interrupting my thoughts. He was almost begging.

I could feel the strength had been drained from my legs. If I tried to stand they would be so wobbly, like a person who had had too much to drink and couldn't walk straight. I had never experienced that sensation, but had seen others who had. I gave a small nod.

His arms tightened around me the minute he had me secured in them. I leaned into his safe embrace as he took me to where the guest rooms were located. My head nestled on his warm neck. He placed me on one of the beds, carefully pulled back the covers, then lifted me up and eased my legs underneath.

As I lay there, he fetched a servant to bring some warm water and liquor to wash my head and some bread and stew for me to eat. I was grateful to him for thinking of food.

"What time of day is it?" I asked.

"Evening. When did he- How long were you out there?"

"I don't know," I said just above a whisper.

"No one comes up here, Naia," he said, really talking to himself. He was trying to put it all together. "He wouldn't go this far, would he?" He paused and looked at me with uncertainty and hesitated before continuing. His eyebrows were scrunched together and he was pacing back and forth when, suddenly he sat down on the edge of the bed, clearly uncomfortable.

"Naia, tell me. Please?" He begged, reaching to move some hair out of my eyes, clearly set on hearing the answer directly from my mouth.

I knew I couldn't say what really happened, there was no point. It would just put me at more risk. So I lied.

"Quinlan, I fell," I said quietly. "I have been through a great ordeal, you know that, and must have collapsed, stumbling into the wall and falling. It has been since yesterday since I've eaten anything, a full meal at least. That would explain everything."

"Yes, it would, wouldn't it?" Quin stated, clearly not believing a word I was saying. *He knows the truth.*

"So your story is, you fell from malnourishment and landed hard enough that you hit the wall, started to bleed and passed out, to be found by me hours later?"

I couldn't tell him. I couldn't risk Javil finding out I had ratted him out. Even though Quin had already seen him abuse me before, I felt this was the next level.

"I… Yes, that is what happened." I finally got out. I couldn't do it. I just couldn't.

I could tell he didn't believe me based on the hesitancy in his eyes. As he was about to confront me again, the servant came through the door with the requested items.

"Sir, here are the things you asked for," she said, placing them on the table next to the bed. "Is there anything else you need? Would you like help cleaning her up?" she asked, looking over at me.

"No, that will be all, thank you," he replied firmly, and she left, shutting the door behind her.

We were alone again.

He grabbed a cloth and dipped it in the water bowl, wrung it out a little, and then sat down on the edge of the bed, reaching across my body to reach the gash on my head.

He sat there in silence, as he lightly dabbed the cloth on my wound, trying as hard as he could not to hurt me.

He sighed and gave me a pained look. "You need stitches, Naia."

That was the last thing I wanted to hear, but he was right. It had been hours, and there was still blood trickling from the wound. I had probably lost too much blood already. He saw another servant pass by in the hall and asked her to fetch Zahir as quickly as she could. She nodded in obedience and took off down the stairs.

While we waited for Zahir to arrive, he took a damp cloth and held it against my head wound with his left hand, while he held my neck with his right, lightly rubbing his thumb across my face where my jaw and ear met.

His shoulder length brown hair danced in the rays of the setting sun that shone through the window. His dark brown eyes were intently watching me, making sure I was ok. I couldn't take it anymore, his arms flexing as he tensely dipped the cloth in the water, his soft smile *telling me everything would be okay.* I started to panic. My breathing intensified and I started to thrash around a little.

Quin took that as my being in more pain, so he gently started stroking my arm and whispering encouragement to me.

"Stop touching me!" I shrieked, finally breaking. It was all too much, everything. The attack on my village, the attack on the castle, King Zaxton being murdered, me being abused, and then being smothered in affection. I couldn't take it anymore. *I want to go home.*

"Naia, I… I'm sorry, I thought…"

I started sobbing, Quin started to come to my aid, but hesitated unsure what to do after my outburst. He resorted to sitting on the edge of the bed, facing out, his hands in his lap and his head hanging low.

"Quin. No, it's not your fault. I am sorry," I managed through sobs. I just got so overwhelmed and I couldn't breathe, and I couldn't think and I…"

"Naia," he said, cautiously placing one hand on mine. "You don't have to apologize. I understand." I nodded and turned away. I felt so badly I had yelled at him.

There was a knock on the door and Zahir entered with the suture kit. I winced, knowing what was to come. I had spent the day yesterday stitching up warriors, I was not looking forward to the pain that awaited me.

Zahir took one look at me and then motioned for Quinlan to follow him outside. Quinlan did not look happy to leave me, but he reluctantly followed.

They whispered for a while. I couldn't make out what they were saying, but when they walked back in I noticed Quinlan seemed really aggravated.

Zahir approached my bed slowly and reached out to take the cloth off my head to inspect the damage. I flinched when he made contact with me, and Quinlan lurched forward in protective mode, even though Zahir was only doing his job. I looked over at his worried face and gently smiled, assuring him that I was okay.

Gently brushing away some hair that had fallen in the path of the gash, Zahir looked at me and then at Quinlan. He spoke, preparing me.

"Naia, this is going to hurt. Quinlan is going to have to hold you down while I do this. Are you going to be okay with that?" *He knows. He knows I didn't really fall and had told Quinlan. Oh no.*

Quinlan walked over and sat on the bed opposite Zahir and looked at me troublesomely. He didn't want to do it. Hold me down. It was going to kill him. I gave him an unconvincing nod of encouragement, and he placed a hand lightly on my neck where it met my shoulder, and then immediately removed it. It was where the bruise was forming from when Javil had choked me. "Naia," he breathed. "This... Zahir, I can't do this. I can't knowingly be a part of something I know will cause her excruciating pain." He grunted, walking away.

Zahir looked at him, understandingly, but said, "you don't have a choice Quinlan. Like she doesn't. She needs help; we have to help her even if it will be uncomfortable for us. For her, it will be worse." He turned to me. "I am sorry, Naia, but you need to hear the truth. This will be terribly painful, but I know you can do it, and we will be here the whole time. Quinlan, hold her," he repeated, firmer this time, but still had understanding in his tone.

Quinlan hesitated, then put each of his strong hands on both of my arms at my elbow, and pushed down on my biceps with his thumbs to secure me. His breathing was so heavy. His eyes, pained. I closed my eyes. I couldn't look at the pain on his face. I hated that he was hurting for me. I thought I was ready, but when the needle hit my skin- I wasn't prepared for what was going to happen.

Piercing pain. Stars. I screamed, thrashed around, and screamed again. That was only the first stitch. By the third, Zahir had instructed Quinlan to move behind me so he was straddling my body. His legs wrapped over top of mine locking down my knees. His left arm held both my arms at my sides, and his right hand held my head firmly at my jaw.

They had put a leather strap in my mouth to bite down on and muffle my screams so as to not disturb everyone else in the castle as much as possible. Sweat poured from Quinlan's face. He held me firmly, but yet with gentleness as I sobbed, whispering in my ear that everything would be okay, the pain would be over soon. Oh, how I wanted to believe him. How he managed to hold me there for seven stitches, I had no idea.

Zahir finally finished and sat back in the chair, exhausted from his efforts. Quinlan held me in his arms, softly stroking the side of my head that wasn't covered in stitches. "It's done, it's over. I'm here, Naia. I'm here."

I cried and cried. I had been strong all day. I was in the protective arms of a man, who I was pretty sure would do absolutely anything for me at this point, and I was safe. So I cried. And that was okay.

JAVIL

What did I just do? I thought as I walked up to the overlook to make the announcement about my father. I had been angry before, but I had never hit a woman, not before her. That was beneath me. Enemy or not. *If Picel finds out,* I need to swear her to secrecy. No one could know it was I who had done it. What would that say about me, about how this place was run? Granted, Picel was King, not me, so that was in my favor, but I was in charge until he was able to take over completely. I had messed up big time.

I made it to the top of the steps and rounded the corner to the balcony, the overlook of the courtyard. Every castle member and castle staff was there waiting there for me. I stepped out and began to speak.

"Unfortunately, I bring grave news today. You might be wondering where my father, the king is, or even my older brother. The reason I am standing before you today is because King Zaxton is dead. He was murdered last night in cold blood. The Crown Prince was gravely injured in the battle and is to remain in his chambers until released by Zahir. Therefore, that leaves me to run things until Picel is fit to do so. I know this is not what any of us planned. You all know my feelings about being in charge or the acting king, but even though this isn't what any of us wanted, it is how it will be. Any questions, comments, or concerns will be directed to me for the time being, not Picel. Is this understood?"

A murmur of yesses went through the crowd. A man yelled out from the back. "Will there be a service for King Zaxton, Sire?"

"Yes, I will be conferring with my brother today or tomorrow, and we will let everyone know when final arrangements have been made." I paused. "Anything else?"

"Will King Picel have a coronation?"

"Again, I will speak with him and keep you all posted."

"Is he going to survive?" A voice called from the right.

I glared in the direction of the voice, but my mother's voice rang in my head just then, and said, *Don't do it. Stay calm.* So I answered him by voicing Picel was looking good, and he was getting better day by day.

I made my way back to Picel's room to sulk. I hated being in charge. I hated Picel for getting hurt, and I hated myself for allowing it to happen. I had failed my job, and now I had to do his and mine.

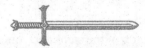

I met Quinlan in the hall outside Picel's room.

He looked awful. He glared at me and then walked towards the guest area, slamming the connecting door behind him. *What's up with him?*

I followed him and saw him going into one of the smaller guest rooms that was usually used for a teenager or two of a merchant visitor.

I peeked inside and saw Quinlan talking to Zahir while someone lay on the bed… *Her.*

I burst through the door.

"Naia, what on earth could you possibly need so much that is keeping Quinlan and Zahir from doing their jobs?" I yelled at her, not realizing she was asleep and couldn't hear me.

Quinlan growled, lunged at me, shoved me into the wall, and then grabbed my throat, pinning me against it.

"Why did you do it?" He screamed, which woke Naia in a fright. She started whimpering for Quinlan to stop, but he didn't listen.

Zahir was on top of us in an instant, prying Quinlan's hand off my neck and dragging him away. I gasped for air, clutching my chest, trying to get a breath. Quinlan was furious and punched at me, but hit Zahir across the jaw and sent him flying and colliding with the doorframe.

"Enough! Stop, stop, stop!" Naia's cries loudened. "Please!" But none of us were listening. We were in too deep, rolling around on the floor, acting more like boys than the warriors and royalty we were. We were pretty evenly matched though; the fight could have gone on for a while if Zahir hadn't been in the room. He was clearly a medic, not a warrior, but he surprised me. He threw a mean punch. I grabbed Quinlan, getting elbowed in the ribs in the process, and Zahir grabbed me, separating us again, blood trickling out of his mouth from Quin's punch.

"You selfish jerk, What has she *ever* done to you?" Quinlan screamed, throwing another punch as Naia begged him to calm down, but he didn't let up. I was livid.

"You know who she is, Quin! How dare you take her side, protect her. What kind of Captain are you? You are the King's Guard! Act like it! Enforce the rules!" I stepped back. "Get her out of here. I don't care what *you* do, but *she* is not welcome here!" I yelled, pointing aggressively.

"I don't care who she is, Javil," Quinlan growled. "She had nothing to do with any of it. I don't even think she knows who she is," he said, now looking at her and walking over to her, taking her face in his hands as she cried.

"What is this?" I growled.

Quinlan froze, he knew he had crossed the line. Standing up for her was one thing, but touching her, comforting her, that was a whole other level of betrayal to me and he knew it.

"Get out of my sight," I growled, my eyes darkening, staring hard at Quinlan. It wasn't an option.

"I'm not leaving her, Javil."

"Quinlan, this is an order from your acting King. Do as you're told. *Now.*"

Quin glared at me, then sighed, dropping his hands from her face, and reluctantly walked out of the door, looking back at me, then Naia, worried of what I would do next.

Naia reached for him and whimpered as he left. She looked so confused and scared. Quinlan was right of course; she didn't have any idea of who she was, but I didn't care. She was a threat, and I would treat her as such.

I started pacing slowly, trying to figure out what to do with her. I could send her to the dungeons, kill her, put her to work. I knew Picel fancied her, not in a romantic way, but in a 'you saved my life, and I am grateful' kind of way.

"Sire," she said timidly. "Please… I"

But I didn't wait to hear what she had to say. I didn't have to listen to it. I walked out without another word.

24

PICEL

Naia never returned to me. I was starting to get worried when Javil came bursting through the door to my room. He was furious.

"What happened, Javil?" I questioned, but he looked at me for about ten seconds and then stormed back out.

What was that about?

Javil had been acting so strangely. I knew he thought Naia was an enemy, even with what Father had told us, but she had been nothing but kind and caring, a servant to me. I liked her. I wished he would see reason. She'd lost her family like we'd lost ours. We understood each other, but since Javil had found out who she was, not even I could change his mind, and I usually had that ability. He usually listened to me.

Javil came back a while later, and we started discussing the recent events and the plans for father's burial.

"Whoever murdered Father is king. Why would they murder him and not claim their place?"

"I don't know, but we have to be prepared for another attack or something else to happen," Javil warned.

Javil and I decided that Father would want a burning, so an enemy wouldn't be able to disrespect his body in any way. Exhuming a body was quite common, and we needed to protect our father from that at all cost.

It was to be held in one week's time, to the west of the Oasis so that we could see the setting sun as our father went up in flames. We decided on having a public burning for our father and a private coronation for my becoming king. I wanted the people to be able to grieve their king's death- later on we could have a bigger celebration next year when I was originally supposed to have been crowned.

After Javil left, Zahir came up to help me get used to walking again. "If you are going to get better, you need to gain your strength," he said. "It is going to be painful, but you will heal so much faster."

And he was right–I did.

"Picel, Your Majesty," Quin said, knocking on my door.

"Quin, enter, please!" I said. I was working on getting out of bed at the time of his arrival.

"Picel, do you need help? Can I be of assistance?" He inquired as he opened the door and saw my footing waiver.

"No, no, I am quite all right. Zahir said it is good for me to struggle at times. It builds strength." Quin nodded. He looked troubled.

"Quinlan, what ails you?"

He paused contemplating if it was worth telling me his problem. "I…" He hesitated.

"Quin, what is it? Talk to me please. I know I am King, and you are now my guard technically, but aren't we still friends?"

He paused, "this is a matter for my king and not my friend. It… it concerns your brother."

"What is wrong with Javil?" I asked, beginning to worry.

"There is nothing wrong with him per say, but more something that he is doing that is wrong. I hesitate to bring this to you, Javil is my friend, but people's lives- a girl's life is at stake."

"Quin, tell me," I commanded. I knew what he would say, and I feared the repercussions of what I would have to do to make it right.

"Javil is, he…" He sighed. "Javil is abusing Naia. He is hitting her, throwing her into walls, strangling her… I know you have seen it a little… but it is worsening and I can no longer tolerate it. Something must be done!" Quin said as he paced my room.

I sighed. "I feared this is what you would bring to me."

"I know that he's your brother, and that puts you in a really hard place but, Naia, she doesn't deserve what he's doing to her. She is just a girl."

"I know, Quinlan, I know. I will see Javil's punishment fitting of how he has treated her. Maybe it will teach him."

"I doubt it," Quin mumbled under his breath.

I let it slide. I doubted it too.

25

JAVIL

hree lashes to my back. That is what Picel gave me for how I was treating Naia. He let Quin do it. He enjoyed it. How dare he. I am his superior! I am his Prince. I hated Picel for letting him. Naia is a threat! She deserved what I had done. She deserved it.

The day of the burning came a week after Father's death, and I was getting ready in my room. I was buttoning up my undershirt when there was a knock at the door.

"Come in," I answered.

"Javil?"

My heart leapt. It was Picel. He was out of bed!

I got choked up as I said, "Come in."

He opened the door and I immediately bowed, getting onto one knee. My Brother, my King, was standing before me. Alive and well. Mostly.

I stood at his request, completely in awe of Picel's presence.

"Picel, I... wow, you look magnificent."

He was wearing a black tunic suit, lined with gold and designs on all the openings and was detailed at the neck with a v-shaped golden line that followed the buttons down to his sternum. His pants were black as well and were tucked in just below his knees into almost knee-high golden boots laced in black leather. He wore a belt that could carry his sword and a dagger for back up. To finish off the look, he had on a gold cloak that brushed the floor as he walked and leather gloves to cover his hands. *Magnificent.*

"Are you almost ready, Javil? We need to start going to the burning site."

"Yes, just give me five minutes."

"I'll meet you at the stables," he said.

A burden lifted from my shoulders. My brother was alive. He was King. I didn't have to deal with any of this, anymore, if I didn't want to. It was not my job now. However if he asked, I would assist in whatever my brother needed.

In burning the dead, usually it was just the family who attended, but today it was the King The whole Kingdom of Arilos showed up, minus the guards who were on duty at the castle. *A perfect time for an attack,* I thought, but quickly shoved the idea away. Today was not the day to think of worse case scenarios.

My father had already been laid on the rock platform when we arrived, his wounds not visible, in respect for him. Picel and I walked silently to the front of the platform and Quinlan gave me a concerned look as he approached from behind.

Father had been put into a royal blue suit that was similar to mine- white pants and his crown. Picel and I decided no one should wear that but him. I laid his crest necklace on his chest. A Lion. The King of the Pride. A tear slipped down my cheek as I placed my hand on his chest where someone had stabbed him endlessly. We still didn't know who. Thankfully his face hadn't been injured, so the people could see him one last time.

Picel and I paid our respects and moved aside allowing the rest of Arilos to pay their respects as well. As the day went on, you could barely see my father under the many flowers and gifts which would go up in flames alongside him when nightfall came. Until then everyone mingled. There was music playing and a feast, celebrating the life of King Zaxton.

"I remember one time when Javil and I were little." Picel spoke to a group of us. "It was after dark and we wanted to go for a swim. Dad and Mom were throwing a banquet of sorts and Javil and I were getting restless.

I think Javil was four... Do you remember this, brother?" He asked, looking at me and I shook my head.

"Ah, then you are in for a treat... Javil didn't really know how to swim- like I said, he was four. We were at the oasis after being told not to leave the castle walls and, having been told time and time again to not swim without an adult. Well, being almost nine, I decided I was adult enough to take care of myself and my little brother. We were wading in the shallow end when we hit a drop off. I could swim, but Javil went straight to the bottom. I managed to sprint to the front screaming my head off and Father, in his best formal wear, came barreling out and dove into the oasis in his entire get up. He got Javil out, gave us the sternest talking to, and walked back into the banquet dripping wet. He locked us in our rooms for the night and went back down to the festivities. He was livid. I still can't believe he jumped in fully dressed like that."

I laughed, picturing the scene. *I wish I remembered that.*

"Do you remember the time our father told us that he had been struck by lightning before he became king?"

"Yes! I can't believe he survived that. That is how he met Zahir, did you know?"

More stories about Father went around the people, laughing, crying, and yelling at times, not angrily, but in the way of people trying to get their stories straight.

Nightfall came and we went back over to where my father had been laid, wood now surrounded his resting place. I grabbed the oil and drizzled it over my father's body. Picel did the same. Once he was properly covered, Picel went for the flame. He hovered the torch over his head for a moment and listened to the crackle of the flames. This was the last time we would see our father. It was almost unbearable, but it was time to let him go- time to move on. He dropped the torch and the night sky was lit up once again. The people left a few at a time for the next few hours until it was Quinlan, Picel, and I.

We sat around the flames, obvious tension between Quilan and myself. The silent glares, the short sentences.

Finally, Picel had had enough.

"What in the world is going on with you two? You have barely spoken a word to each other the last few days. What happened?"

"Ask *him*," I said coldly, gesturing at Quinlan.

He sighed deeply and put his head in his hands.

"Picel, I fell for her."

"Who?" My brother curiously asked. As far as I knew, he had no idea what had been going on, other than that I had hit Naia and was punished for it.

"Naia, the servant girl, the... you know."

"Oh," he said. I looked at him, clearly annoyed, and he sighed.

"And you don't like her, Javil, because?"

"Not like her? Picel! He is hitting her and throwing her into walls!" Quinlan yelled before I could speak.

"Don't play dumb, brother," I interrupted. "You know exactly why I don't like her."

"So you are hitting her?"

I was getting much more aggravated.

"Seriously, Picel, why don't you care?"

"I do care! About how you are treating her! Tell me, has she done anything to lead you to believe she has ulterior motives?"

"No."

"Has she lied to you or deceived you in any way?"

"Not that I am aware of."

"Has she tended to everything that has been asked of her? Stitching up soldiers and tending to both you, me, Father, and Quinlan in our times of need?"

"Yes," I responded glumly.

"Then I have no reason to worry and neither do you. Let it go, brother. She is not her mother." Picel said with finality.

"But Quinlan..." I started

"Quinlan has chosen a lovely woman to fall for. Let him be happy." Picel finished. And that was it.

We sat in silence for a while as there was nothing more to say. We wanted to respect Father, but also didn't want to talk to each other. No words were said until there was an unsettling noise in the dark night behind us.

26

JAVIL

Getting attacked by villagers that night was the last thing any of us expected. Picel whipped around, sword flying from its sheath. It was up and in position above his shoulders in less than two seconds. He swung high and hit flesh. The man cried out and landed on the ground next to us with a thud. Dead.

He was quick for someone who had only days before been allowed to leave his bed. I was impressed. He was surely a fighter.

"We needed him alive!" I yelled. "We needed information. Picel, come on, brother, use your head!" I screamed, still frustrated at the conversation from earlier.

"Good thing there's more where he came from," Picel responded, grunting as he took out another guy. This time he went low and made contact with the man's leg. The man wailed and fell to the ground. I grabbed some rope from my travel bag and tied him up, tying off the wound so he didn't die from blood loss while we fought the others.

In the dimness of the dying fire, I could make out five other enemy warriors closing in. I hadn't had much time to train since I had to tend to my brother, but I had enough practice. It was like riding a horse. I immediately went to Picel's side, and we stood back to back, with Quinlan in front of us.

All five men attacked at once. I made sure I took on two, and Quinlan did the same so Picel would only have to deal with one in his weakened physical state. I crossed blades with one, while spinning backwards to kick the other. On my way back around I lost my grip on the other sword, and was about to raise mine to strike again, when I took a blow to my jaw. I fell to my knees and Picel moved in front of me, blocking me from a deadly blow. He screamed in aggravation. He knew he was not going to let anyone get to me. He was king. He was the strongest. At least that is what he portrayed to our enemies, though at the time it was far from true. They would never know he had been near death only days before. Quinlan moved to Picel's side as I struggled to stand back up, but it was too late. The enemies had overtaken Quin and Picel and were tying them up. They had me pinned down.

Picel tried to make a move forward to escape, but was stopped with a spear at his throat. I froze, not wanting to make any sudden movements that could risk my brother's life. We were at odds about Naia, and I was mad that he had allowed my beating, but he was still my brother. I would still protect him at all costs.

"If you interfere, the king will die," the enemy told him. "I would back off if I were you."

Picel looked at me, making sure he had heard the man correctly. *They thought I was king.* I was okay with that. I gave a slight nod and he hesitantly stepped back.

"Very good choice," another warrior said. "We don't wish to kill you. Our leader has requested to see you."

I looked at Picel who was seething in anger. He was trying not to blow. I was his little brother. It was in his blood to protect me, too. He couldn't this time without risking all our lives, and it was killing him.

I turned back to my captors and spoke confidently with no waver in my voice. Strong, brave, a king. *Or so they thought.*

"I will go with you willingly. No fight, if you let my brother and the other warrior go," I stated. Clearly they didn't want me dead, at least not yet. I needed to see what they wanted, and I knew Picel or Quin would get in the way if they tried to come with me.

The enemy men stepped aside to confer while Picel and Quinlan shouted words of opposition, clearly not in agreement with the offer I had made, but it made sense. Picel was needed to run the castle. Quinlan's job was to protect Picel. Not me. I stood in silence, my hands at my side, awaiting the enemy's decision.

"It will be as you have asked, but know that we will not untie your companions; they will have to do that themselves," he said as he took all the weapons we had and shoved them into a side bag of horses that had appeared with more enemy riders.

"Fine," I said.

"Javil, no, what are you thinking? They will kill you. You can't do this! I forbid you to do this! We will fight our way out!" Picel begged angrily.

I looked over at Quinlan and raised my eyebrows in question. Would he oppose me? He slowly lowered his head in respect of my decision. Though, clearly not liking it either, he understood that I was protecting the King.

They grabbed me then, tied me up for good measure, and threw me on top of a horse led by another rider.

I looked back and saw Picel and Quinlan already attempting to undo their binds, but it was no use. They were too tight. They would have to walk back to the castle and have someone else do it for them. I hurt for my brother. Having our father die, then having me taken by the enemy, I still hadn't figured out who, but I didn't have a choice. If I wanted my brother and Quinlan to survive, I had to go with them. I knew Picel would be angry at me, but he would get over it, and he would be alive. That's all I cared about. I also knew he would begin immediately planning a way to get me out, but doing that would take some time. For now, I would be a prisoner of war.

NAIA

I didn't like the fact that Quinlan had to leave me to go to the burning, especially with how things were between him and Javil, but I understood. He had been the King's Guard and his most trusted warrior other than his two sons. They were all best friends, well, they had been until I came along. But he still needed to be with them. If not as friends then as their guard.

After he left, I fell asleep. The next morning I managed to get up and walk around the castle a little bit. The scare from the night before with Javil had shaken me to my core. I was so glad he was not in the castle for the day.

I went to the kitchen and Pepper was there. She looked to be in her mid twenties and was the youngest niece of Zahir. She told me that they didn't get to talk much, but was glad to be in the same location as him. Her father and mother were still in Joris and she sent them part of her wages each month. She had landed herself a job in the castle kitchen when she was only fourteen. Zahir promised King Zaxton that she would work hard and make delicious food, and she had proved him right.

"Hey, Pepper… Do you have any scraps I could have? I haven't eaten since yesterday," I asked.

"Naia! Really? Yes, here, take this," she said, handing me a piece of freshly baked bread. "I'm baking it for the fallen soldiers' families. You know, the ones who died in the battle last week? I know it is a bit late, but I thought maybe they might appreciate it, you know?"

That girl was so sweet. I really liked her. She had blonde hair and wore it tied back at the base of her neck every day. She was young, but was phenomenal at her job, and had already been promoted to the second in command. I hoped she would be able to either run the kitchen or have her own little shop someday. Everything she made was delicious.

I bit into the bread. It was the perfect amount of crunchy on the outside and soft on the inside. I held it to my nose and took a big whiff.

"Mmmmhh," I moaned. It smelled like home on my birthdays when Mom made bread just for me.

"Thank you, Pepper. It's scrumptious!"

"Really! Oh good, I am so glad you like it."

"Pepper, I like everything you make! We all do!"

"You are too kind, Naia! Well, I best be getting back to it. I don't want to get reprimanded for not having dinner ready because of making so much bread for the warriors' families."

"Sounds good, Pepper. I'll see you later," I said and almost skipped through the door. She always made my day better.

I could get used to this. I knew I would have to work and tend to the warriors, the King, Javil… I shuddered at the last name. I quite liked his not being around. I felt relaxed. Safe.

I made my way down to the infirmary and found Zahir working away on warriors who needed bandages changed, stitches removed and what not.

There was moaning and yelling all over the place. So many were in pain and in need of relief. I walked over to Zahir and asked if I could help in any way.

He happily sent me to work re-bandaging some men who were almost healed, but wanted to take extra precaution so infection didn't set in. I lathered the flax and honey concoction on their scabs, put a mint leaf over the wounds, and then wrapped them back up, sending them on their way.

I finished re-wrapping them all pretty quickly, and Zahir asked if I wanted to assist him in removing stitches from some men. I hesitated, knowing that what they experienced, I would soon have to endure, but ended up agreeing to stay and help. I would want people there for me., I needed to be willing to do the same.

We were halfway through when the guards at the gate started yelling and rushing around. We weren't close enough to hear specifically what was going on, but it seemed like a pretty big deal.

Zahir instructed the injured warriors to stay where they were. He told them it was essential to get these stitches out immediately to minimize the risk of infection.

He turned to me.

"Naia, kindly go peek outside to see what the commotion is. I need to tend to these warriors, but would like to know what is going on," he requested gently.

"Of course, Zahir," I replied, and walked out to the courtyard.

The King was waving his hands about, screaming at men to go do different things. I thought I heard him say *prepare for war*, but I wasn't sure. I looked to his left and saw him there. Quinlan. He was tied up, but there were guards working on getting him loose. I almost ran to him, but thought better of it since, one, Picel was right there and I wasn't sure if he would approve of Quin's and my relationship-whatever we were, and two, it was not the place for a woman at the moment. At least a woman with no battle experience like me.

Quickly, I went back to Zahir to update him.

"Picel is enraged, but in a scared sort of way. Quinlan is tied up, and there are ropes on the ground where Picel is standing. Javil is nowhere to be seen."

"Oh no," Zahir replied gravely. "Javil must be in the hands of an enemy."

"What? Are you sure?" I asked, almost relieved, but having a mindset like that was selfish, even after what he did to me. *Even after all the pain.*

"It's the only thing that makes sense, especially if Picel is yelling *to prepare for war.*"

"Oh," I said. "So what happens now?"

"Well, Picel will probably implement a plan and then send men to go after his brother.

"Will he not go himself?" I asked.

Before Zahir could respond Picel came bursting into the room with Quinlan. His body was so tense, you could see his veins bulging on his neck and arms.

"Tend to Quinlan," he growled at me.

This was the first time he had spoken to me in such a way. Usually he was patient and had a little sense of humor, but this was a different situation. His brother had been captured and taken to enemy territory. He was not thinking about being nice. He was King, and he had a job to do.

Quickly I obeyed. I hooked my arm under Quinlan's and assisted him to Zahir's bed in the back room. I wanted Quinlan to have some privacy from the other guards. For some reason he still hadn't been untied. I found a knife and started sawing away at the ropes. We didn't say anything as I worked, but we kept giving each other lingering silent glances. We could hear Picel in the background ordering Zahir to hurry so he could start looking for his brother.

Picel then walked in and said in a softer tone, "please hurry, Naia. We need to be on our way as quickly as possible."

I nodded in understanding; he quickly turned and left, not looking back.

"What happened, Quin," I whispered, dabbing a wound on his arm with a wet cloth. I was getting to take care of him now. I liked that.

He winced as the liquor made contact with his skin, but then began to tell me the story of the night prior. Enemies attacking, Javil being taken, the enemy thinking he was King and then Picel being forced to let his brother go. It was basically the worst case scenario, other than if Picel, or all of them, had been killed.

"Are you okay? I mean, obviously not, but do you need anything? Can I do anything?" I asked, brushing his cheek with the palm of my hand, and rubbing my thumb under his eye. I left it there and he shuddered, slowly looking up at me. He took my hand in his and moved it off his face, placing it in his lap.

"Naia," he said softly, then inhaling, and slowly letting it out. And then, one single tear slipped from the outside corner of his eye.

I don't think I had realized how much we cared for each other until that moment. He had been with me through some of my hardest moments, and now I was here for one of his. I wrapped my arms around his neck, sitting beside him, and let him cry everything out, because soon he would be required to be tough again, to be a warrior. But here in this moment, he was a man who had been through a great ordeal and needed to weep.

"Naia, I failed him. I failed my King!" He whispered, burrowing his head into my neck as tears fell. *Is he confiding in me?* "How can I ever live with myself again? Call myself the King's Guard? I'm a failure! I should be locked up. Hung!" He said, sobbing even harder.

"Quin," I said, gently stroking the back of his head. "The King is safe though- he's here, safe in the castle."

"Not Zaxton. I did the same thing my father- " his voice trailed off and he pulled away to look at me. He was distraught. I couldn't imagine what was going on inside his head. He was right. He had messed up. And it couldn't be fixed.

I didn't know what else to say. I just sat there, rubbing his head, his neck, his back. Trying to make it better, knowing there was nothing I could do to fix this for him.

After a little while he spoke again.

"Picel knows about us," he said.

I looked at him with so many thoughts flooding my mind. *Us? Picel knows? What?*

"There's an us?" I asked, trying to hide a forming smile.

He looked at me, completely embarrassed at his forwardness. I'd wondered if he was interested in me, but up till then there had been no discussions about it.

"Oh, um. Only if you'll accept my long drawn out request to court you," he said, wringing his hands together in his lap and looked down at the ground.

"Really?" I said with a soft smile. Then remembered what he had said earlier. He nodded.

"Picel knows?" I asked worriedly.

"He approves," he said with a slight smile. "Javil still doesn't, but Picel is fine with us courting. At least he didn't say he wasn't."

"Us," I said, resting my head on his shoulder and taking his hand. *Quin is mine.*

Zahir was considerate and shut the door back into the infirmary so others couldn't come in and ridicule Quin for what happened. Not that they would, but there was always a chance. He was already the one who didn't defend the king, who ended up being murdered. He didn't need to be known as the one who let the prince get kidnapped too, even if Javil did deserve it.

Picel came back an hour later and requested Quinlan join him in the study. I told him, respectfully, that Quin was resting, and needed to continue to do so, and that respectfully, he should too, and that I would send him up when he awoke.

Picel nodded hesitantly, but listened to my request. I wasn't ranked above him, obviously, but working in medicine with Zahir allowed me to make recommendations that people, including the King, usually listened to.

Quinlan stirred a few minutes after Picel left. I walked over to the bed and gently wiped some sweat away that was forming on his forehead. He tossed and turned, moaning and mumbling in his sleep. I wondered what he was dreaming about, not something pleasant, that's for sure.

He awoke with a start and saw me sitting there, next to him. He sighed in relief. Was he dreaming about *me?*

He sat up and leaned in quickly, waited a second, and then very gently touched his lips to my forehead.

"What was that for?" I asked softly, my heart beating twice as fast as normal.

"Thank you," he said, giving me half a smile.

"Um, the King is asking for you." I murmured nervously, not sure how to respond to his intimate gesture.

"Ah, yes, we have matters to attend to," he remembered, snapping back into reality.

I carefully helped him to stand, assisted him in taking a few steps, and then allowed him to leave, but only after promising he would take the stairs slowly. He shut the door, leaving me alone with Zahir.

"Are you alright?" He asked softly.

"No," I paused, "but I have to be, because he is not."

"It's okay not to be okay, too, you know?" Zahir replied and went inside his own chambers leaving me alone in the infirmary with my thoughts.

28

PICEL

Quinlan and I talked for hours, trying to figure out what to do, how to rescue Javil, even though we didn't know where he was. Because of that, we were getting nowhere so I sent him back to his chambers.

I paced the floor in my room as I tried to figure out how I could have gotten into this situation in the first place. *Naia showed up, Arilos was attacked, I was injured, Father was killed, I became king, Javil was taken. Naia showed up, Arilos was attacked, I was injured, Father was killed, I became king, Javil was taken. Naia showed up, Arilos was attacked, I was injured, Father was killed, I became king....*

I grabbed a clay pot that was on my night stand and chucked it across the room, barely missing a servant who had just entered. She yelped and quickly retreated before telling me why she was there. I felt awful, I wasn't trying to hit anyone. Anger was not how I usually handled things. I had spent too much time with my brother. Mother would not be happy if she were here. She would tell me to take a breath, take a step back, use my thinking brain. I didn't know how to do any of those things at the moment.

I leaned my hands against the wall. This was all too much. I didn't know how to do this. I wasn't supposed to be in this mess. Father was still supposed to be here. I wasn't supposed to be alone.

I immersed myself into my battle plans again, trying to figure out how many men to send to go after Javil, where to even send them, if I should go myself, if I should send one or two people. Then I realized something. They had been carrying Rowynalyn blades. *Javil is in Rowynala.* And then I realized something else. *Naia.* She was from there. Maybe she could go talk to her people, see if they knew anything, and find out what they wanted. That was only if she were willing. I wasn't going to force her into a dangerous situation, even though I had a feeling she would agree.

There was also some potential leverage I had that she wasn't aware of yet. That could make a difference too.

As I was trying to figure out how to make the whole plan work, there was a soft knock on the door.

"Majesty?" *Naia.*

"Come in," I said gently. *Perfect timing.*

"Um, I'm sorry to bother you. I know I am one of the last, probably the last, person you want to see, but a servant came running into the infirmary with a shard of clay in her arm saying you were throwing things, and she didn't want to come back to bring your clean garments. I told her I would take care of it," she said, peaking through the crack in the door.

I walked over to the door and grabbed it just above where her hand was and pulled it open an inch more, peeking through and looked down at her. I inhaled. *She is so young.*

"Why are you one of the last people I want to see?" I questioned.

"Um, well," she stuttered. "Because of…" she paused.

"Because of you and Quin? And because my brother hates you? You think I will side with him?" She nodded.

"I don't hate you, Naia. Truly. I actually was about to come find you to ask a huge favor…" I paused before continuing, making sure I knew what I was asking of her before I did so, going over the consequences of what she might go through, but I saw no other option.

"Yes, your Majesty?" She asked.

"Please stay with me for a while," I said, not ready to ask this tremendous favor of her, but more so not ready to tell her what comes with that favor. *Her presence is so calming.*

She hesitantly opened the door and slowly walked in, her hair pulled back in a bun. She wore a maroon dress layered with a cream apron that was spotted with stains, probably from caring for me and my brother. *And Quin.* I gasped for air at her beauty. It was incomparable. Like my mother's. *I missed her.*

"Majesty, are you okay?" She asked. "Is there something wrong with my attire?" I cleared my throat and forced my gaze away from her, not realizing that I had been staring for as long as I could.

"No, no, you look… Beautiful," I whispered.

"I don't feel beautiful, majesty, but thank you."

I motioned for her to come sit at the table with me. After offering her some fruit, which she gratefully accepted, I decided it was time to get the conversation over with.

I leaned down so my thumbs were resting under my chin and my hands covered my mouth and nose.

"Naia, I need to ask, I hope you will consider, ahhh." I stopped again. This was too much. She wouldn't be able to handle it. She wouldn't want to, especially after what I had heard about Javil abusing her. I couldn't ask, but I had to. *She might be my only hope. But I can't send her into the fire.*

She looked at me expectantly, waiting for my plea.

"Naia, I'm here, humbly asking if you would consider going on a rescue mission for my brother." I hurriedly continued before she could shut me down. "Please, you might have a chance at negotiating with the people of Rowynala. That is who I think has taken my brother." She looked at me in complete disbelief as expected. As she should.

"Naia, I know what he has done to you, but I am begging you. You might be my only hope to get my brother back. Please." I said getting on my knees next to her chair and grabbed her hands in mine. "I will send Quinlan with you as your guard plus as many of my warriors as you want. No harm will come to you." I said, knowing I wouldn't be able to keep that promise, but I had to try to convince her.

"Picel," she started. "I have no power. I am but just a villager. My people are not violent. I have no idea why they would have taken your brother or wanted to kidnap you, the King. None of this makes sense."

"You really don't know," I whispered to her, almost shocked. I thought she had been playing it safe, but she was completely clueless.

"Naia. you have more power than you think." I said, staring her in the eyes, not sure I was ready to tell her the truth, but it was my only option. She was my only hope at safely getting my brother back or even at all. I wasn't sure what the consequences would be if I told her the truth, I could lose everything, but, for the sake of my brother... he was the only family I had left. I was willing to risk it all.

NAIA

"Naia," he said hesitantly. "You are the rightful heir to the throne. You are the True Queen of Arilos." He wasn't serious. *Me, Queen?*

I jolted backwards almost falling back on my chair, but Picel tightened his grip on my hands so I stayed upright. I stared at him, completely taken aback in disbelief at his words.

I had grown up in a village, tending to herbs and fruits, eventually learning the trade of medicine. I was no Queen! That would mean… that would mean that my mother was supposed to be Queen before me. She would have told me. *Right?*

I thought back then to the boat. *Naia, it isn't safe here for me to tell you. Please,* she'd said. Then I fast forwarded to the King, King Zaxton, before the battle that had taken his life. *I knew your mother, Naia.* Maybe she knew King Zaxton before his father took over; not after.

Then my mind turned to the men who had shown up at Edwin and Ingrid's house who claimed they were looking for my mother... why? Because they knew that she was the rightful queen and they wanted her dead? Maybe. My mind kept whirling as he spoke to me frantically.

"You really don't know anything? Would your mother have told someone that could have said something to an enemy? Someone who hates both our families? Causing them to attack your village and then the castle?"

"I have no idea. She never talked about any of this." I changed the subject. "You really want me to go rescue your brother? My abuser?"

"I... Please, Naia, consider it. It would mean everything to me. You have to realize how much I am risking by telling you this. I am risking my throne and what I have trained for my entire life. You have every right to take the throne from me, but I am trusting you to do the right thing. So far, that is all I have seen you do. You are kind and compassionate, loyal, and strong. If you asked me to give you the throne after this, I would, but right now I am begging you, please help me save my brother. He is all that I have left."

I looked at him, shaking my head. I pulled my hands from his grasp and fled. It was all too much.

I ran into Quin's room next door and collapsed against the inside of the door frame as it shut behind me.

"Naia! Are you okay?" He said, rushing to my side, taking me into his arms without hesitation. He was so tender with me. It was something I had never expected from a warrior of his level, but I cherished it.

"Did you know?" I sobbed.

"What?" He asked, confused.

"That I am the True Queen of Arilos? Did you know?" I asked, shoving him backwards off me. His eyes widened, then saddened, and he took a deep breath, contemplating how to answer my question.

"Did you know?" I repeated again, tears streaming down my cheeks creating wet stains on my dress.

"Yes," he replied softly, inching closer again, reaching for my hand, missing it as I pulled it back away from him. He touched the hair that was falling out of its tie in front of my face instead. *Such a sweet gesture, but the wrong timing.*

"I wanted to tell you, but I was commanded to wait. It wasn't my place. You have to understand that. King Zaxton, may he rest in peace, made it clear I was to protect you, but not say a word. Picel asked for my silence as well."

"So was any of this real? You and me?" I asked, angry at him for keeping this from me.

"Of course it's real, Naia! I attacked Javil, the Prince! My Commander! I took a beating for you! I still have the bruises to prove it!" He said, clearly frustrated.

He took another deep breath and moved slowly towards me again, sliding himself down the back of the door so he was seated next to me.

"Naia, I really care about you. I would do almost anything for you, apart from anything that goes against what I am commanded by my King," he paused and turned to face me, his hands moved to cradle my face as he knelt before me and kissed my forehead softly and tenderly. I looked at him for a moment, but had to look away as my feelings in that moment were too much to bear.

"You. Hold. My. Heart," he said, pausing after each word, and moved his hands to the back of my neck, his thumb guiding my eyes to his.

"I do?" I whispered, leaning my forehead onto his.

"Yes." He breathed, pulling me into his arms, pressing me against his chest. I let myself rest there for a moment, safe in his warm embrace, but then pulled back to look at him trying to convince myself that this was real. *Is this even possible? Has he fallen for me? Completely? And not just because I was the true heir to the throne?*

I reached up, smiled, and brushed a piece of hair that had fallen into his eye as he looked down at me. We lingered there for a moment, our gaze focused on each other, neither of us wanting to let go. Neither of us breathing. That moment- I wanted it to last forever. But I had to be sure he was serious. I broke the silence.

"Really?" I asked, still in disbelief that I had captured this man's, this warrior's heart.

"Yes, Naia." He groaned in frustration that I didn't believe him, and he pressed his lips onto mine.

I gasped and he smiled against my lips. He pulled away slowly, looking into my eyes with such love, sincerity, and protection. I knew then that he would give his life for mine in a heartbeat if he had to.

30

PICEL

I went to Quinlan's room and paused. *How am I going to play this?* I knocked. There was no answer. I peeked inside to see Naia sleeping soundly in his bed, but Quinlan was nowhere to be seen.

"My King?" A voice said from behind the door. *Quinlan. They were together... Right.*

"Can I help you?"

"Ah, Quin, I was just looking for you." I said a little too energetically.

"Were you just watching my woman sleep?" He questioned, and though I was King, a fight sparked in his eyes.

"I am sorry, it was not my intent. I was looking for you, but she just looks so peaceful, I couldn't help it. I am sorry for overstepping." I apologized.

"What did you need, Your Majesty?" He asked, moving to block Naia from my view.

I beckoned him outside, not wanting to disturb Naia and also not wanting to make Quin angry by looking at Naia anymore, even if it was accidental.

"Quin, I am going to get right to the point. I have come here today to assign you a mission.

"To rescue Javil," he responded.

"Yes." I hesitated. "But I am also sending Naia, if she is willing. She hasn't agreed to go, yet, but I hope..." I stopped, seeing the anger in his eyes, but I was his King, so he didn't question me. "You know she is our best chance at getting Javil back," I continued, treading carefully. "You saw the Rowynalyn blades." He nodded.

"But Picel, are you sure? They are the ones who potentially murdered your Father, captured your brother. What they could do to her... it terrifies me, even if they are her people." He confessed and then said words I never expected.

"Picel, I love her. If something were to happen..." His voice grew quiet. *Love?*

"Like something happened to my Father? The King, who you were supposed to protect?" Instant regret flooded over me. I shouldn't have said that, but it was too late to take back.

He looked at me very carefully before answering, hurt and anger flooding his eyes, but he did not lash out.

"Your Majesty, with all due respect, I don't think it wise, and I don't want to put Naia in danger, especially being the rightful Queen, but if it is what you command, and she agrees to go, I will see it through."

NAIA

I agreed to go to Rowynala- with only Quinlan, no other guards. He alone could protect me. I trusted him. Selfishly I also wanted time alone with him.

Unfortunately, since we were leaving that meant I needed to have my stitches removed a few days early. Zahir said that it would be fine, but I really didn't want to deal with the pain.

It was as excruciating as I thought it would be. I writhed in Quin's arms, screaming in pain. After what seemed an eternity, it was over. I never wanted to go through that again.

It was the early hours of the morning and we were just under halfway to Rowynala. I was riding behind Quinlan, my arms wrapped around him. I was enjoying our peaceful ride. Quinlan was in protective mode. I could see his silhouette constantly scanning the desert's dunes for danger. The forest line was just appearing in the distance. From there we would have to travel another mile to get to the waterfall, then find a path up in the scattered starlight. In the forest, the trees covered most of the sky, but seeing the desert under the stars was one of the most beautiful things I had ever experienced in my life. Billions of stars and galaxies spanned the sky. Hues of blue and purple scattered throughout showcasing where different galaxies ended and others began. I wished I could enjoy it more, especially being out there with Quin on horseback, but that would have to wait for another day.

As we rode I prayed we would be protected and that even though we were most likely being sent to our death, God would somehow spare us. *I know You can.* I thought, looking up at the vast sky. *You are big enough.*

My thoughts changed direction. *Queen? Me?* I couldn't even comprehend the thought. *I am only twenty! Picel is almost thirty and even he is nervous for his new role. And Picel is sending me on a mission that could end my life before it even began! Was he really trying to get rid of me? Was that his plan? What am I supposed to do?*

I buried my head into Quin's back and breathed deep. I felt so safe with him and I knew God would take care of us, even if things weren't going according to my plan. *Maybe especially since things weren't going according to my plan! Nothing had recently.* I wanted to enjoy this time with him even if just for a few minutes.

"Quin?" I said, leaning up on the inside of my knees so I was at his ear level. He turned his head slightly, not taking his eyes off the path before us, but it signaled that he was listening.

"Can we stop for a minute?"

"Out here? In the open? Naia, we are on a rescue mission. On a quest from the King. No, we need to keep moving," he said, all warrior-like. I smiled.

"Please?" I asked gently, squeezing his torso a little tighter. "We don't know what is going to happen. Can we please spend just five minutes together under these magnificent stars? Alone? There are always people coming and going at the castle or we've had to be secretive. We have never been allowed to just be."

Slowing the horse down to a walk, he sighed.

He was going to stop! Yes!

Once he found a place he deemed safe, he slid off Aseria, our horse, and took my waist in his hands, lowering me down slowly, held in his strong arms. My arms wrapped around his neck and I looked at him. Hopeful. Once my feet were on the sand he pulled me in close. My arms moved under his, and I clung to him as he did to me. My head was at his neck, his hands were around my waist. No air was between us. I felt each inhale and exhale he breathed, so tense, so scared. He held me like he might never get to again. *So I wasn't the only one who needed this.*

"Naia," he whispered in my ear.

"Mmmh," I replied softly, not wanting to move from my protector's arms.

"Can I kiss you?" He pulled away from our embrace so he could see my face, searching my eyes for a yes. He hadn't asked last time. Maybe he realized how big of a deal it was for me, especially after being treated so badly by Javil.

"Naia," he said again, his forehead moving against mine and he exhaled. Our noses touched, he leaned in a little more, still not touching my lips.

"Are you giving me a choice?" I teased in a whisper, knowing now he wouldn't put his lips on mine until I gave him permission.

He growled in frustration, clearly getting impatient with my delaying him and his desires, but he held back. He was so self-controlled. A gentleman; Though I had barely nodded yes when he moved his head the last centimeter fulfilling his desire to have his lips on mine.

Sparks flew. The last kiss we had shared was innocent, new, quick. He had just told me that I held his heart and would forever. This time, this time was different. This kiss was an *I will protect you until my last breath* kind of kiss. Passion-filled. I never wanted it to end. I never in a million years thought I would experience something so wonderful, especially with someone as amazing as Quin, but I pulled back, knowing we couldn't stay.

He hesitated, clearly wanting more, but respected my choice and rested his right hand on my face, his thumb at my ear, and his fingers curved around my neck. His left hand had intertwined with mine. And in that moment I wanted nothing more.

"I love you," he said softly. And going against my better judgment, I leaned in again, gently brushed his lips with mine and pulled away again.

"I love *you*," I replied. He sighed. It was a sigh of longing, of contentment, of fear.

We stood there in silence, looking into each other's eyes, memorizing them, holding each other. It didn't matter to either of us that we had switched places. I used to be the servant and he was the King's Guard. Now it had been discovered that I was technically supposed to be Queen, so he would report to me if that ever came to be or would he be King along side me? I didn't care. I would be his either way.

"We need to keep moving," he said after a while, pulling me in tighter, pressing my body into his, then releasing me.

"But we didn't get to look at the stars," I replied, half serious, half completely content with what had already taken place in the middle of the desert. With Quinlan. My Heart.

He chuckled and jumped up on the saddle, swiftly pulling me up behind him. I resumed holding onto him, but this time it was different. I don't know if it was the kissing or saying we loved each other for the first time, but now, no matter what happened in Rowynala, we would always have this memory to look back on. Forever.

A couple hours later we made it to the base of the waterfall. It was almost sunrise and the mountain was slowly coming into view. We walked along the bottom for a while until we found a path that would lead us to the top. It wasn't straight up, but it was pretty close. We had to lean all the way forward in the saddle. I squeezed Quin's torso and the horse's back, and he squeezed the horse's neck to try to avoid sliding off.

It was then that I realized how much life I had missed. I had always been confined to my village. I was never able to explore like the others, and now I knew why. My mother had been protecting me. I looked too much like her. Maybe other villages in Rowynala *were* violent. I still wish I knew the whole story, but Picel had only been able to fill me in on the bits and pieces he knew. He wasn't around when everything went down between our parents and grandparents.

By daybreak, we'd reached the mountain's summit. Quin brought Aseria to a stop to scout the area, and I looked around and admired the Rowyn trees that glinted in the sun rays that peaked through and bounced off the leaves onto the forest floor below. I missed seeing it like this.

Aseria must have heard a noise in the distance because she reared and sent Quin and me tumbling off. Thankfully a tree stopped us from going back over the edge, but my back would be bruised for sure. Aseria took off back down the hill and disappeared into the trees below.

I shuddered, hoping she was uninjured and could make it back to the castle. I wondered what Picel would think of having her return riderless. He might worry and send the whole guard.

The headquarters of Rowynala was about an hour walk from where we were, so we set off, hoping to be there by the time the sun had just finished cresting the horizon.

When we arrived at the edge of the village, everyone stopped what they were doing and all eyes looked to us.

Picel had put me in a fancy navy dress and some pretty cream flats that were now covered in mud from the hike - so much for presenting myself like a Queen. Quin was weaponless except for a dagger that he had strapped to his arm under his cloak; he wore the lion crest on his tunic to alert the village that the King had sent us.

I held out my hands, to show them I carried no weapons and slowly took a step forward. Bad idea. Instantly, we were surrounded, being held at sword point, and were escorted forcefully to a cottage on the far end of the village.

We passed a few other cottages but what drew my eye were wooden cells that were scattered through the trees, barely visible. They were made from thick trees and had been tied together with rope and lined with moss. I tried to slow down to scan the cells for Javil, but he wasn't there. *Where was he?*

They propelled us forward and we quickly arrived at the main building. It was made from forest logs and was lined with moss. The logs were sealed tight to keep out cold air, an actual living place, not like the open cells. Once inside I saw it was not as much of a living space as a gathering place. This must be the place this village goes to fellowship. We had one of these buildings, that is, before it was lit up in flames.

I was brought to a chair in the center and was motioned to sit. Quin was forced to stand behind me, which I think he approved of. It gave him a better shot at protecting me if the need arose.

Two men grabbed my arms and tied them behind me to the chair. Quin started to fight as a warrior in love would, but was quickly knocked unconscious. I wailed, hearing him collapse behind me, unable to go to him.

"Please, we come in peace!" I started, but was quickly silenced when I heard footsteps directly behind me.

They were heavy, thumping across the ground. One step was longer than the other. Did he have a limp? The steps were purposeful though, never getting in my line of vision. *I have heard those footsteps before.*

"Why are you here?" the man asked coldly, his voice muffled. I was about to tell him the plan, when Quinlan awoke suddenly.

"Naia, he isn't Rowynalyn! He will kill you if you tell him! Please don't say anything!" he warned.

Quin was smacked across the face by a warrior, sending him crashing into the ground again with no way to stop himself. I heard a crunch and a groan, and realized he must have broken his nose. I could hear him screaming for me as some guards grabbed him and dragged him outside, away from me through a door in the back.

"Why are you here?" The stranger repeated, pacing behind me, still not letting me see his face.

I figured my best option would be to tell him the truth, even though Quinlan had warned me against it. It is how I was raised. Honesty. I wasn't going to stop now.

"I am here to make a trade," I stated somehow confidently.

"A trade? For whom?" He asked curiously, though I figured he already knew.

"Myself, for the release of the King," I barely remembered they thought that Javil was king or that he was Picel.

"And what makes you think that I will make the trade? Who are you to demand such a request?"

I looked straight ahead and lifted my head up just a little. If I was going to pull this off, I was going to need to play the part. Scared or not.

"I am Naia, Daughter of Luria. I am the True Heir of Arilos."

JAVIL

My face was wet and my head was throbbing. I sat up and brought my hand up to wipe my face. Sticky. Not water. Blood. I was covered in blood. *What had they done to me?*

My hand went down to the ground to feel what I was sitting on. Dirt. *Great.* The only place I knew that had this much dirt was the Forest. *Rowynala. Lovely.* I knew that though, before, it had just set in completely when I had awakened.

I wiggled my feet and ankles and somehow there were no ropes around them. Only my hands were bound at my wrists, probably to keep me from attacking anyone again.

I had come into Rowynala swinging. It was *my* job to protect Picel and I had done that. He was okay, angry with me, but okay. I paced, well more like dragged myself back and forth trying to come up with an escape plan, but tired quickly, seeing as I had been almost beaten to death. I knew I had bruised ribs and a gash on my head. I could feel the pressure of both. My legs were weak, but that could just be from lack of nutrition. I had lashes on my neck at the shoulder going towards my chest and a few on my back as well; adding to the ones I had already received from Javil. It was some of the worst pain I had felt in my life. Hours went by, maybe a day or two. I really had no idea.

I heard a yell outside. I jumped up to my feet, as quickly as my wounded body would let me, and started to yell out to whomever was there. I needed to talk to someone, anyone, a guard, another prisoner. Shouting out, I demanded to have someone come speak to me. No answer. *Come on!*

The door flew open and light flooded the room. I was in a small dirt and rock cell that was about ten feet underground. I couldn't reach the top standing or jumping. It was about fifteen feet wide by fifteen feet long. I could pry off some rocks and try to dig my way out, but my hands would be in shreds after a few hours, and I wanted to keep those so I could fight, if I could get these horrid ropes off.

As I was contemplating my options, someone tossed down a rope ladder with logs for the steps and ordered me to climb out. I did so and was met with a lovely punch to the face, sending me flying back down the ten foot drop. I gasped for air, but couldn't seem to catch a breath. The wind had been knocked out of me completely.

A guard yelled down for me to climb back up, but I was so light-headed that when I stood, I only collapsed again.

There was laughter above me and a different rope was flung down. This one looped. I was told to loop it under my arms and they would pull me up. I hesitated, but did what I was told, not wanting anymore trouble.

They dragged me up the side of the pit, leaving many scrapes and gashes on my body from the rocks and roots sticking out of the dirt walls. I barely held back a scream as that motion reopened wounds they had given me previously. They flopped me onto the grass above, blindfolded me, and slammed the door shut. Then they forced me to stand and shoved me forward.

NAIA

The True Heir of Arilos…

At those words, I was forced out the way we had come in and was half dragged to a clearing in the woods. I was guarded by three warriors, one on each side, and one behind me.

I heard a commotion behind me and then saw *him* as they entered my line of vision. Javil was being dragged across the ground. He looked horrible.

I heard a yell to my left. Quin, being shoved towards me, wounded and bloody. He had been beaten… badly. I took a sharp breath in as I made eye contact with him. I noticed him mouthing something to me; *be strong, remember, My Heart.* I had to bite the inside of my cheek to keep myself from calling out. I tasted blood as I bit down too hard.

I stood up tall and faced straight ahead. I took a breath and, as I exhaled, the village guards brought both men up to me within an arm's length. I could touch them. My abuser, and the love of my life both beaten and bloody before me.

They hadn't hit me or beat me in any way yet, and I didn't want to see what Quin would do if they tried. He would probably end up dead. I shivered in fear of it actually happening.

"Choose, girl," the man spoke from behind me again. He was in their line of vision, not mine. They both tensed up at his voice *or the sight of him?* Especially Javil. *Did they know him?*

"What am I choosing?" I asked, as steady as possible.

"You are choosing who will die. I won't tell you when, or how, but you will be solidifying the death of one of these men. Like it or not."

"No, Absolutely not," I said without hesitation.

Quin painfully looked at me. He knew I couldn't make that choice. He knew what I would do.

"Are you sure? Because if you don't choose, I will."

I forced myself to look at Javil, then made my way to Quin. He looked so helpless, weak. He was unable to do anything to make this any easier for me. He couldn't protect me anymore.

I knew the choice I had to make. Javil had abused me and I was in love with Quinlan, but the choice was obvious. Quinlan, reading my mind, widened his eyes and slightly shook his head, begging me not to.

I stood taller and, staring straight at Javil, made my choice.

34

NAIA

"Me."
Me.
Myself.
Naia.
I will give my life for both the man who hurt me,
And the one who will love me forever.

QUINLAN

Every part of my body told me to try to rush to her, to beg her not to do it, to give my life for hers, to remind her how much I loved her, but I remembered my mission, to save Javil, save the prince. And she knew that. She had done well.

I stared straight at her, tears filling my eyes.

Javil gasped next to me, stunned at Naia's willingness to sacrifice herself for him after how he had treated her back at the castle.

The guards grabbed me, and started to drag me away from her. *No, please!* I tried to say. *Let me say goodbye!* But all that came out was a pitiful moan. I was in too much pain to fight. Emotionally and physically. *I'm sorry Naia. I failed you.*

Thud. I took a blow to my ribs. *Thwack.* Another to my jaw. *Smack.* They hit me with a heavy log. *Crash.* They threw me into a pit and locked the top.

I can't breathe. Naia... Nai....

36

JAVIL

*S*he didn't choose me.
 Why didn't she choose me?
I deserve it.
I should be the one dying, but she chose herself.
I owe this girl everything.

37

NAIA

wanted to lunge after Quin, but decided against it. I saw the direction they had taken him. If I could escape, I would be able to look for him. Not that it was likely.

Finally, the man showed himself to me. He was terrifying. A large man with a dark beard. He had dark straight black hair and wore a hooded cloak. I could see a scar across his cheek and he walked with a limp. He wore a red tunic and black pants. Flykryn. *He was the servant that told me King Zaxton wanted to see me….*

"Do you know who I am?" He asked, chillingly.

"You killed King Zaxton," I questioned, my voice barely above a whisper.

"Did I?" he smiled cunningly.

"Ahiam," Javil said, coolly. Saving me from having to respond further.

He was terrifying. Yes, he walked with a limp, but I could tell the rest of him was still strong. His neck was so thick and muscular and the rest of him followed suit. And his face was aggravatingly handsome.

"Oh very good, Nephew! I didn't think you would have any idea who I was." The man named Ahiam applauded.

"Unfortunately I do," Javil snarled. "Father warned me of you. Almost too late, but I know enough."

"Then you know what I am capable of?" He asked coldly as he stepped towards Javil.

"Yes." Javil said angrily. *What had happened?*

"You know that Naia isn't the only Heir to the throne?"

"Of course she is," Javil scoffed, but looked at me as if I knew what Ahiam was talking about. I didn't.

"Ah, actually. There is someone else," Ahiam revealed.

He waved his hand and they brought someone else out of the woods. She was covered in dirt. You could hardly tell what color her hair was. She wore a maroon gown that grazed the grass below her; its sleeves and hems were lined in gold, but had been torn to shreds. She was barefoot, her feet cut and bleeding. As she got closer I saw she was bound by rope at her wrists. She also had a black eye.

As she approached us, I gasped when I realized I knew this woman. She had raised me, loved me, tried to protect me.

Mom.

"Choosing yourself was not an option I gave you, Naia," Ahiam said, pacing in between me and my mother. "Pick one of the men to kill or I will kill her while you watch," he threatened, gesturing at my mom.

"No!" Javil yelled at the same time as my mom.

Thwack. They were both smacked across the face. *Why was he defending me all of a sudden?* I knew what my mother would want, even if it killed me to say. She would want the royal family safe at all costs.

"No. I choose me." Mom's eyes widened, trying not to panic at the thought of losing her daughter, her last child.

"Fine," Ahiam said, raising his spear, ready to strike down my mom. She stood there, unmoving.

"Wait!" I wailed. Seeing him actually about to kill her changed things. He wasn't bluffing. I knew I had to try to do something to stop it from happening. He smiled, as if he were not surprised that I was having second thoughts. My mother remained motionless.

"Please, let me have till morning to decide," I begged.

"So be it," he said, after thinking it over for a moment. "Tonight, your consequence will be spending the night with the man who loves you, who is destined to die after the beating he has just received from my men."

Ahiam turned to my mother, "My brother, swore that he would make your life miserable, Luria. Though he is dead, by your Zaxton's hand. Now I get to carry his promise out. And I will not fail. *That* is why I haven't taken my throne yet. But I will. You'll see."

"Please," Mother begged. "My daughter has done nothing to deserve any of this. Please just take it out on me!"

"You had your turn… now it is hers."

Before my mother could protest, I was grabbed by two men and brought deep into the woods where I had seen them take Quin moments before.

We arrived at the pit where Quin had been taken to and they flung the door open. In the noon sky, I could see Quin laying on the ground, motionless, covered in blood. I gasped as I choked back tears. This was my fault. I couldn't cry. I wouldn't. I needed to be strong - for him.

I did cry out in pain, though, as I was tossed into the pit. The door at the top was quickly shut and Quin and I were left alone in the overwhelming darkness.

38

PICEL

What was I thinking? Sending Naia and Quinlan into the fire like that? What kind of a King was I? Granted they had agreed to go, but only at my request. Naia had no battle experience, and Quinlan would die protecting her in a heartbeat. It was hopeless.

I paced back and forth for days waiting for some sort of word from them, that they were on their way back, that they had succeeded, but it never came. They never came. But their horse returned… riderless.

39

JAVIL

Light flooded my eyes as my blindfold was ripped off my eyes, taking some of my dark curls with it. I winced and looked to my right. Luria, the Rightful Queen of Arilos, Naia's mom, was beside me. She was silent. I flinched as my uncle started talking from behind me.

"The whole thing played out perfectly, you know. You and Picel were busy with the battle which allowed me the opportunity to sneak into the castle as a wounded guard. I tried to pin it on Naia, but your brother managed to convince you she wasn't a part of it. It would have been more fun the other way." *He did it. He killed Father. He murdered the king. His nephew. For what?*

"Why?" I growled, anger filling my soul.

"Your father took everything from me. After what he did. He killed his own father. To avenge *her*," Ahiam sneered, pointing at Luria. Her breath caught. *Did she not know that? Or had she tried to forget?*

Ahiam continued, "Zaxton should never have gotten to rule Arilos. Never! It's my turn. I knew that you and your brother wouldn't hand the castle over to me without a fight so I had to plan another way to acquire the throne. I had to use a pawn. You."

"You won't win. Arilos will *never* be yours."

"And how not?" He questioned, spreading out his hands in front of him. "I have you, your guard. Your father's first love, *and* her daughter. The only person I need to take down is your brother, and then I will rule Arilos!"

I tried to stand, but he shoved me back down, putting his meaty foot on my sternum so I couldn't move.

"Ha, good luck with that," he laughed, signaling one of his men to grab me and pin me against the wall. I squirmed, trying to break free, trying to catch my breath. It was no use.

"Let him go, Ahiam," Luria spoke from behind me, her voice trembling.

He looked at his warrior and waved his hand. I dropped to the ground gasping for air. *He respected her? No that wasn't it. There is a history there. He said something…"you had her turn". What had he done to her?*

"Luria, are you really trying to command me," Ahiam laughed. "How have you been? How is your father? Oh… right… he is dead."

Luria's eyes darkened as she focused on Ahiam. I knew then that I should never mess with her. She would be a force to be reckoned with.

"Unhand him! He is only a boy! He wasn't alive either when everything went down! He is no more a part of this than my daughter is. Don't blame him for his fathers choices."

"His father crippled me! It is his fault I walk with this limp," Ahiam roared pointing to his mangled leg.

"That fault is your own. You hurt me so Zaxton hurt you. It might not have been right on his part, but you have to take responsibility for what *you* did."

"What I did? I don't know what- Oh, you mean what I did to *you*," he sneered. I shuddered at the sinisterness in his tone. This man was pure evil. And *I* had done things. I wasn't any better, but this man had no regrets whatsoever.

Luria's face tightened as if remembering what she had been through all those years ago at Ahiam's hand. And even now, she was having to endure him again. I was beginning to realize that maybe there was more to the whole story than what I had pieced together.

"I need to admit something," I said to Luria, my voice raspy, just above a whisper. I couldn't tell her all of it, but I would get a head start. Maybe someday I could admit everything I had done, but it wasn't time for that. I wasn't ready.

Luria looked at me, studying me, and tilted her head.

"Okay," she said simply.

"I have caused Naia a lot of pain. She-she should have chosen me for my uncle to kill. There is no question about that. I need you to know that I… I am sorry about everything, especially now… only now… after her offering her life for mine." I waited for her to respond, not knowing what else to say.

"You hate her because of her lineage? Because of me?" She asked at last. I hesitated. Then, knowing I had to say something, I looked her in the eyes and answered with one simple word.

"Yes."

"Why?"

"Does it matter?" I didn't want to talk about it any more. I didn't want to think about my mom.

Luria studied me for a moment and then asked a question that tore my heart in half.

"Do you regret what you did to my daughter?"

"Yes," I didn't hesitate to answer. "She never once disrespected me. She knew that I was her authority and she kept serving me as such despite my actions. I don't get it."

"I know you don't… You will." she said simply, and curled up, leaving me to my thoughts.

I heard her crying as she fell asleep. As she was able to get into her own mind and look into her thoughts, her memories of what had happened before were able to rise to the surface. I hated falling asleep for that very reason. I didn't want to think about things, but going to sleep seemed to be the time when thoughts awakened. Whether you wanted them to or not.

40

QUINLAN

The trap door flew open and I heard a soft gasp from above. Someone was thrown down and they let out a cry as they collided with the ground. Then silence.

"Quin?" The voice whispered.

Naia.

"Quin, what did they do to you?" She sobbed softly, a quiver in her voice. The door had shut. We were in complete darkness. I couldn't see her. I needed to see her.

Naia.

My soul flooded with emotions, relief, anger, fatigue.

Out of habit, I reached for where her voice was coming from and attempted to stretch my arms out to get to her, but remembered, too late, my broken ribs and torn flesh. I tried to whisper her name, but managed only a strange gurgling sound causing her to panic.

"Quin! Where are you! Quin, I am so sorry! Quin!"

"Ssshh, ssshh," I struggled to get even that out.

Unable to make big movements, I crept towards her an inch at a time until I finally grazed her face with my hands.

She flinched. I slowed down, not wanting to scare her, but also yearning for her touch. Her warmth.

Taking the pain that came with it, I pushed myself up so I was leaning against one of the corners of the walls. I couldn't keep myself from screaming in pain.

Naia tried to tell me to stop, to keep still, but all I wanted was to have her wrapped in my arms again. I kept at it until I was positioned how I wanted to be. I reached my arms out to where I knew her to be, despite the pain, and guided her so she was leaning into my chest against my shoulder. She exhaled softly as she rested her head against mine. I was her safe place. Her rock. Her heart.

We sat there in silence, my arms around her waist, for what seemed like hours.

Eventually, getting stiff, she shifted into a new position and I let out a mix of a grunt and a mangled moan.

"Quin, what did I do? Are you okay?" She panicked. Didn't she know I would rather have her in my arms and be in pain than have her not in them and hurt less?

"I'm okay, I'm okay," I barely managed to get out.

"Quinlan, tell me the truth, please," she pleaded.

"There's a lashing on my back…mmm… where your arms just grazed, and, aaahh, on my shoulder where your head is, but I'm okay, I promise. I'm just, mmm, I'm glad you are here." I managed to say in between labored breaths.

She sighed, then whispered something heart breaking in my ear. Something I couldn't imagine her having to think about. Something I didn't want her thinking about… Ever.

"He said you are going to die tonight," she whimpered. "He said… that they had beaten you so badly that you would die here in my arms and that would be my punishment for me not playing his game," she said, nuzzling into me further, forgetting the wounds I had just told her about. I grimaced, but I didn't mind. I understood the feeling of not being able to get close enough to someone. The feeling of wanting to be able to crawl into their soul.

"What? Mmmh, no, Naia, no. That isn't going to happen, not tonight, not ever." I said pulling her in tight despite the pain radiating through my body. I would always fight for her. I would always have her back. No matter the cost.

And then she surprised me. She tilted her head up and, after finding them, softly placed her lips on mine, lingering for a second and then slowly pulled away. My eyes widened in surprise, but I was delighted.

"What was…?" I started to say, but she cut me off.

"Please don't say anything- just hold me," she said tiredly. "I love you, Quin."

"I love you, Naia," I whispered, but she was already asleep in my arms.

I didn't have the heart to tell her my whole body was asleep and on fire. I eventually slumped over and fell asleep too, the pain numbing as my mind did.

The next day I was still alive. When she woke up, I asked her a question I had been dreading, but needed an answer. "Naia, I know you don't like talking about him, but I need to know," I paused, thinking the unimaginable… Did he? Did Javil, has he ever…?" I held onto her a little tighter and harshly exhaled, worried at what she might say.

"Did he?" I asked again.

She took a shaky breath. "No," she sighed. "Not that."

I breathed a sigh of relief. I would kill him. I didn't care if he was my brother in arms, my Prince, even if he were King. If he had… no. I wouldn't have cared- he would be dead.

Hours later, the door burst open again. It was light out. This time there were three guards with daggers strapped to their upper arms, and they jumped down into the pit with us.

They rushed in and pried Naia from my grasp, throwing her against the wall by the door. She yelped and collapsed to the ground. Not unconscious, but in a lot of pain.

I tried to lunge for her, at them- either would have worked, but my pain held me captive. I was stuck on the ground as they hurt her. One kick, then another. I couldn't take it anymore.

"Enough! Leave her alone!" I shouted, helpless.

Thwack. I took a blow to my jaw. As I took the hit, Naia cried out, partly because she hated seeing me get hurt, but more so because the guard had smashed his foot down on her arm as he threw the punch at me. Despite all the pain coursing through my body, I lunged and placed myself between the man and Naia, arms up, ready to take whatever they threw at me. They would not hurt her again. Not if I was there.

"Enough," a voice at the top of the door said. His tone conveyed that he didn't care in the slightest. He was stopping the torture simply because he wanted to speak..

Naia froze. It was Ahiam.

"You're alive, I see." He said, unenthusiastically.

"Yes," I snarled.

"Pity," he replied, then turned to Naia, who was still lying on the ground in pain.

"Well, let's get to it," he said, waving his hand at the guards to lift Naia out of the pit.

"Get to what?" I growled, still shielding Naia.

"You know... her choice." He smirked. "Her choice to die for you and the Prince. I shall see it carried out," he said waving his hand at a guard, then shoved me away from Naia. She was completely defenseless as they roped her arms and hauled her out of the pit.

One night went by, then another, and Naia was never brought back to me. I feared that she had really been killed. The door opened seemingly every twelve to fifteen hours and something edible was thrown down to me. I had no idea what it was, but it was bitter and soft. I could barely get it down, but I knew that I needed any form of strength if I ever got out of here to go after the man who had stolen My Heart from me.

JAVIL

Luria and I had the chance to talk a little bit more before I was dragged out of the pit. We talked about my life growing up in the castle, what her life in Rowynala had been like, and a little bit about what had happened between her and my father.

I was shocked to hear how their story ended.

After my grandfather had killed her father, Jorah, she was separated from her mother. She and her guard took refuge in Rowynala for a while and then, after some intense events took place, they ended up settling there after her mother had passed from an illness.

I was speechless as she told me her whole story. It was the most tragic one I had heard yet. Naia's was close, but it didn't surpass her mother's.

Luria had just asked to hear about my father's death and burial when the door flung open and a ladder dropped down.

"Climb, boy," the voice said. Not an appropriate way to address his Prince, but I obeyed for the sole purpose of not wanting to be hit again.

As I exited, I saw Naia being dragged into the clearing where we had been earlier. I wasn't sure how long it had been.

They grabbed my arms and half dragged me to where she was already kneeling on the ground, her eyes covered with a piece of cloth. She was silent. *What had they done to her?*

"Hit the girl," I was instructed by my great uncle as they brought me up next to her.

"What?" I retaliated backwards. "Never again," I looked at Naia, a promise in my eyes.

"Again? Oh, oohhh, you've hit her before?" Ahiam exclaimed almost gleefully, clearly intrigued by my statement. "Hit her," he demanded, and stepped closer to me. "You know you want to," he teased.

"No, Ahiam, I won't hit her again. She doesn't deserve it and never has," I said, turning to Naia. Though she couldn't see me, I knew that she was aware of my gaze.

Ahiam thought for a moment and then spoke, staring directly into my eyes. "Either you hit her or *he* hits you," He said with a smirk, motioning to a really muscular warrior whom I knew could knock me out in two seconds flat.

I knew what I had to do. I could redeem myself- or start to; show Naia that I *had* changed. If we made it out alive, I wanted to look her in the eye someday and tell her I not only regretted my previous choices, but that I went the whole way to try to make up for them. I wanted to try to somehow pay her back for saving my life. Twice.

"Come at me." I taunted, turning to the burley guy. "Give me your best shot." He punched. I blacked out.

The next thing I remembered, I was in a dirt circle, people were cheering, and someone was handing me a sword.

42

NAIA

I heard the hit as the guard's fist collided with Javil's face. *Javil took a punch for me? Maybe he really could change.*

"... but I want to give another option before I do to make it more interesting."

"Hmmm?"

Apparently Ahiam had been talking, but I wasn't listening. I had been through so much. They had taken me from Quin and had practically starved me for two days. Then they put a cloth over my eyes and dragged me to a field where Javil had refused to strike me. I couldn't think-let alone make a choice like what Ahiam was asking.

"I will take that as a yes," Ahiam said, turning on his heels to leave. I still had no idea what I had just indirectly agreed to.

"I will give you a chance to say goodbye," Ahiam said sorrowfully and had his guards throw me back into the pit with Quin.

QUINLAN

I rushed over to where she had landed just as the door slammed shut again, leaving us in the overwhelming darkness.

"What happened, Naia? Are you hurt?" She whimpered and crawled into my outstretched arms.

"He didn't hit me. Javil didn't hit me!" She cried. *What?*

She felt so small. I could feel her bones. When was the last time she had eaten? Were they trying to starve her to death or just torturing her before they actually killed her?

"He said he would let us say goodbye, Quin. What does that mean?" I shuddered against her, pulling her in tight against me. Her heart was pounding so fast.

"I don't know, My Heart, but I know that I will fight for you with every breath and every ounce of strength that I have. I won't let anything happen to you." I took her face in mine.

"Quin, you can't promise that. You have no control over what happens. I... I don't know what to do! They have you, my mom, and Javil! Any choice I make will hurt someone."

"Naia, this shouldn't rest on your shoulders. None of this is your fault. Nothing that has happened is your fault. Do you understand?" I said, kissing the top of her head as she had reburied herself in my chest. "I've got you," I whispered.

"Time's up!" a voice called from above and we were both roped and dragged out into a dirt patch surrounded with curious villagers, wondering of the events to come.

We didn't get a chance to say goodbye.

44

PICEL

have to go after them.

I made sure the castle could handle my absence and set out to Rowynala with a group of my best warriors.

I instructed them to wait at the edge of the forest for my return. I didn't want anyone else getting hurt. My plan was to sneak into camp and release them one at a time, so as to not cause a scene, but they didn't listen. They wouldn't send me into enemy territory without backup. Good men.

We made it to the headquarters around noon. I was not prepared for what I saw when I arrived.

Javil and Quinlan were face to face in an open dirt field, both armed, both already beaten to a pulp, though I guessed not from each other. A girl was weeping in the front of the crowd. *Naia.* She was hurt too. I cringed at her visible wounds. I couldn't bear to think of what wasn't seen.

A man shouted from a makeshift throne set up to overlook everything, and my attention turned to him. I knew this man. He looked like... oh no. Ahiam. Ahiam who had nearly killed my brother, who I presumed had set the fire in Rowynala, and who I assumed killed my father too. I quivered in fear.

Hiding in the trees I inched closer as the fight began. I had to come up with a plan and fast.

45

NAIA

I couldn't bear to watch… but I had to. Quin and Javil both looked so close to death. I didn't know how they were still standing. Javil and Quinlan, *oh, my Quinlan, we didn't even get to say goodbye*, stood face to face eight paces apart, walking in circles, swords in hand, waiting for the signal to fight.

Quin glanced at me and gave a small smile, trying to encourage me even as he walked, already gravely injured, into his probable death.

It was clear that Javil was the stronger of the two. Though, it confused me that Ahiam was willing to let Javil live being an heir to the throne; a threat. The fight was just for the theatricality of it all. The torture. Javil would end up dead sooner or later.

The horn blew, and the fight began. Both men knew that if they didn't fight the punishment would be my death. Surprisingly, Javil didn't seem to want that anymore. Something had shifted in him when I had offered my life for his. I had become one of his protected.

Quin made the first move, grazing Javil's arm. Javil winced and returned the favor by nicking Quin's cheek. Quin grimaced but surged forward forcing Javil to back up. I was surprised he had that much energy left in him. *Adrenaline. He was fighting for me.* I put my hands over my eyes and peaked through. I didn't want to see the whole picture. I didn't want to watch the man I loved fight and possibly die. It was too much to bear. I could see the rising anger in Quin's eyes as he went after Javil. This was his chance to get back at him for hurting me. This was his chance for revenge.

They sparred back and forth for a while, giving each other little injuries that they could sustain and continue to fight. I knew even though Quin was mad, he didn't really want to kill Javil. Eventually Ahiam had had enough of the light swordplay and gave an order that they end this quickly- the Kill Order.

All of my breath went away. I couldn't move and couldn't turn away all at the same time. Either way, someone was going to die. I loved Quinlan and couldn't bear to witness his death, but Javil was Picel's brother, someone I was starting to care about. I couldn't imagine having to tell Picel that his brother was dead. It was a lose lose situation and I hated it.

"It's okay," I heard Javil whisper to Quin. "Do it. I deserve it. You know I do. Quin, DO IT!" Javil screamed, falling onto his knees, opening his arms, and hanging his head. He was offering his life for Quin's? I knew that they were friends, like brothers, but Javil dying for Quin? That I didn't see coming.

Quinlan hesitated and then raised his sword to strike. I leaned forward as he did, waiting to see if I would still have the love of my life in a few minutes. The guard behind me must have thought I was going to try to make a break for it, because he placed his hands on my shoulders ordering me to stay back. As if telling me that no matter what happens, there was nothing that I could do to either change it or fix it.

As Quinlan moved to bring the sword down on Javil, he made eye contact with me, mouthing *I love you, My Heart.* He turned back to Javil who stood before him. But instead of striking Javil, in a split second he dropped his sword to the ground below, grabbed the dagger that was still under his tunic somehow, and drove it into his own chest, immediately dropping to the ground.

I screamed. My vision blurred. I don't know if it was from shock or from tears. Probably both. I tried to breathe, but I couldn't get a deep breath. I felt like I was suffocating.

The guard behind me released his grasp on my shoulders and shouted something. I was too dazed to put together what it was, but heard more shouting so I looked up and tried to focus on what was happening around me.

Fights were breaking out everywhere. I saw flashes of gold and heard a thundering voice run past me. *Picel.* "Naia, go to him. He needs you." He himself was headed for Ahiam.

Springing into action, almost blindly, I rushed to Quin's side as people were falling all around me. As I approached him, someone was running from where he laid. *Who was that?*

After I saw him up close I only had one thought. *He can't die alone. He can't die alone. He can't die alone.*

"Quin, Quin, what were you thinking? Quin, please, please don't leave me," I sobbed over his body.

Somehow he was still conscious, though I feared he wouldn't be for long. There was a lot of blood. He raised one of his hands and placed it on my head. I could *feel* his breath struggling as he inhaled and exhaled with great difficulty.

"Naia," he gasped. "Our job was to save Javil. You did that; now it's my turn," he said as he started coughing. Blood. *No.* "I love you with every fiber of my being," he continued, pain in every syllable. "Don't forget me, please."

"Never, Quin… I could never," I said, gently pressing my lips onto his, giving him one final kiss as he breathed his last.

Out. In. Out. In. Out…

46

PICEL

After I saw Quin fall, I signaled my warriors. We attacked full force and took out the intruders in the Rowynalyn village pretty quickly. It was clear that Ahiam was there without invitation. He didn't have a lot of reinforcements in Rowynala, which was his first mistake. His second... messing with my family.

I sent a few men to get Naia, Javil, and Quin's body, while I went straight for Ahiam, whose eyes widened as he saw me. He started to say something, but I didn't give him a chance. He would pay for Quinlan's death, and my brother's and Naia's injuries; though, not by a death of his own. Not yet.

I knocked Ahiam out with the hilt of my sword. He grunted and collapsed like a fallen rag. I jumped on him and secured him with ropes on his hands and feet and shoved a gag in his mouth. I didn't care that he was in his sixties. He was a dirty rotten scoundrel.

I sent him off to the dungeons of the castle with my best warriors. He was getting up there in years, but I would take no chances of an escape. I gave my warriors strict instructions to keep him passed out by any means necessary. The only thing they couldn't do was kill him.

I scanned the scene playing out before me. Naia was crying over top of Quin's body while Javil was standing off to the side talking to someone. She looked just like Naia. I was still trying to place who she was when it dawned on me. It was Luria, the woman my father knew, Naia's mom. I breathed a sigh of relief. At least after losing the love of her life, Naia had her mother present with her.

I started walking towards Javil and Luria, but Luria excused herself and walked away to tend to Naia. She gave me a slight nod in passing and I returned the motion. *Does she know who I am?*

"Are you okay?" I asked Javil as I walked up to him. He looked horrible. I had never seen anyone look as bad as he did. He looked worse than I felt after the last battle.

"What do you think?" He said back, not angrily, but defeated.

"Did you know Quin was going to do that?" I asked.

"No," was all he said.

I knew that had to be hard for him. He was the protector, it's in his blood, though it was Quinlan's job. He would beat himself up over this for a while.

I placed my hand on his shoulder and he jerked away from my touch. I had others to check on and knew that it wasn't the time to talk, so I gave him a small nod and walked away.

I made my way over to Naia, who was still draped over Quinlan, and Luria, who noticed my arrival. This time she gave a small curtsy, acknowledging that she knew who I was. In return, I gave a small bow signaling my respect for her. So there wouldn't be two battles today then. Good. Naia had already been through too much. I didn't need her to witness a fight between myself and her mother.

"We need to get her out of here," Javil said, approaching from behind me. *Since when did he care?*

"Yes, that would be wise," Luria agreed, turning to me for confirmation. I nodded. We needed to get her home, but first I needed to make a hard stop.

"Picel," Javil said quietly. "A word."

He guided me off to the side and spoke words that I had been trying to avoid.

"Picel, taking Quin is just going to slow us down. And we need to get Naia to safety and fast. We don't know how many Rowynalyn's will fight for Ahiam. We need to leave his body here."

My body tensed. Quin was my best friend, my best warrior. I hated the thought of leaving him to rot in Rowynala, alone, but Javil was right. Naia was fading and though he didn't want to admit it, Javil was too.

It was custom that when a warrior fell, an entourage of warriors, and sometimes the king himself, would go to the warrior's home to tell the family in person of the fallen.

Javil wanted to take Naia with him on his horse, but I insisted that she ride with me. I was appreciative that he was protecting her, but I still didn't trust him to not hurt her if something went wrong. We set out through the woods, hoping to arrive at their cottage by nightfall.

47

NAIA

I tried to move. I couldn't. I was trapped. Panicking I started to thrash around, but someone quickly tightened their grip around me, pulling me in tight against their chest and whispered in my ear, "Breathe. You are safe." I winced, my injuries causing me pain with each movement. *Why were we moving so much?* As I calmed, the voice spoke again.

"Naia, hey, it's okay, I've got you. You are safe. We are going home. We just have to make one quick stop first."

Picel.

I realized we were on horseback riding through the forest of Rowynala. That's why I was being jostled around so much. I faced Picel from the front of the saddle. He held me so carefully, so tenderly. I buried my head against his neck, safe in his arms, and fell back into sleep.

"Naia, how could you! You had the chance to save me and you didn't! I thought you loved me! I thought that I held your heart!"

"You do! Quin you ARE my heart! I love you more than anything! Quin! Stay with me, please!"

"Quin!"

48

PICEL

I laid Naia on the ground outside and passed her off to Luria's care. Taking a deep breath, I knocked on Quin's parents door. His father opened it and his knees buckled. He knew. *He knew.*

"Ingrid," he called, his voice tight. "Ingrid honey, we have company."

"What, well who could it be at this hour? Not those travelers again. They scared that poor girl away. I wonder what has become of her," she rambled as she made her way to the main room where we had gathered.

She entered carrying a bowl of something and, when she realized I was there, it crashed to the floor, sending shards of clay flying in all directions. The bowl's contents splattered on the ground and on the bottom of her already dirty dress.

"Oh my," she said, fear creeping into her eyes as she looked each one of us over. "Oh, no," she whispered, seeing the crest of Arilos upon my chest guard. She knew. *She knew. But I still have to tell her. I have to tell her that her son, her only son, her only child, is dead.*

"Ahem," I started, not really knowing where to go from there. How was I supposed to do this? Quin was one of my closest friends- not just a guard- he *meant* something to me personally. *Tell them that, Picel.*

"Ma'am, Sir, uh I don't know how to tell you this, I don't know where to begin at all, uh, maybe you should sit down?" I tried, but they just stared at me, waiting for me to drop the news that they already knew. *They just need to hear it.*

"Quinlan is gone." *Tell the whole story Picel.* "He died, protecting my brother, the prince, and the love of his life-Quin's life. He pierced his own flesh in order to keep the Prince alive and the blood off his hands. Javil and Quinlan were forced to fight to the death with the girl watching. It was brutal, tragic, and I give you my deepest condolences. His life should not have ended that way. He was… Quin was one of my closest friends, but as his parents, I can't imagine what you are feeling."

I bowed, taking a step back to give them some space to process everything, but what his mother did surprised me. She walked over to me slowly and gently placed her hands on my face. All of my men were on guard, but I subtly lifted my hand to keep them back. This woman would not harm me.

"Thank you," she said softly through tears, "Thank you for coming to tell us yourself. That is very honorable, Your Majesty."

I hugged her then, Quinlan's mother, for a few moments before she let go and made her way back to her husband, who spoke next.

"The girl, what happened to her? Did his death really save her? Is she okay?"

"Yes, she is. Well, she is alive at least. She is in grave condition, and she is completely distraught as well. We need to get her back to the castle as soon as we can to get her help," I said.

"She is here?" Ingrid gasped.

"Yes, her mother and my brother have her outside. We were not sure if as things are, you would wish to see her or not."

"Bring her in, please!" Ingrid cried. "It is still winter. She must be freezing! Get her in here by the fire. There is no reason for you to travel back tonight. And I have herbs that will help her heal quicker."

"Are you sure it won't be too much trouble?"

"By all means, no!" She said, heading to the door.

When she opened it, she found Javil and Luria crouching next to Naia on the ground. Naia's face was turned toward her mother, hidden from view. Javil had laid out a blanket for her to rest upon to protect her from the cold dirt and leaves below.

Ingrid gasped and took action immediately, instructing Javil to pick her back up and bring her to the fireplace, where Edwin was setting up a makeshift bed for her to lie on. I didn't like him holding her, I wasn't even sure if he was well enough to, but I stepped back as he walked her through the door and gently laid her down. Before he stepped back he traced her jawline with his thumb. My body went rigid as I saw him touch her like that. He had no right. Not after what he did to her.

Ingrid brought out another quilted blanket and handed it to Luria to wrap around Naia as well. Her face contorted into puzzlement as she looked at Luria, but she shook it off and busied herself cooking dinner for everyone. I begged her not to, but she and Edwin insisted.

Edwin went out to his little stable and carved up one of his lambs for us. It was some of the best meat I had ever had in my life. No offense to Pepper.

We ate in silence, not wanting to disturb Naia's slumber so Ingrid quietly whispered, "What is her name? The girl that my son loved and saved?"

I hadn't realized that Naia's name hadn't come up yet but, then again, we had been more focused on Quin's death.

"Naia. Her name is Naia," Luria spoke softly on her daughter's behalf. Both Ingrid and Edwin gasped and looked at each other. Frozen they looked at us, tears forming in Ingrid's eyes. I realized that their small motion had caused my warriors to move in, ready to strike if needed.

"Drop your weapons," I commanded quickly. "You are causing fright in an already broken household." No one moved. "Drop your weapons," I said louder.

As they backed away, Ingrid slowly stood and approached where Naia was laying and brushed a strand of hair from her eyes. Seeing her face for the first time fully, she gasped again.

"Edwin, Edwin, it is her!" She exclaimed! "It is the same girl whom you found all that time ago! Who had lost her family! Edwin, she is okay!" Even through the dirt and the bruises she could tell that it was Naia. I was impressed.

"Ingrid, I don't know if *okay* is the right word, but yes, it is her, and she is alive and Quinlan saved her. It's a miracle."

"You know her?" Javil asked, standing up to walk towards them and then knelt down next to Ingrid. He took Naia's hand in his.

"Yes, she came to us after she went over the waterfall the night of the attack on her village. Some men came to our house looking for her mother Luria, she must have heard and then disappeared. She had lost her whole family… but you," she said, turning to Luria. "You are her mother?"

"I am," Luria said softly.

Realization set in Edwin's eyes. "Wait. I know you… Luria? Your Majesty!" He said and dropped to his knees and bowed his head. "What happened to your family was a tragedy. I am so sorry, I… I should have done more. If I had more courage to stand up to Ishvi… You and Gibor kind of just disappeared."

"We had to for our safety, and the safety of the castle. I didn't want to leave, but Zaxton…" her voice trailed off. "Edwin. I don't, and never have, blamed you for anything. You refused to hurt me even though it could have cost you your life. I owe you my *life* for that. Truly. And Ingrid took care of me when I was close to death. You have done nothing but help me and my family."

Edwin choked back a sob and brought his sleeve up to wipe the tears forming in his eyes.

"But you should still be Queen! It is your rightful place!"

I tensed as Luria glanced my way, and then back at Edwin. "The King and I have yet to discuss this, my friend," she said calmly. "Though, I will say, I have no intention of claiming the throne for myself, if that helps with anything, Your Majesty," she admitted, "I grew to enjoy my life, and am not at a place where I am wanting to reclaim my throne, but if my daughter wants it for herself…"

"It shall be hers," I interrupted and cleared my throat. "If Naia wants the throne… it shall be hers."

Luria looked at me kindly and smiled. We were unified again. I know my father would have been pleased. A thought crossed my mind as we finished dinner and made our way to our sleeping quarters for the night. *This is what it can look like when pride falls.*

I smiled and drifted off into a deep slumber, thankful for my brother, for Naia, and for Ingrid and Edwin who, even after finding out about their son's death, graciously welcomed us into their home.

Javil wouldn't leave her side. Not even to sleep. He slept with one arm draped over her body even though he was in bad shape himself. They had beaten him to a pulp.

I winced as I looked at his body. Ingrid and Luria had convinced him to stand next to her for a few minutes while they tended to his wounds. He had stripes across his back, and bruises lining every inch of him. He should be dead. I was still curious about the motives of Ahiam in letting him live. Maybe he wouldn't have if I hadn't shown up with my men.

Ingrid was ready to offer me Quin's old room, but I politely declined. There was no way I could sleep in the bed of my recently killed friend. I offered the bed to Luria and she graciously accepted. She was a lady; a Queen. She shouldn't be sleeping on the floor anyway.

I resorted to sleeping on a bale of hay Edwin had set up outside for himself when he wanted some fresh air. It had been a while since I had slept under the stars. Granted, there were branches and leaves blocking most of the view, but it was the thought that counted. It was cold, but I had a blanket and my cloak, so I was alright.

Early in the morning, I heard a rustling noise and was jolted awake by a crash to my left. I sprung up grabbing my sword and, in turning around, faced Edwin standing there mouth agape.

"Your Majesty, I am so sorry to disturb you," he said frantically. "I get up at this hour to tend to my few animals before the sun completely rises, and I like to assist my wife with things around the house after she wakes up. It is the only time I get alone. I apologize, I didn't realize you were out here."

"Oh, you are quite alright. I am just a little on edge from the events of the last few weeks," I admitted, lowering my sword and sheathing it.

"Mmm, you have been through a lot haven't you, your Majesty?"

"Please, Sir, call me Picel,"

"Only if you call me Edwin,"

"Edwin. If you or Ingrid need anything, and I mean anything at all, please do not hesitate to reach out to me personally," I changed the subject.

"It is an honor, your Majes- Picel," he corrected.

We sat in silence for a while until we heard the women get up, and then made our way inside to help with the morning chores.

Luria and Ingrid were deep in a conversation when we walked back in.

"She needs to be queen. Your family needs to take the throne back."

"That is her choice, Ingrid. I won't force her. I like Picel: he is doing a marvelous job like his father before him."

"Ahem," I cleared my throat as we walked towards them. "Good morning, ladies. How are we fairing this morning?" I asked with a smile that was directed at Luria for the kind things I had overheard her saying. She smiled and went to the stone oven to stir what was boiling in the pot. It smelled so fresh...mint? She was boiling mint for Naia and Javil's wounds. It must have been done because she took the pot off the stove, wrapped it in a cloth so she wouldn't burn herself, and brought it over to where Javil was still passed out. Naia was still under the protection of his arm.

"Sire, Sire," Luria said quietly, as to not disturb her sleeping daughter. "Javil, wake up, we need to redress your wounds."

"Mmm," was all he got out.

I moved in to help, knowing how stubborn he could be.

"Brother, get up," I commanded, gently nudging his ribcage. Wrong move. He was up in an instant and despite his injuries, had me pinned against the still scorching stone oven. I screamed in pain as my calf was burned by the sizzling stones.

Out of instinct, my hands went to his throat and I brought him to the floor gasping for air.

"Enough!" I yelled in his face. "Enough! Javil, until you get a hold on your emotions, I am separating you from Naia. you are a danger to us all if we can't touch you without you attacking. What if that had been Luria? Or Ingrid? What would you have done then? They could be dead! You are lucky it was me you attacked."

"I'm so sorry," he struggled to say under the pressure of my thumb on his throat.

"What?" I said, releasing him, though I already knew what he had said. I wanted him to say it again.

"I am so sorry," he repeated, sitting up. "I was dreaming. You *know* not to wake me up when I am asleep. Especially after an attack. You have no idea what I've been through and what she went through," he said, gesturing to Naia. "Give me a minute to heal from it all. *Please*," he pleaded.

I thought for a minute, debating my choices. I knew that he would hate me forever if I kept him from Naia, but I also knew that if he were to hurt her, I would be at fault. One of the hardest parts of being King was making those kind of decisions, especially when it revolved around my family. I turned to him and sighed. Knowing that what I would say next could change everything.

"Javil, you aren't to be alone with Naia unsupervised. You will not stay with her at night and you will not keep her company during the day unless someone is there to chaperone you. I am sorry, but after the choices you have made you have to earn back your trust, with me and with Naia. I also don't want you taking care of her without her permission, and right now she is not able to give that. If you do, spend time alone with her, and I find out, there will be severe consequences."

Javil glared at me and took a step forward. My guards moved in. "Who are you to decide what is best for her! Her mother is in the room!" He shouted.

"I agree with the king," Luria said softly. "Until you prove that you can be trusted, I don't want you around my daughter unless Picel or myself are there."

"Is that how it is going to be?" Javil spat.

"Yes, brother. It is."

Javil scoffed and stormed out of the house. I heard the pounding of hooves withdrawing away. I guessed that he would return to Arilos and sulk. That was fine with me. I would rather have him angry at me and be away than have him be at peace with me and accidentally hurt Naia or someone else in the house.

Luria slathered some mint on my burn to help cool it down and then wrapped it; it wasn't bad and would heal in a week's time.

A few days later it was time to go home. Time to somehow get back to the normal that never existed in the first place.

JAVIL

They arrived back at the castle a few days later. Naia was still sleeping most of the time. She wasn't doing well at all. She was really sick and had too many infections from the lashes and cuts she had received in Rowynala. I wasn't sure if she was going to make it. And that killed me.

My heart had changed the instant that she willingly offered her life for mine. In an instant everything I had done to her came flying back to me and I regretted it with all my heart. I wished I could take it all back, but I couldn't. What was done was done. I could only hope that she, that everyone, could maybe, one day, forgive me. Then I remembered what else I had done and knew they never would.

I was furious with Picel that he didn't trust me, but at the same time I understood his reservations about me. I just had to prove to him that I really had changed. How I was going to do that I had no idea.

50

NAIA

DAY I (Edwin and Ingrid's cottage)

"Naia, stay with me, stay with me. I owe you the throne, I really do. You saved my brother, even after everything that he did to you. I am so sorry about Quin. Please wake up; I can't lose you too. You were so brave, so strong, so selfless. You are everything a queen should be. Your mother said that she doesn't want the throne; it's yours if you wake up. Naia, please."

Picel.

"Naia, sweetheart, I can't believe that it was you that Quinlan ended up with. After he met you in the marketplace I could tell that he was taken by you. I know him, I never saw you together, but I know that he really, really loved you. Fight for him sweetie, please."

Ingrid.

DAY 2

"Naia, please. I am so sorry for everything. Please wake up so you can forgive me. I know that is selfish, but I need you to. Please. I need to thank you for saving my life and for being willing to sacrifice yourself for me. I didn't deserve that. I don't deserve that. Naia, wake up!"

Javil.

DAY 4 (Back in Arilos)

"Naia, sip on this, please. You have to eat. I want my friend back! Please! Naia?"

Pepper.

DAY 7

"Sweetie, you need to get up and get out of bed. It's been a week. You need to get up. I know you have loved and lost, and that is so hard, but you still have people who love and care about you. Javil and Picel are devastated that you are not recovering. I am scared for you, sweetie. Please, open your eyes! God is still good!"

Mom.

DAY 12

"She is going to die if she doesn't get up soon. There has to be something that can be done."

Javil.

"She is barely getting enough water and broth. I have given her maybe three sips each day for almost two weeks! She can't live on that."

Pepper.

"Don't say that! She might be able to hear you!"

Mom.

"She isn't wrong, Luria. She is so depressed, sick, and injured. If she doesn't start to try, it could very well kill her."

Javil.

"We are doing everything we can, your Highness, but there comes a point where she has to choose to fight. You remember those times, don't you?"

Zahir.

51

PICEL

DAY 15

It was my night to watch Naia. I had talked it over with Luria and we decided it was a good idea to take turns watching Naia overnight or else we would all be exhausted all the time. With me having to run a kingdom, I knew she was right.

It came to a point, though, where I couldn't bear to see her suffering anymore. She was so depressed because of losing Quin and barely eating anything. It killed me to see her in so much pain.

Her body was mostly healed, her cuts and lashes, at least, were scarring up; now we needed to get to her mind. We needed to give her a little push.

"That is it. Naia, I am done letting you sulk," I said marching to her bedside after Luria and I had traded places. "We lost Quinlan too. He was my best friend. I am sad too, but it is time to get up. It's been

15 days, Naia, so I am going to do what needs to be done." I ranted, but also spoke in a gentle tone. I really did care for her.

I placed my hands under her and gently brought her to a sitting position. She fought a little bit, but then gave in as she still didn't have much strength.

There was a light knock on the door and Pepper let herself in. I had asked for her to meet me in Quin's room as we were leaving dinner. I knew that Pepper cared greatly for Naia as well, so she would do anything to help; even though she was the cook. I had her excused from her duties for a while and told her that I would pay her for her help with Naia. She would have done it for free, but I wasn't going to keep her from getting paid.

With Zahir being her uncle, she knew enough about medicine to be helpful in that aspect of things as well. When she entered, I asked her to go to Naia's room and bring a brush and a clean change of garments to my chambers.

Naia had been placed in Quinlan's room to grieve, but she couldn't stay there. Remembering Quinlan and their shared memories was just too painful for her. She didn't say that of course, but she would never make any progress staying there. I knew that from experience from when my mother had passed.

She was too weak to walk. I carefully scooped her up in my arms and carried her to my room, gently laying her on my bed. It was the only place I trusted her to be where Javil wouldn't enter without permission.

She was so light. The only sounds I heard from her were moans and groans of pain and complaint, but I was determined that Naia would get better - no matter what.

As I laid her down I cringed when I saw a scar on her temple and realized it was from when Javil had smacked her and sent her flying into the wall. There were a few lash marks on her arms but, as Pepper pulled her dress down, and I moved my arms, I saw that some bruising still covered the entirety of her back and stomach. *What had she endured in Rowynala?*

Pepper came in shortly after and we got to work. I sat Naia up and leaned her against me, holding her neck delicately so Pepper could brush her hair without pulling Naia backwards. Once her hair was finally free from its knots and tangles, Pepper styled it with a low braid that fell straight down her back, allowing her to lay down and still be comfortable. I held Naia close, my mouth against her ear, softly encouraging her to keep fighting and reminding her of how strong she was.

I tried to be considerate and closed my eyes as Pepper lifted Naia's underdress off her body and replaced it with a fresh one, but did I have to look a few times to make sure I had her positioned in a way for Pepper to get the dress on. It was difficult work changing an almost unconscious person - especially as gentle as we had to be to avoid her remaining few injuries.

After we finished changing her, I laid her back down on my pillow and placed myself gently down next to her. I studied her as she quickly fell asleep, still not fighting for consciousness. She was breathing better, though, and seemed more peaceful. I gently moved a piece of shorter hair that had fallen from the braid and landed across her eyes. As I tucked it behind her ear she spoke.

"Thank you, Pi..." she trailed off before finishing my name. I smiled. *Pi.*

"Of course, Naia." I replied.

Pepper gently awakened me an hour later with food for Naia. It was the middle of the night, but we needed to try and get her to eat something. It was not my intention to fall asleep next to her, but I had been so tired I didn't even remember drifting away into a deep slumber.

I murmured in Naia's ear what I was doing as I sat her up and slid in behind her. I gently held her head up as Pepper spoon fed her bit by bit. Together, with a bit of coaxing, we managed to get Naia to eat over half the broth and drink a full cup of water. By the time she had finished, she was basically asleep again and had nestled up against my neck. Pepper looked at me and smiled.

"I hope it is not out of place for me to say, Majesty, but you two could make a cute pair."

I blushed. "Ah… ahem… thank you, Pepper."

"Of course Majesty," she curtsied and left, leaving Naia and I alone. *I think so too.*

"Picel? Picel?" Naia murmured.

I opened my eyes and turned my head realizing that she had flipped over during the night and was lying on my chest. I fought back a smile. *No Picel, don't think that way. She isn't yours.*

"How are you feeling?" I asked. Some hair had fallen in the path of her eyes so I brushed it gently away as she answered, tilting her head up so she was looking into my eyes. I resisted the urge to continue stroking her head, but oh how I wanted to.

"I am still weak, but I am alright. Has it been you taking care of me?" She laid her head back down against the warmth of my neck and I pressed my lips onto her head. I couldn't stop myself. *Careful Picel.*

"All of us have been, but last night you were in my care," I murmured. She hadn't asked me to move yet so I contentedly stayed how I was.

"Why did you bring me into your room instead of Quin's?" She asked softly.

I took a breath trying to buy time as I thought of a way to explain my thought process to her, but before I found the words, the door flew open. Javil.

"Why is she in here?" He demanded.*So much for not entering without asking first.*

"Good morning to you too," I said, pulling Naia in a little tighter. I didn't like him being near her, even if I was present.

"Why. Is. She. Here?" He said again, taking a step forward.

"I was actually just about to explain that to Naia," I replied, more calm than the time before. I knew that there was no point in fighting him. And I didn't want to scare Naia. Javil was doing enough of that for both of us.

"Then explain," he demanded, folding his arms across his chest. "Explain why you get to take care of her, why *everyone* gets to take care of her but me!"

In the process of Javil coming in yelling, Naia had taken my hand. When Javil demanded for answers she gave it a little squeeze; a gentle reminder to keep breathing. Even in her fear and pain she was trying to help me. I admired that.

"Well, I figured that by staying where she was," I didn't want to say Quin's name so I went around it, "I thought it wise to bring her to a place to make new memories. Ones that won't make her so sad."

"New memories, in your room, with you! All I want is a chance to prove myself that I won't hurt her and no one will let me near her! Also you should have told me! I went to his room looking for her and she wasn't there! I thought that something had happened to her I…!"

Naia had curled up tightly next to me. She clearly did not like Javil's presence anymore than I did. "Picel," she whispered. "Make him go away, please."

Javil heard her words and stopped dead in the middle of his sentence. His voice softened. "Naia, please, I am not going to hurt you anymore. The minute you offered your life for mine I knew that I was wrong about you. I regret everything. Please, please forgive me. I beg you!" Javil pleaded, and took a step closer to the bed. "I want to do better, I want to change. I know that we will never be friends, but I at least want you to trust that I won't hurt you ever again. I need you to trust-"

Naia pressed herself harder into my body, trying to get away from the man that had put her through some of her hardest trials.

"Javil, you need to go," I warned. He stood there, not moving.

"Now, Javil." He was hurt. He scowled and tucked his head into his chest like a child who had just been punished by their father.

"I… I am sorry," he said, noticing Naia's frightful position against me for the first time. "I will go. Forgive me," he said sorrowfully and walked out the door.

JAVIL

"Luria, what am I going to have to do to prove myself to everyone? To you? I don't want to be who I used to be. I don't want to be Ahiam." Luria looked up from her book and studied me for a couple seconds before replying.

"Javil," she said carefully, "Your father made a *choice* to not treat people the way that his father and uncle treated people. I think I can say that you, this far, haven't made that choice. You might be making it now, but trust doesn't form overnight. You have to earn it."

"But people aren't letting me earn it! That is why I am so frustrated!" I shouted. Luria sighed.

"Look at it this way. If you were King and you had a warrior who had just started working at the castle, would you promote them to be your guard on their first day?"

"No, that would be pure brainlessness!" I exclaimed.

"Exactly. You would make them earn their way by the little tasks, starting in training and then working their way up to a village guard and then a castle guard and then, eventually, once they have earned enough trust, you would consider promoting them to be your guard."

"It is like that with Naia. Because of all the choices you have made in the past, you are starting out in training and then, as time progresses, you will gain more and more trust from the little things. Once you have proven able to do the small things, then you will be considered for the bigger things. If you can't be trusted with small, not super important things, then you won't be trusted with bigger things. Does that make sense?"

It did. And I was completely taken aback at how ridiculous I had been in my thinking. I thanked her and left. *The little things. What does that look like?*

53

PICEL

A hiam was still in the dungeons. I had contemplated just letting
him starve and rot away, but thought better. That is something
he would do, not me.

I descended the stairs after lunch to speak with him for the first
time since taking him captive. I would have been more likely to kill
him had I gone down sooner.

He was huddled in the corner, chilled without a blanket to keep
him warm. I banged on the cell bars to wake him up. He jumped,
clearly startled, but quickly resumed a look of hatred on his face- one
I was sure he wore often.

"Ahiam," I said, resentment flooding each letter.

"Nephew," he replied coolly. "What do you want from me? Are
you here to kill me? To torture me?" He croaked.

"That is entirely up to you," I said. I had talked with Javil and Luria the day before, and we agreed to have mercy on him if he would willingly surrender, return to Flykra, and never return to Arilos. I didn't want to be like him.

Javil was a little more hesitant, but he claimed that he was trying to show mercy as he wanted mercy shown so I rolled with it.

"And how is that?" Ahiam asked cautiously.

"If you are willing not to bring further troubles to Arilos, go back to Flykra and never come back, we will let you go peacefully."

"Or," he chided.

"Or, if you are not willing to go in peace or you come back with another army, we will not show such mercy and, you will be tried and executed as a murderer of not only the King's Guard, but the King himself."

"You know about that, do you?" He smirked.

"Yes, my brother filled me in," I said.

"Ah," he replied.

"So what will it be?"

"Can I think about it?" He asked in all seriousness. That wasn't good. I knew he would most likely return with an army if he decided to claim peace, but we would be ready.

"No, you answer now," I said sternly.

"Fine, I choose peace," he said a little too quickly.

I sighed, already preparing for what was to come. War.

"So be it. Guards, see him to the gate and shut the drawbridge," I ordered. They hesitated, respectfully so, but then obeyed.

"Give him a horse for his travels," I called as they left. I wanted him off my land as quickly as possible.

"I don't get it brother. Why won't you give me a chance," Javil asked as I was leaving my room later in the day. Pepper had offered to fill in for me so I could tend to some needed things around the castle and get a bite to eat.

"Javil, you are still so wound up. Your anger hasn't diminished in any way. I have no reason to believe you have changed because your actions around us have not. Therefore, I am not going to trust you around Naia. Absolutely not. Once I see a change in your behavior away from her, then I will consider allowing you to be supervised around her again."

"Picel…"

"No, Javil. That is my final answer. Do not argue with me."

He was angry. I knew that, but I wouldn't risk Naia's safety again. I already regretted asking her to go to Rowynala. I wouldn't ask her to be around my edgy, unstable brother, too.

54

NAIA

I missed Quinlan so badly, I thought about him every minute of every day. I cried for most days but Picel rarely left my side.

Mom was glad that he was taking care of me. It allowed her time to get readjusted to life in the castle. It had been years since she had stepped foot inside. I didn't know all of her story, but I knew that it had been a devastating departure. At least looking back, that is what I gathered from King Zaxton's response to me being there. Not that she didn't want to take care of me or be there for me, but she had suffered at Ahiam's hand too and for her it was a second time. I couldn't imagine having to go through everything twice.

As King, I didn't think that Picel would have the time to take care of me, but he made sure that he did. He fed me until I was strong enough to eat on my own. He helped Pepper change my dress every day and night, held me as she brushed my hair, and then held me when I was able to brush my own.

By the end of the third day with him, I was able to walk a small lap around his room. The fourth I walked two. He held my arm the whole way, but made sure I put all my weight on the floor. He was just there to make sure I didn't fall, supporting me every step. Literally.

He hadn't made any advances on me since the night that he brought me to his room, when he kissed my forehead. I knew though, that he was doing everything he could to hold back. The intensity of how he looked at me while I tried new things as I recovered is what gave it away. He was so afraid that I would fall or relapse back into my detachment from the world.

At the end of the fifth day, he encouraged me to walk the hall outside his room. I walked down and back and paused when I passed Quin's room. Picel had given me space to make the walk alone, but was close enough that if I started to fall he could catch me. I wavered at the memory of Quin and started to tilt. Picel instantly appeared behind me, grabbing my waist to support me as I waivered. He then turned me around into his arms and I broke. Tears escaped and I started shaking, barely able to stand on my own.

"I know, Naia, I know. I am so sorry. I miss him too," he whispered, stroking the back of my head and pulled me in tighter for more support. I welcomed his embrace and we stood there- mourning together.

It was weird. The same hall that had caused me so much pain just weeks ago was now the hall where I was being rebuilt again. I only hoped that my trials were nearing their end. As I stood there in Picel's arms grieving Quin, I wasn't sure how much more I could take.

55

PICEL

"No, no, you want to duck, then jump. Here, watch me again," I said to Naia as I tried to teach her sword fighting. It had been a couple weeks and she was finally regaining her strength. If she was going to become queen, which she hadn't yet decided, she needed to know at least basic fighting skills. It seemed though, that the sword was not her strength. Her mother was an archer, so maybe we would try that next.

The weight of holding a sword was still hard for her, so I decided that the best option would be to use the training swords, also known as 'sticks'. She thought it was silly, but I assured her that using sticks would help her with the muscle memory she would need in a battle.

"It's too confusing- I can't do it," she complained, sitting down on the stones that were warming from the heat.

Spring had hit in Arilos and it was a beautiful sight. The cacti were in full bloom making it very easy to gather their fruits and spindles. We used every part of the cactus. Pepper would use the paddles in stew and the fruits with everyday meals. She said that soon she would make cactus sweets!

Mom used to make cactus sweets when we were kids. It was a birthday tradition for me as my birthday was in the early spring. I begged her for it all year, but she always told me that the best things are worth waiting for. I looked at Naia and smiled softly, not realizing what I had done until she looked at me, puzzled, and gave a shy smile in return.

We had become good friends, Naia and I. It was nice. She was a good friend to have.

Part of me wondered if she was developing feelings for me, as I had her, but then I would second guess myself and think that she would never fall for me after loving Quin. Quin had been her whole heart. I couldn't compete with him in any way.

Luria was helping her learn the ways of life as queen, or at least what it could be like if she accepted. Though Luria was teaching her more etiquette like posture and dancing. Oh, how I loved watching her dance. She flowed effortlessly across the floor. She was a natural. Luria said Naia had gotten her ability to dance from her father because she herself was never one to be good at dancing.

"May I have this dance?" I said one day as I approached her practicing alone in the ballroom.

She smiled and held out her hand in acceptance.

We danced for a few minutes until she spoke softly next to my ear. "Picel," She said.

"Yeah," I whispered, anxious for her next sentence.

"You know that we can only be friends, right?"

My heart sank. I had hoped, maybe, just maybe that she had moved on enough to consider me as an option, but I was wrong.

"Naia, I…"

"Picel, I love being your friend, and I will always be here for you, but…" she paused, not wanting to say the next sentence… so I finished it for her.

"Your heart is still with Quin."

"Yes. It would be too hard to be with you after loving him. I still have so many feelings swirling around from his tragic death. I' just not ready to fall in love again," she said, her voice shaking. "And being in the same wing as… Picel, I couldn't."

In the same wing as Javil. That is what she didn't say. Her own quarters were in the guest hall, but she had been staying with me. I knew then that she might always be afraid of Javil. Scared of what he could do, how he could respond to the news if we got together. I understood, but oh how it stung. I took a deep breath and looked into her eyes.

"I understand, Naia." And I did. She was right. It made sense. I pulled her in close one last time, kissed her knuckles, and walked away.

56

NAIA

I went to the lounge room and found my mother, working on a dress for herself. It was a light blue fabric that would match her warm skin tone. She rarely made things for herself; I was glad she was working on a project that would benefit her.

"Hi, sweetie!" She said enthusiastically as I approached her chair. "How is your day going?"

"Ugh," I replied. I could be myself with my mom and I really was thankful for that.

"That bad?" She asked. "What happened?"

"Oh, nothing. I just had to tell Picel that I could never be with him. It was horrible. He understood, but he wasn't thrilled."

Mother looked at me curiously and thought for a moment before replying. She liked Picel. I knew that she would be a little disappointed in my decision.

"I see," she paused, "what made you decide that? If I may ask. Do you not trust him?"

"Of course I trust him, but if I let myself remember, let myself dwell on what happened, at his brother's hand; what happened to Quin, then I can't leave my bed. I know he has been there for me since Quin died. I know that he swears that he won't let Javil hurt me again, but if I think about it…" I choked back a sob. "If I think about it, any of it, I have to think about Quin dying. I can't do that, I just can't, Mom."

"Oh, Naia," Mom said, taking me into her arms. "Ssshh, ssshh, it's going to be alright. Someday. Remember, God's got you. He knew everything that was going to happen. He is still here with you now," she paused as if deciding whether or not she was going to say something or not. She did.

"Did you get to meet King Zaxton before he died?" She asked softly. *So they were close.*

"Yes, I did. He was lovely. You were friends?"

"Is that what he told you?" She said, turning to look at me. There was a glint of sadness in her eyes.

"He wouldn't tell me anything. He said that I wasn't his daughter, only because I asked, but that I wasn't ready to hear anything else."

Mom chuckled. "He was so wise. He was probably right then," she said, stroking my face. "He was so good at judging those things, but I think you are ready now," She said, and began the story of not only how she and King Zaxton met and fell in love, but also how she ended up falling in love with my father and had me and Rhyson. It was a extraordinary story; one I would cherish for the rest of my life.

"I tell you this to remind you of God's hand in everything, Naia. If that hadn't happened to me, then you probably never would have gotten here to Arilos. You might not have even been born! I would have never gotten as close to your father as I had, and wouldn't have married him. You might not be as strong as you are. You might not have met Quinlan or Picel or even Javil. If Zaxton and I had worked out, everything would have been very different. I am glad it turned out this way, because then I got to be with you, Rhyson, and your Father, while they were alive. I wouldn't have traded my time with you or them for anything. And we don't know what God is going to do next but, we can trust that it is a part of his completely perfect plan. He doesn't make mistakes and He never fails. Remember that."

I sat, wrapped in my mother's arms for a while and we cried together. We cried for our lost loved ones, we cried for the hard things that happen in life, but we finished with a prayer, thanking God for everything that He had blessed us with. It was much needed time with Mother, and with God.

"Mom, I have one more question," I asked tentatively. I knew that it would be a hard one for her to answer.

"Go ahead, sweetie," she said.

"What happened after... the waterfall?"

She sighed deeply, looked down pursing her lips, and slowly nodded her head as if preparing herself to tell me the story. I hadn't heard yet about Rhyson's death and I didn't want to, but I needed to know. I still wasn't completely sure if Dad was alive or not, but it had been so long and we hadn't heard from him so there was a pretty small chance.

"Oh, Naia, it was awful," She said, wringing her hands together. "I almost had a hold of your brother when he got caught on a rock and went under. I tried to free him, but the rapids pulled me away... I was barely able to grab a fallen log as I was about to go over the edge. I saw you and your father go over and I was sure that you hadn't survived. I... I should have gone to look for you... I am so sorry," she said as tears streamed down her face.

"After losing my father, and Zaxton and your..." her voice trailed off. "I suppose I trained myself to just... move on."

Not wanting to upset her any further talking about our families' deaths, I asked how she had gotten to Rowynala's headquarters.

She went on to tell me that she had gone home, but the fires had completely destroyed it. She dug around searching for anything that was salvageable in the remains of the village, and then made her way to the headquarters. Ahiam had taken over and, unfortunately, remembered who she was and took her as a prisoner. She didn't go into how she had been treated. I think it was too hard for her to re-live, but I already knew first hand what she had probably been through.

"What is it like for you being back at castle Arilos?" I asked cautiously. I didn't want to make things harder for her than they already were. She thought for a moment before finally speaking.

"It is strange. Everything is exactly the same, and yet so different at the same time. It is definitely hard not having your father here, or Dot, his sister, but it still feels like home. I still hear my father's voice booming down the halls and my mothers's soft spoken answers. It seems like yesterday that I left, but also it feels like a hundred years. I... it's...." She started to cry. I couldn't imagine the processing she was having to do. I wrapped my arms around her and we sat there for a while. For the first time in my life I was comforting my mother.

PICEL

After being rejected completely by Naia, I told Luria that I needed to take a trip. I didn't tell her why, but I asked if she would make sure the castle stayed running properly while I was gone. After she agreed, I left.

I decided to go visit Edwin and Ingrid to see how they were doing after hearing of their sons passing. I fiddled with a piece of rope as Edwin told me what Quin had been like as a kid.

"He was a spitfire. He always wanted to become a guard for Arilos. He knew that we would be compensated if he worked for the King. I warned him against it, as it is a dangerous position, but he was too stubborn. I told him that we had more than enough wages from your father, who was still sending payments for saving Luria all those years ago, but Quin didn't care. He wanted to be like me."

"He was so good at his job," I said. "But, he was an even better friend. He was always there for both Javil and me. We put him in the middle a lot, but he handled it so well. He always listened to both sides, debating for days sometimes, deciding whom he most agreed with. Sometimes it was Javil, sometimes me. It would just depend. And Edwin, you should have seen him with Naia. He loved her so much. He would have done anything for her. And he did. I will respect him forever."

"I wish that Ingrid could have seen him in love," Edwin said. "She was really sick when she birthed him. We didn't think she would make it through labor, but praise God she did. She got to watch him grow up into a fine man but, the one thing she always wanted was to see her son wed a beautiful girl. After Quinlan met Naia the first time in the market, it was all that she talked about for days. *Quin needs to marry this girl.* That was all she wanted, and he was so close."

"So close," I repeated. "It was an unexpected tragedy no one could have ever seen coming. We have been at peace for so long. I still don't get it, but here we are, too many deaths later. Still standing." I sighed. This conversation had taken a dark turn. We needed to make it lighter again.

"Ahem, so what is Ingrid making for dinner?" I asked.

"Ah, she is making you her famous chicken and dumplings. It will be the best thing that you have ever tasted in your life!" Edwin said, rising to go inside.

"I believe it!" I laughed. "I will be in in a moment," I told him. "I need a minute to think, and pray."

"Take all the time you need, son," Edwin said, gently patted me on the shoulder and walked inside.

I had never been much of a prayer. I believed in God, but I didn't talk to him as much as I should, but there in the woods, processing everything that had happened in the last month, I bowed my head and prayed.

"God, I know we don't talk often, and I am sorry. That's on me, but I need your help. I have a Kingdom to run now that my father is gone. I'm scared. I pretend that I know what I am doing. I make decisions that seem right, but things always end in disaster. So many people have died, and I think I could have stopped it if I had come to you for advice first. Please forgive me for my ignorance. Please forgive me for my pride." I paused, thinking it silly to ask the next part, but went on anyway. I was already praying, why stop now? *"There's this girl, God. I really like her, in fact, I think I am in love with her. Naia. You know who she is."* I chuckled to myself telling God who one of his children is, *"Please help me to be patient in waiting for her. I don't want to ruin anything with her or with my brother. Help me trust you."*

"Picel, honey, dinner is ready..." Ingrid called from the door.

"I've got to go, God. Thank you for listening," I said, and stood to go to dinner.

"Ingrid! Edwin was right! This is the best meal I've ever had in my life! Thank you so, so much!"

"Oh, you are too kind, Picel," Ingrid said, smiling from ear to ear. It was the first time I had seen her smile this big since Quin had died. It was nice to see joy returning to her.

" May I ask you something, Picel?" She asked as I took another bite of dumplings.

"Of course, Ingrid, anything," I replied, food dripping out of my mouth. I paused and wiped my mouth with a napkin. "I am sorry; that was not polite of me; My mother taught me better than that. Forgive me."

"Oh pish posh," Ingrid said. "You can eat as messily as you would like here. Please, don't feel obligated to be perfect. Here you don't have to be King," she smiled.

"Thank you for your kindness, Ingrid. What was it that you wanted to ask me?" I said, trying to quickly get the subject off my eating habits.

"Ah, yes," she said, pausing to glance at Edwin who encouragingly nodded.

"Would *you* ever consider Naia as a wife?"

I spit the dumplings all over my plate, and my eyes widened. "Ingrid, I..."

"I caught you off guard. Your Majesty, I am sorry," she panicked. "It's just that she is such a sweet girl and I think she deserves someone as kind as you. I know she is quite a bit younger, but I have been thinking. If she can't have Quinlan, I think that he would want you to have her. Not that she is property, but I think he would trust you to take good care of her. Tell me you have thought about it?"

This kind of talk would have never been allowed at the castle. Having a villager speak so boldly to the king would not have been tolerated for even a second, even by my father. But I loved it. She was becoming a second mother to me. I would listen to anything she said.

"Ingrid, I have thought about it, yes. Naia means a lot to me. She got me through the hardest time of my life, but she needs space right now. She is still, as we all are, trying to move past Quinlan's death. She told me that she could never be with me because I make her think of Quin, which makes sense, but I want her more than anything."

"Do you love her?" Ingrid asked. It was blunt, but her tone was soft and loving.

"Yes," I said, looking down. "Deeply." It was weird admitting that out loud. Especially to Quin's mom.

"Then go get her," she said, and continued eating her dumplings like the conversation had never happened.

58

NAIA

I moved back into my room while Picel was away. I hoped that we would still be okay after what I had told him. I knew it couldn't have been easy for him to hear. I was nervous for his return, and anxious to see how things were between us.

"Naia, he is back," my mother whispered through my door one afternoon. My heart fluttered. I gathered my composure and went down to greet him. I was surprised to see him smile when he saw me.

"Hello, Naia," he said casually.

"Majesty," I replied with a curtsy. His eyes saddened at my greeting.

"Have you been well in my absence?" He asked, pushing the sadness away. "No trouble with anything?" *He meant Javil.*

"No, no trouble at all," I said with a small smile. "I moved back into my room," I admitted. It was better he found out sooner rather than later. Before he could answer I continued on with my thoughts. "I am much stronger and I think it will do me good to be in my own room again." He cleared his throat. I knew that he was disappointed, but I needed my space.

"Picel, I am so thankful for all your help, truly, I just…"

"No, I get it," he said gently. "Really, I do."

He couldn't keep his eyes off of me. Every time we passed in the hall, in the dining area, or in the courtyard. Picel was watching me. I knew it. Javil knew it too, and I could tell he was not happy about it. He glared as Picel watched me. I didn't know what to do. So I kept my head down and stuck with Pepper.

We had become good friends since my return from Rowynala. She had helped Picel a lot in taking care of me and I loved her company. She had a bright positive attitude that I needed to help me heal. *God does bring the right people to you.*

"He is watching again, Naia," she would say.

"Don't look, Pep," I would return most times.

It had been a while since Quin's death and I had processed a lot since my talk with mom, but I was still hesitant to fall in love again. And I had already told him no. What if something happened to Picel? What if I lost him too? I couldn't do it twice.

Knock knock knock. "Naia? Can we talk?" It was Picel. *What could he want? Surely not...*

"Is everything okay?" I called from my room. "I'm sort of in the middle of something, can it wait?" I asked, forgetting I was talking to the King of Arilos. *Can it wait... ugh.*

"Uh, um, yeah, yeah. I will talk to you later," he said, and started to walk away.

I really wasn't doing anything important other than trying to take a nap, but I didn't want to face him. I didn't want to see his face all hurt and sad. And I needed to minimize the tension between him and Javil as much as possible. Keep the peace. I knew that Javil had been wanting to assist me with things, but I still wasn't comfortable with that and Picel wouldn't let him near me anyway. It was best if Picel and I just remained friends. *Right?*

I was just about to fall asleep when there was another knock. "Naia, please... Naia?"

"Come in," I sighed. I sat up on the edge of my bed, pulled the sheets over me to keep me decent, and waited for him to enter.

When he came in, he stood by the door for a moment, contemplating his choices. He was holding something that was blue.

"What is it, your Majesty?" I asked softly. There was clearly something on his mind. Something that was troubling him. I wanted to be there for him, but I needed to keep things formal.

"Naia, I am Picel to you, always," he corrected gently, finally starting to walk towards me. As he reached my side, he took my hand and handed me a blue flower. A forget-me-not. I looked at him, puzzled.

"Ahem," he started nervously. "Naia, this is a flower, the same flower, well, not the same one, but the same kind.... Aagh." he said and started to leave. He was nervous.

As he turned back around he noticed what I was wearing and immediately averted his eyes. "Um, were you trying to sleep? I am sorry, I will leave…" he faltered, starting for the door again.

I stood, not caring about my state of dress, I was decent enough. I stepped towards him and gently grabbed his hand. *Naia what are you doing?* My brain screamed. But I kept going. He tensed.

"Picel?" I whispered.

He pulled his hand away and went to sit on my bed, but then got up again and started pacing. I had never seen this side of him. Not since I was recovering. He was restless. He was usually so sure of himself, so steady. I didn't know how to respond. He was making *me* nervous.

"Naia, um," he let out a deep shaky breath.

"Picel. Breathe," I said. "Look at me." He didn't. "Picel, what is going on?"

I moved towards him and gently cupped his face, directing him to look into my eyes, willing him to talk to me. *What am I doing?* He didn't talk. Instead He grabbed my face delicately in his hands and put his forehead against mine. My stomach fluttered. His breathing was so heavy. Our noses were touching, but our lips weren't. This had happened to me before, with Quin, out under the stars. *Quin.*

I breathed out and pulled away. It was too soon. I wasn't ready.

"Picel we are just friends," I whispered, hesitantly looking at him.

He tensed up again and slowly moved away from me and sat down in a chair across the room, his thumbs rested under his chin, and his fingers covered his nose and cheeks.

"Naia, I…" he said as his eyebrows furrowed. "I'm so sorry. I…I know what you said, but Ingrid…."

"Ingrid? You've talked to Ingrid about me?" I asked, stepping closer to him.

"She brought it up and I… I just wanted some advice. I didn't mean to overstep, truly," he shook his head, embarrassed.

"You talked to Ingrid about me?" I repeated, my voice soft. I was stunned. *He cared about me that much?*

"Yes," he breathed, looking away from me.

"Why?" I inquired, taking another few steps. His jaw tensed. I was worried that *I* had overstepped, but he reached out and took one of my hands in his. I didn't pull away.

"Because you are so important to me. I know that you said we can only be friends, but Naia, I want more than that. You deserve to know that. And I am willing to wait for you to be ready, however long that takes," he squeezed my fingers in his.

As he did, a wave of emotions flooded me. I knew that he was drawn to me, that there were feelings, but the depth of those feelings I wasn't aware of.

I closed my eyes and, as I did, he stood, gently placing his lips on my forehead. I tensed, but then, for a moment, leaned into him slightly before pulling away from his touch.

I knew I still wasn't ready for anything yet but, after finding out that he was vulnerable about his feelings for me, and that he was nervous about it, I was willing to give him a chance. But I wouldn't tell him just yet. I needed to figure things out for myself first, and that, I knew he would understand.

59

JAVIL

Their looks at dinner were unbearable. It was harder than I thought it was going to be. I could tell that there was something forming between them, but it had intensified overnight. She smiled at him, he looked away, back and forth, over and over.

I glanced at Pepper who was trying to hide a smile as she looked at Naia. She knew something and I was going to find out.

"Pepper, hold on a second." I said as she was leaving the kitchen after cleaning up dinner. "I wanna talk to you about something."

"Sire? Is everything okay?" She asked hesitantly, taking a few steps back getting closer to the wall as I approached her.

"Can you tell me what is going on with Picel and Naia? I have seen their glances and my curiosity is getting the best of me. I... I'd like to know where they stand."

"Sire, it isn't my place," she whimpered, colliding with the wall behind her. "I am not at liberty to say. Respectfully, if you wish to gain information, you should talk to the King or Naia herself."

"Is that so?" I said, taking one more step and bending down until my eyes were lined up with hers. "Tell me," I growled, growing impatient.

"Javil! What is going on?" A voice said from behind me. I hadn't heard Naia enter the room as I had been too focused on getting information from Pepper.

"Pepper, are you okay?" Naia asked, disappointment flooded her face as she approached us. I knew instantly I had let her down. Any trust that I was trying to form with her had vanished the instant she saw me cornering Pepper. She took another step towards Pepper and I. That is when Picel entered the room.

"No," was all he said as he looked at her, his brow scrunched. His hand reached for Naia's arm to pull her back. I wanted to be offended that he didn't trust me, but I couldn't be because I didn't trust myself.

Naia being Naia, gently placed her hand over Picel's, moved it away, and took another step towards me.

"Naia, please," Picel begged. He didn't want to risk anything happening to her - not again. He had fallen hard for her. And based on her lingering eyes and tender voice around him, it might not be as quickly but, she was falling too. I had my answer.

"Picel, it's okay. He isn't going to do anything with you here. I am safe. I promise. Let me talk to him."

I was surprised that she was even in the same room as me. Our time together had been limited since our return to Arilos, and I knew that she was still terrified of me. Maybe having Picel in the room gave her a new found courage to face me, especially when I was cornering her best friend.

She was sounding more and more like a queen every day. I was impressed at how quickly she picked up on everything. Maybe it was just in her blood.

Picel reluctantly took a step back allowing Naia to come toward me. That surprised me too.

"What are you doing?" She asked softly. "I thought you were trying to do better. What happened?"

What *had* happened? I had no idea.

"Are you two together?" I asked Naia, avoiding her question. I knew, deep down, but I wanted her to say it. I was still looking at Pepper. I couldn't look at Naia, not when I already knew the answer she would give.

"Is that what this is about?" She asked, moving so I could see her better. "Javil? Answer me. Please." I heard Picel move a few steps forward, ready to intervene if I blew.

I said nothing, but shifted my gaze to the floor. I felt so ashamed– especially because of the grace she was showing me- the grace she had always showed me. Picel would have thrown me to the dungeons immediately if he had been the one to enter the room first.

No one moved. They were waiting for me to answer, but I didn't have one.

"Naia, it's time to step away," my brother said at last, reading my mind. I was about to break. "You tried, leave us, please," he said, gently guiding her away from me and towards the door. "I will come find you later," he promised her as he shut it quickly behind her.

"Javil," he said, walking slowly towards me and Pepper. "Let's take a walk or a ride, huh? Come on, let's go," he said, cautiously. "Leave

Pepper alone." I nodded, but anger boiled inside of me. All the feelings I'd held in about Picel and Naia getting closer, Quin's death, Father's death, and even Mother's death- I couldn't stop myself. It was all just too much. I sprang forward, grabbed a knife that was sitting on the kitchen counter, and disregarded everything that Picel had reminded me of days before, and drove it into my brother's chest.

Forgiveness. I was going to need that again.

60

PICEL

I was too stunned to even cry out in anguish. The searing pain flooding my body by my brother's betrayal was as unbearable as the pain of the physical wound he had inflicted.

I looked at my brother, stunned; then collapsed to the floor holding my chest.

"No, no, no! What did I do? NO!" Javil panicked. "I just stabbed my brother–I just stabbed the King!" He muttered to himself.

Seeing her chance to escape, Pepper bolted for the door. I heard her footsteps receding as she left. I hoped she would get help, but I would understand if she didn't come back.

I could feel blood seeping from my wound. It was bad. I didn't have much time to get the bleeding under control before I would be unconscious or dead.

"Picel... I... I am so sorry... I..."

"Javil," I groaned. "You can beg for my forgiveness later. You have to stop the bleeding, please. I can't leave her. I beg you," I managed.

"Right, right," he said, ripping off my shirt part-way to gain access to the wound. I winced as he wasn't very gentle; but he didn't have time to be, and he knew it.

Javil had just started applying pressure to the wound when Pepper, Zahir, and Naia came rushing through the kitchen door.

Naia screamed my name and surged forward. She instantly knelt down next to me, removed her apron, and made a makeshift pillow for my head. *I love her. Even if she will never love me back.*

She stroked the base of my neck where it met my chest, just above the shirt that Javil was using to keep me from bleeding out. Shivers ran up my neck and I relaxed as her gentle hands soothed the pain just a little bit.

"Sire, you need to go," Zahir said sternly. "You can't stay here. I won't allow it."

"Yeah," Javil mumbled and gave control of the situation to Zahir, thankfully without a fight.

Zahir knelt at my side to tend to my wound. He quickly removed the shirt completely to assess the damage and cringed. If Zahir was cringing, it couldn't be good.

"Naia, are you strong enough to keep pressure on the wound if we walk Picel to the infirmary?" He asked her. "I need to bear the weight of his body. You shouldn't be doing that." He told her and I silently agreed. That would quite literally be too much weight on her shoulders.

"Yes, I can do that," she said confidently.

"Good. Let's go," Zahir said.

With his and Pepper's help and with an excruciating amount of pain, I was able to sit up and stand with most of my weight on Zahir. He made sure that he had a solid hold on me, and then we began the long trek to the infirmary.

As we made it through the door of the kitchen, Naia ordered Pepper to clear a path for us and to make sure the bed was set up for a chest injury. Gasps from servants rang out as we passed by. There was no way to really avoid the people of the castle. Before the day was over all of Arilos would know that the king had been injured. I prayed that the attacker would remain a secret. If it didn't, I would be forced to give my brother the most severe of consequences. He would have to be executed.

Zahir was going to have to cauterize my wound to stop the bleeding. He got out an instrument with a wooden handle and a skinny metal rod sticking out from it and placed it in the fire. I flinched as he brought it closer with its tip red from the heat of the flames. *That thing is going to go inside me? Aahh.*

Pepper had taken over keeping pressure on my chest so Naia could sit at my side. She cradled my head across her lap holding my left arm at my side while stroking my hair with the other as she leaned over whispering encouragement in my ear this time. "You can do this. I'm here. It's going to be alright. You are going to be fine." I think she was saying that for herself as well as me. I wanted to believe her but, when the five guards came into the infirmary to hold me down, I had my doubts.

"Your Majesty, are you ready?" Zahir asked, his voice strained, clearly not wanting to hurt me, but knowing that he had no choice if he wanted me to survive.

"As I'll ever be." I grunted, baring my teeth down on a strap of leather that Zahir had provided for me. I was going to need it.

61

NAIA

As Zahir cauterized Picel's wound and I heard his pained screams, I flashed back to the time Quinlan had to hold me down for my stitches after Javil had thrown me into the wall. It seemed like years ago. But it had only been months. Shivers ran down my spine just thinking about it. It was the most unimaginable pain I had ever experienced, and this was going to be ten times worse for Picel. His wound was so much bigger.

He tried so hard to hold back the screams, but he couldn't do it. At first his whole body went rigid. His hands grasped the sheets under him for support. Then he started to fight to get out from under the guard's hold on him, thrashing into me and, at one point, ramming into my jaw with the top of his head. I choked back a scream of my own.

I sobbed with him as Zahir inserted the cauterizing rod into his wound again and again to make sure he got every piece of flesh fused together. I hated seeing Picel in this much pain.

I could hear his flesh sizzling as it burned. The smell was awful. It took me back to the people who had been burned alive in my village. I wanted to throw up. Too many horrible flashbacks were happening all at once. I almost couldn't bear it, but I wouldn't leave Picel's side. He never left mine.

The depth of his wound caused the cauterizing process to take twice as long as it normally would have. Long, agonizing moments later, Picel finally passed out from the pain and eventually fell into a deep sleep. I silently thanked God that he didn't have to feel it anymore, at least until he woke up again.

Zahir gave me strict instructions to keep the area smothered in honey and the mint leaf concoction as it was vital to Picel's healing without infection. Even then, it wasn't guaranteed.

"Mmmm," I heard the next morning. *He is awake! He made it through the night!*

I sat up slowly and started stroking the top and sides of his head with my fingernails. He gave a small moan of approval, so I smiled and continued as I spoke.

"How are you feeling?" I asked, moving to graze his cheek.

His eyes fluttered open. He turned his head up towards mine and instantly focused on my eyes, my lips, and then my eyes again, as I was laying behind him, holding him up.

"What are you doing here?" He groaned as the pain became more noticeable with being more alert.

"You never left me," I said softly. Now it's my turn to not leave you." As I was finishing my sentence he lifted an arm up over his head and moved a piece of hair that had fallen over my eyes and nose, grunting as his movement caused his chest muscles to stretch and strain his injury.

"Picel, stop, you're gonna-"

"Am I hurting you, laying on you like this?" He asked, his voice deep and husky from sleep. My heart fluttered at the sound of it. *You are just friends Naia.*

"Pi, I am the last thing you should be worrying about right now," I scolded, gently putting his arm back into a position that wouldn't cause so much strain on his wound.

"But am I?" He asked again. I wasn't going to win this one, so I told him the truth.

"My legs are completely asleep," I admitted, trying to move them a little bit, but prickly pain surged through them.

"Why didn't you say something?" He muttered, trying to move, but I gently held him down.

"I didn't want to cause you any more pain, Pi."

"Help me sit up" was all he said.

"Picel," I protested.

"Please, Naia. Please," he begged.

I sighed and rolled my eyes, starting to adjust us both into different positions. With me out of bed, Picel was sitting up by himself. Once he was situated, he took my hands and guided me to sit facing him on the bed. My feet almost touched the floor. He kissed each knuckle and then rested my hands on the side of his chest that wasn't injured.

I tensed up a little, not comfortable with his gesture, and not wanting to accidentally do something that would hurt him more.

"Naia, I wouldn't be *here* if it wasn't for you," he said, continuing the conversation we had been having before. "You have saved my life three times over. I wouldn't be alive at all if you hadn't shown up here. God knew that. He has used you to save me," he said, pulling me closer so I was laying right next to his fresh wound. I was so scared that I was going to hurt him, but he didn't seem concerned in the slightest.

"Naia," he whispered, looking down, searching my eyes for an answer to a question he hadn't even asked yet- an answer to a question he had wanted to ask for longer than I realized.

And I gave in. I don't know if it was how softly he was talking to me, how badly I subconsciously wanted to, if it was the intimate moments we had shared recently; having to take care of each other in different ways, if it was how safe he made me feel every second of every day, or if it was simply because I had completely and irrevocably fallen for him, too. I tilted my head up so it was an inch from his, and he slowly leaned down and closed the gap so just the tips of our lips were touching.

After he pulled away, he looked at me and smiled. It was the kind of smile that you saw when a child received their hearts desire for their birthday, or the kind of a smile that a man gives a woman he is completely in love with. *Oh...*

62

JAVIL

"*When are you going to learn that life isn't about you, Javil? You are so selfish, so prideful. How could you do this to your own brother? He came to rescue you!*"

That is what Naia had said to me as they rushed Picel to the infirmary. I deserved that. She *was* getting braver.

I racked my brain for some logical explanation for what I had done to Picel. There wasn't one. I had failed him. I had failed Naia. I was hopeless. Destined to always be the bad guy. I just couldn't help it.

Leaning against the corner of the wall with arms outstretched, I tried to breathe. Picel could have ordered my execution, banishment, or to be sentenced to the dungeons, but he hadn't. *Why? Had Naia stopped him?* I was about to lay down when there was a knock at the door.

"Who is it?"

"Zahir, Sire. May I come in?"

Picel. Has something happened?

"Yes," I said quickly, eager to learn of the condition of my older brother, my King.

"Will he be okay?" I asked the moment Zahir stepped through the door. "Please tell me that I did not kill my brother. Please tell me we have not lost another King."

"No, he lives," Zahir said somberly.

"But?" I returned, catching his tone.

"But he faces a long journey. He shall not be ruling Arilos anytime soon. He will need a week of bedrest, and then we will slowly start adding daily activities back into his life."

"And I am supposed to rule? I am supposed to take over as King of Arilos?"

"No," a voice at the door said. "No, I will be taking my place as Queen."

Naia

I took a step towards her, wanting to apologize and wanting to fix the problems I had just caused.

"No, Javil," she said firmly.

"Naia, please." I begged.

"No. You have had chance after chance. You have been forgiven time and time again without major consequences. This is too far. This I won't tolerate." She lifted her chin and stared into my eyes. "Go. Now. I am banishing you from Castle Arilos. Immediately."

Naia allowed me to pack a small bag under the watch of five warriors, my warriors, and then they escorted me to the castle gate. I didn't even get to say goodbye to Picel. *Did he know she was doing this? He couldn't have. He wouldn't allow it! Would he?*

"Naia, please," I pleaded. "Please don't do this." Tears filled her eyes. *So it hurts her to do this to me? Then why do it?*

"I have to- For Picel's safety and my own. This is my final decision, Javil," she stood her ground.

"Naia," I tried again, but she turned her back on me.

"Go," she said, pausing as she walked back inside. Then the guards slammed the gates behind her. Leaving me alone, outside of my only home.

63

PICEL

I woke up to Naia curled up and crying on a chaise next to my bed.
Her sniffles sounded like she had been crying for a while- the tight,
no room to breathe kind of cry. I reached out slowly and touched the
top of her head with the back of my hand letting her know I was there.
She jumped, not expecting my touch, but her crying calmed.

"Naia, what happened? Are you okay? Are you hurt?" I asked
almost all at once. And then, "Did Javil hurt you?"

She broke again. *I'll kill him.* I wanted to jump down next to her
on the floor and wrap her in my arms, but my body refused to coop-
erate, keeping me captive to the bed.

"Naia... Naia, come here. Hey, come here. I can't come to you so
you're gonna have to come to me," I said softly. "I know we aren't officially together, but I need to comfort you. It is in my blood," I begged.

"I'm scared of what you are going to say, Picel," she sobbed. "I did something, and it's changed everything. You are going to hate me. I… I don't know how to fix it!"

I tried putting myself in her shoes and how she could be feeling. What was causing her to respond like this? And then I knew. Why did I even have to ask? It was Javil and how he had treated her in the past. *Oh Naia. My poor girl.*

"Naia, I'm not going to hurt you," I whispered. "That's what you're afraid of, isn't it?" I asked. She hesitantly looked up at me, tears streaming down her face. *Yes.*

I exhaled slowly and carefully sat up, trying not to strain my wound too much. I shouldn't have done that but, right at that moment, Naia was all that mattered.

"Come here," I said, patting the mattress next to me. "Come sit down. Please."

Reluctantly, she stood from the chaise and placed herself next to me. I circled her hand with my thumb, assuring her that I meant what I said- I wouldn't hurt her.

"What happened?" I asked again as calmly as I could manage with the pain shooting through me. And the rage that was starting to boil, wondering what Javil had done.

She took a shaky breath, her eyes darting to the door as if she was expecting someone to walk through at any moment, but said no words.

"Naia," I said, pulling her against the good side of my chest. "Just lay here. You don't have to say anything yet, take your time," I concluded. "Have you *seen* Javil?" I asked. I shouldn't have. I knew better.

She started shaking uncontrollably. I wasn't sure if she was seizing or having some kind of episode. With my wound as fresh as it was, I wasn't able to offer her anything but the comfort of my arms.

I pulled her in tighter, murmuring in her ear that she was safe and protected. But it did nothing. She continued shaking and pressed into me harder.

Thankfully, Zahir came to check on me and saw her distress. He gently moved her back to the chaise and coaxed her into taking a breath and drinking some water. They shared some words and then he came over to me.

"Picel, did you tear anything?" He asked, starting to lean over to inspect the damage.

"I don't think so. But it does hurt."

"That is to be expected but, Picel, you need to rest. You can't risk anything right now. I know you want to take care of Naia, but you have to focus on *your* healing. Do you understand?" I nodded and looked over at Naia. She had the look of someone who was about to throw up. Her face was pale, her eyes dazed, and she was rocking back and forth.

"Zahir, what is wrong with her?" I asked. He looked at me for a second, contemplating his next sentence.

"I am not at liberty to say. That information needs to come directly from her I am afraid," and he turned to leave. "Naia, soon, and be careful with him, please," was all he said before seeing himself out.

I caught her eye, but in embarrassment, *or fear,* she turned away. We sat in silence for a while until she finally turned to face me, tears in her eyes again.

"Picel," she said, standing up and walking closer. "There is something I need to tell you, and I am not sure what you will think.

I was still sitting up, so I patted the spot next to me again and she sat down, rubbing the silk in nervousness as she did.

I was getting nervous myself. She was making it seem like she had done something unforgivable.

"Zahir went in to see Javil to let him know how you were doing. I was on my way back to you when I heard Zahir say that you wouldn't be up for a few weeks and I panicked. He was telling Javil that they would need someone to rule and I just couldn't let him."

"Okay," I said, my voice clearly strained.

"I stepped in the room then and I told Javil that he wasn't welcome at the castle anymore... I banished him. But before that..."

I squinted at her, stunned, confused. She looked at me expectantly, awaiting my response. I knew I had to be careful, because she was already in a delicate state, but I needed to know more.

"You banished him because... you didn't feel safe? He did something else to you? Either option would be fair, but why didn't you talk to me about it first?"

And then it hit me... she didn't have the power to banish him, not unless... "Naia..."

64

NAIA

"Picel, I took the throne. I am Queen of Arilos," I said before he could say anything more. Fear spread through me rapidly. My body was starting to shake again and I felt like I was going to faint. I put my hand on the headboard to steady me.

Picel put his arms up and rested them on his head and gave me a pained look. I wasn't sure if it was from physical pain or emotional pain. Probably both. We had talked about it a few times, but I ultimately told him that I really didn't want the throne. I don't know what came over me. I just wanted Javil gone. It was too dangerous to keep him around.

"What… Why did… Naia…" he stammered. He was angry. He was angry, but he didn't want to scare me so he was holding it in. "You… banished my brother, you didn't even let him say goodbye? You… you… gaaahhh."

"Picel, I was not going to risk your life again!" I wailed. *What a great way to start being Queen...*

"Picel..." I pleaded.

"Did people hear you?" Anger boiled through his words. He couldn't hold it in forever.

"Yes," I whispered. *It's over. Whatever this is, whatever Picel and I had or were starting to have is done.*

He inhaled sharply.

"Okay... we can figure this out. People will understand that you said it out of fear and you really didn't mean it. I can take the throne back. Everything can go back to how it was."

"Picel how will that make people look at me? My reputation will be ruined. And if you demand to take back over, how will that make people look at you? You will lose their respect too!"

"Get out," he commanded.

"Picel, please! I need you to support me. I need you to understand that I did it because it was the only option to keep you safe! You weren't going to punish him–he is your brother! You were going to let it slide again! Put us at risk again! I wasn't about to let that happen. Picel..." I whispered, kneeling next to him, taking his hand in mine and bringing it to my mouth. "Please, don't hate me. Please understand."

He looked at me and breathed deeply. His jaw fluttered as he contemplated his choices.

"Okay." He said softly, after an eternity. "Okay, I will stand by you. You have my full support. Naia, all I want is for you to be safe and to feel safe, but next time with something this big, can you *please,* talk to me about it first?"

"Of course, Pi. I am sorry I didn't. Truly. I was just thinking in the moment of what I..."

"I know," he said, bringing my hand to his lips and kissing it softly. "I know."

"Naia, you made a choice, a necessary choice, but it completely changed the trajectory of Picel's life. Everything he has ever worked for, the only family he had left… all stripped from him in a second without any warning. I expect nothing less from him. Give him time and he will come around. He does love you, Naia. I know it," Mom encouraged.

Things had been a little tense with Picel since I had taken the throne from him. He had been helping me get acclimated to the ways of being queen, but it was off. He wasn't himself. How could he be?

I loved my mom for being honest, even when it was hard, even when I didn't want to hear it. She was there– whispering truth in my ear.

I knew Mom was proud of me, but she knew I was hurting. She tried to hide her overflowing excitement of me being queen as best she could, but as we talked, every once in a while a smile would sneak out onto her face.

She had helped me get ready in the morning, and had pinned my hair in a loose bun with a few loose curls hanging out. I wore a deep blue day dress that just grazed the floor when I stood. It had a slight v-neck and sleeves that went down to my wrists. It was beautiful.

She was about to leave when there was an unexpected knock on the door. Pepper wasn't supposed to come for another hour, and Zahir was out of town for the weekend. No one else was supposed to be up in this hallway except the guards; they only knocked if they had previous permission or if it was an emergency.

I looked at Mom quizzically. She gracefully walked to the door and opened it widely. It was him. Picel was in a cloak and a light tunic. He looked as if he were going somewhere.

"I'll leave you two to talk," Mom said, glancing at me. But I was only looking at Picel standing there before me.

He gave a slight nod of his head towards me, and then softly closed the door behind my mother, whispering something to her as she slipped out. She placed her hand on his arm, gave a small smile of encouragement, and was on her way.

He walked in and sat in a chair by the window. He motioned for me to sit in the seat next to him. I sat down, not knowing what to expect as he rubbed his forehead with his fingers. The silence between us was aggravating. I didn't know if he wanted to talk first or if he was waiting for me.

It had never been like this between us before. Conversation had always come easily for us. He was the only one, besides Quin, that I didn't have to hide myself from. I could just be me. But that had clearly changed. Finally after what seemed like hours, he spoke.

"Your Majesty, I am sorry," he started, and I jerked my head up to look into his distant eyes. I was not expecting that response, *"Your Majesty"*.

"Picel, I am only Naia to you. Nothing else, please," I said softly, reaching for his hand, quoting the same words he had said to me just a week before. I couldn't bear hearing him refer to me in that cold, detached way. As I made contact with his skin he pulled away.

"Naia," He said, his posture and voice softening just slightly, as he realized the hurt in my eyes from his rejection.

"I..." He looked at me then at the ground, then back at me. His eyes were sad.

He was wearing a cloak and had set down a burlap bag at the door, I'm guessing filled with clothes and resources for travel. *He was leaving.*

"Where are you going?" I asked softly.

"To Rowyala. I'm going to stay with Edwin and Ingrid for a time. I just… I need to think, and I can't do that here. And since you took the throne, that means I can leave. Will you be okay without me?"

My heart sank. I had driven him away. But at least he was talking to me; letting me know his plans. I understood his need to think. Maybe with him gone for a spell, it would allow me to think as well.

"I think I can manage. I have Mom. Are you leaving now?" I asked, trying to be brave.

"Yes, that is the plan," He said, starting to stand.

"Picel?" I said as he turned to walk out.

He stopped dead in his tracks and turned back to face me. He slowly walked over to me and took my face in his hands as he knelt down, softly kissing my cheek- right next to my lips.

At that moment I knew that I wanted him the same way he wanted me. As his lips almost brushed mine I completely melted. I didn't want him to leave.

"I will come back. I promise. I just need time to process everything. I will come back," He breathed in my ear as he pulled away.

"Picel," I started. "Picel I want…" but it was too late. He was already out the door.

65

JAVIL

I went to Flykra. Maybe I could trap or even kill Ahiam somehow and regain everyone's trust. But how?

I wouldn't turn from Arilos. I knew that I deserved what Naia had thrown at me. She was more than right to banish me. I was honestly surprised that I hadn't gotten a worse punishment, but I knew that torturing people wasn't how Naia wanted to live. I only could hope that I would someday have a way to redeem myself to her. *For everything.*

I traveled through the treacherous mountain pass that looked directly over the edge to the jagged rocks and ice below. I shuddered. If I was to slip and fall… I shook the thought away.

When I arrived at the entrance to Ahiam's fortress I was greeted by a swarm of warriors. I expected as much from Ahiam. Nothing less.

"Javil, to what do I owe this… inconvenience," he said gruffly.

"Ahiam, I am in need of shelter. I was cast out of Arilos and hoped you would...."

"Hoped I would, what...," he laughed. "Take you in like a lost puppy? Like your Father before you? Begging for refuge when *he* was thrown out of Arilos? No. I don't think that is what I will be doing. What I have planned for you will be so much greater than assisting you. In fact... you will be assisting me. Unlike your father, who refused to help, and ended up dead."

Anger surged through me and a low growl erupted from my throat. How dare he bring up my father like that. I tried to rush at him, but was held back by the guards who were behind me.

Ahiam's voice grew louder. "If you don't help me, Boy, I will make sure that your brother meets his end for good. Do you really wish to be responsible for his death?"

I froze. He hadn't heard that Naia was queen, but then again how could he have? I could use that to my advantage... but how?

I raked my thoughts trying to come up with something, anything believable that wouldn't get me killed. My uncle was ruthless. I know that he would kill me on the spot if he didn't believe my story. I had to form my words carefully. I had to make it believable. Words *and* actions.

"I was hurt badly by my brother; he ruined my pride." My voice seethed with bitterness; anger. "He ruined my reputation. He doesn't trust me and he won't give me a chance to redeem myself. If that is who he thinks I am, then that is who I will be. I am in," I said, nothing but confidence in my voice.

"And we could use the girl, Naia, to draw out Picel. If she is put in danger, he would stop at nothing to save her," I informed him, hoping that I wouldn't regret it. I just needed him to believe me.

"Is that so?" Ahiam said, moving closer to me. I could feel his breath on my skin.

"Yes, you have my word," I replied easily, I wasn't lying about that part.

"And how would you put her in danger?" Ahiam asked. He was intrigued. Good.

How *was* I going to do it? Naia was scared of me, or hated me. Probably both. She would never willingly come with me.

"See it done, whatever it is," he ordered before I could answer. "Or else you are dead."

Either I make this plan work and save everyone or I die. They would all die; in the most awful of ways. All thanks to Ahiam's hand and my ignorance. *Why did I come to Flykra?*

When the guards at Castle Arilos saw me approaching, the alarms sounded loudly. I was a threat and a danger that had to be stopped. *Not quite, I am really your only hope.*

"Stop!" A guard yelled from atop the castle gate.

"Come no closer," another yelled.

"Alert the Queen!" cried a third.

I threw my hands up in surrender and dismounted my horse, throwing myself on my hands and knees in surrender.

"Please!" I yelled. "I have just returned from Flykra. I have a warning for my brother and Her Majesty. Ahiam is coming to kill Picel *and* the Queen if he finds out what is going on. Ahiam wants the throne and he will stop at nothing to claim it. I need to speak with one of them, please, before it is too late!" I sat up and looked at them, hoping, praying, that they would believe me. If they didn't… No, I couldn't think about that. I wouldn't.

There were murmurs above me as the men conspired what to do. I had been waiting for a while when the gate finally opened. I couldn't believe who was standing before me. *Naia herself.* I had thought Picel would greet me, seeing as he was so protective of Naia, but I was wrong.

I dropped back down to the sand below me.

"Your Majesty," I groveled.

"Javil," she said with no emotion whatsoever. "Please stand and face me."

"Your Majesty, I am…"

"Do what you are told, Javil," she said a little louder. She was confident. I was proud of her.

I stood, and looked her in the eyes.

"Thank you," she said. "Please come in, but know if you touch me…"

"I won't. You have my word," I promised as I followed her inside.

We walked to the lounge that was already lined with guards along every wall. They were my friends, my fellow warriors, but they didn't look at me like that. Their looks said "kill on command."

"Sit," Naia instructed. I did. "Javil, what is really going on?" Of course she wouldn't believe me. I expected it, but I had to try to tell her. I had to get her to believe me.

"What I told your warriors is the truth, Your Majesty. I swear it. Ahiam is coming after Picel because he thinks that he is still king. Once he finds out you are Queen, he will kill you, too, or worse. Where is Picel? We need to warn him!"

"He isn't here. We- we had a falling out, and he left to get some space to think."

"Naia, where did he go?" my tone was panicked.

"I'm not sure I should tell you that," she said hesitantly.

Of course she wouldn't want to; the last time I had seen my brother I had stabbed him in the chest, but I still had to try to get an answer. I slammed my fists on the table, immediately regretting it. She jumped, rightfully startled at my outburst, and the guards surrounded me with swords pointed at my throat.

"Your Majesty, I am sorry. Please," I stretched out my hands, trying to convey that I meant no harm. "This is life or death. *Your life, my brother's life,* is at stake. The future of Arilos hangs in the balance. Please, Naia. I was angry! I really don't want him dead. Tell me where he is so I can warn him- at least about the danger that you are in. He would want to know that. He would want to come back to help protect you!"

She pondered for a moment and then said the words I had been praying that she would say.

"Guards stand down," The way she looked at me conveyed *her* thoughts. *Can I trust him?* I held my breath waiting for her reply. She sighed and nodded at last.

"He went to Edwin and Ingrid's house to breathe. To heal. He needed to get away from everything, understandably so," she sighed.

"Thank you, Your Majesty," I whispered softly, and set out to retrieve my brother. There was hope. Naia had given me another chance.

66

PICEL

"Picel, honey, come here, come here," Ingrid said as she ran out of her house, seeing me approach.

I had sent a scout with a letter announcing my upcoming arrival a few days before to prepare her.

She had made cheese from a cow they had acquired after Quinlan's death. That was one thing that Edwin requested, and I was more than willing to provide. Ingrid had also gone to Joris before I arrived to buy grain to make bread. It was so soft on the inside, but had that nice, crispy crust. They didn't have any fresh meat which was totally fine. We had some greens and strawberries along with the cheese and some milk.

After we ate, I was helping Ingrid clean up the kitchen, when there was a pounding on the door.

I tensed. No one knew I was here except Naia. Ingrid and Edwin looked afraid; they clearly weren't expecting any company. I motioned for them to go into the back room, confident I could handle whoever was at the door and still keep them safe. I only hoped that whomever it was, was alone.

I grabbed my sword, my chest still healing from the stab wound from my brother, and stopped for a moment debating my options. The wound was closed and scarring, but I was still weak. I had no chance of winning if this guy was stronger than I was. And if they knew that I was, or had been, the king, I was at another disadvantage.

I quickly threw on my cloak and covered my face so as to not be seen, drew my sword, and opened the door.

The figure on the other side was cloaked as well. The sun had set, so I couldn't have seen his face even if he hadn't been wearing a cloak. I saw his body tense, probably surprised that Edwin didn't open the door.

"Who are you, and what do you want?" I said in a deep voice, trying to disguise who I was.

"Picel?" the voice said hesitantly, seeing right through me.

Javil.

67

JAVIL

He lunged at me. I didn't have a sword, but I instantly grabbed Picel's sword from his hand and threw it out into the darkness. He pushed me out of the house and punched me square across the jaw. I winced, but so did he. *I deserved that.* He came at me again, this time going low, aiming for my legs. I saw his shadowed figure bend over and surge forward, bringing me crashing to the ground. I grunted as he scrambled up on top of me crushing my windpipe so I couldn't breathe. *I deserved that too.*

"Picel!" I heard Ingrid shout from inside.

"Ingrid, hush!" Edwin yelled back.

"Picel, Picel, please! I'm so sorry, I'm sorry," I croaked, trying to get a breath. He was not backing off.

I was almost at a point of blacking out when he released his grip on my throat and sat down next to me.

Finally he let me up and sat down next to me.

"You *stabbed* me," he stated aggressively.

"I know, please forgive me," I begged. "I acted rashly, I was angry! You and Naia… I… I was angry," I repeated.

"Clearly." He gritted. He glared at me for a moment, but then reluctantly reached out his hand. I lifted mine and he clasped it, but only for a moment.

"Fine," he growled, and walked back inside, leaving me on the ground to get up on my own.

"Can I please tell you why I am here?" I asked as Picel paced the gathering room. Ingrid and Edwin were awkwardly sitting in the dining area watching the scene between us play out.

"Why are you here?" Picel spat. He was clearly unhappy, which made sense since I had driven a knife through his chest.

"I went to Flykra," I admitted.

"TRAITOR!"

Yeah, Probably not a good thing to start with.

"No! Picel, I had nowhere to go. I thought…"

"You thought what? That you could become all buddy buddy with our evil uncle and win him over to our side?"

"I am trying to gain his trust. He thinks I…"

"What? That you are some poor innocent kid that needs a home? You are a *warrior*, a *prince!* He isn't going to buy it!"

I paused, shoving the thought to stab him again aside, and instead told him why I had come in the first place.

"Ahiam is coming to kill you. He doesn't know that Naia is Queen, but when he finds out…" my voice trailed off. Picel could figure out the rest of my sentence.

Picel looked at me, debating if he could trust my word and my actions. I hated that he doubted me but, until I could prove to him that I could be trusted, he had every right to question me. He spoke as he opened the door. I knew that he wouldn't leave Naia alone, being in danger.

"We need to go back to Arilos… now."

He paused and scowled at me, I felt his hesitancy.

"You can trust me," I assured him, and disappeared into the night without giving him a chance to think about it.

68

NAIA

Everything was spinning out of control too fast. Picel was gone, Javil had been to Flykra and had come back with a warning - and I was Queen. Nothing was as it was supposed to be. I paced the balcony outside my room and cried and cried and cried.

A night after Javil left to go find Picel, Ahiam and his men came. They forced their way into my room, killing the guards that had been stationed outside. I tried to fight them off but it was no use. I hadn't had enough training and the men were too strong.

Beatings, violation of my body, more beatings. Ahiam resorted to just beating me, but his guards... what they did.... The thoughts and images and pain that kept running through my mind and body was overwhelming, yet all I wanted to do was shut them out - an impossibility.

"Where are your men to protect you, your Majesty," they mocked. "They have either died or betrayed you."

I screamed and cried, but they had shoved a piece of fabric in my mouth to muffle my sound. *No one can hear me... I'm all alone. God, where are you?*

After throwing me down the stairs and violating me one last time, they left me in the middle of the courtyard, bleeding, broken and alone.

My enemies... disappeared into the night.

I didn't know how long I had been out, but heard a voice trying to wake me from my unconsciousness.

"Naia? Naia?"

I whimpered as someone gently moved hair from my face and tucked it behind my ear. I was afraid that whoever the man was was going to hurt me like the others, so I started to struggle against his touch, but he didn't. Instead, he cupped my face in his hands, whispering, "I am here, Naia. I am here." He lifted me up gently so I was resting in his embrace on the ground. I think he was crying. "Picel?" I mumbled, relief washing over me as I realized that I was safe.

"Naia, ssshh, it's okay. I am here," he said again and squeezed me just a little tighter, covering my body with his; protecting me. Shielding me from any more danger.

He came back.

I was zoning in and out of consciousness, but could tell that Picel had started walking up stairs - he carried me as if I were a cherished possession- *his* most cherished possession.

I woke again as he tenderly laid me in his bed and pulled the sheets over my defiled body. I knew it was his bed because mine was farther away. He walked to the door and called out to someone. "Get Zahir and Luria... now...run!"

I heard the scrambling footsteps of the servant descending down the stairs. Zahir ran through the door a few minutes later; my mother was closely behind him.

"What happened!" She exclaimed, rushing over to me.

"She was attacked. Javil was right. I shouldn't have hesitated to come back here," Picel growled in self disgust and frustration. "I never should have left! I left her completely vulnerable! This is all my fault!"

"Pi, it isn't your fault. It is mine. If I hadn't stabbed you she wouldn't have taken over, and you wouldn't have left when she banished me. It's on me, it's all on me," Javil argued.

"Whose fault it is doesn't matter. What I want to know is how did we not know that anyone was inside? How did they even get inside?" Mother questioned.

"Luria, if I knew the answer to that, they never would have gotten in," Picel snapped. His eyes shot up and made contact with my mom. "Luria..."

"No, Picel. You are fine," she answered graciously.

Mom looked at me then, tears in her eyes, knowing she couldn't fix my pain, while at the same time remembering hers.

Picel approached her and spoke softly next to her ear.

"Luria, may we speak in the hall?" His voice was barely above a whisper. I could tell she didn't want to leave me, but she nodded and followed Picel into the hall.

"Your Majesty… Naia, I need to examine you," Zahir said to me softly. "Do you want your mother in here for that?"

I didn't know how to answer. I trusted Zahir, but after the way those men treated me, I didn't want to be touched by anyone, let alone another man. My body started to tremble and I curled up into a ball as tightly as I could, but it hurt too much from when they beat me. I straightened out and closed my eyes, took a shaky breath and then opened them again. It was all too much to deal with. Noticing my fear, Zahir stepped away.

"What if I wait until your mother returns before examining you under your clothes? For now, I'll look at your head, arms, and up to your knees?" He suggested.

I thought for a moment and then gave a small nod. Zahir lightly took hold of my wrist, but I immediately flinched and whimpered.

"Okay, go slow," Zahir muttered to himself. "Naia, I am going to pick up your arm. Is that ok?" He asked, changing tactics. I nodded again, this time only tensing up at his touch, not pulling away.

He examined me in silence, except when he would ask for permission to touch me in new places.

My mother came back in without Picel, and sat down across from Zahir, taking my hand lightly in hers. My heart dropped. *Was he still mad?*

After being instructed by Zahir, my mom started tenderly, and slowly, removing my blood-stained, ripped dress and undergarments until I was laying bare under the covers. She then adjusted some cloths so that only the bare skin of my ribs and abdomen could be seen. Zahir and my mother both stifled a gasp when they saw the damage my body had endured.

I didn't want to look, but I knew it was bad. I could feel it. I could feel *them*. Their hands, their fists, their feet. I could hear their laughter. I could smell the leather of their armor, and could taste the blood in my mouth. I wanted to forget, but the memories were overpowering everything else. It was all I could think about.

I tried to focus on something else; anything else, but it was hopeless. My thoughts were stuck on repeat and there was no escape. No relief.

As gently as he could, after asking for permission, Zahir started pressing down on my stomach to see if it was distended in any way. He determined that there would be bad bruising, but he could feel no sign of internal bleeding. He wasn't sure how the attack would affect my ability to have children later on, that would only be known in time. He then pressed on my ribs to feel for fractures and breaks. Thankfully nothing was broken, but he confirmed I was badly bruised there, as well. I was terrified of the next part because he was going to have to lift the blanket and I was not ready for that. Who would be?

Though I wanted to know if we were okay, if he still was mad at me or not, I was glad that Picel was not in the room when Zahir started to lift the cloth.

Zahir looked to my mom for support; for permission before continuing. I was twenty, almost twenty one, but it made sense that he wanted my mother's consent, as well as mine, for what he would have to do next.

As he lifted the blanket, his face fell.

"Luria," he said, troubled.

My mom went to where Zahir was and looked for herself. She gasped and her eyes darted to mine.

"Naia," Mom said softly, walking back up to my side. "Did these men defile you, did they..." her voice trailed off, not wanting to finish her sentence, not wanting to think about her daughter having to go through such a degrading, violent and repulsive thing.

My silence was all she needed. I looked at her, tears in my eyes, pleading with her to not make me answer her question. I *couldn't answer* her question. I couldn't even nod my head. I was frozen. She instantly stood and walked to the other side of the room, her hands covering her mouth. I could hear her trying to suppress her sobs, but it was no use. Any mother who loved her daughter as much as mine loved me would respond the same way. I knew that she was trying to be strong for me, but her tears made sense.

"My daughter," she cried. "I am so sorry."

I knew she wanted to fix it. I knew she wanted to take me in her arms and make everything better. I knew this was why she had kept this side of her life from me, wanting to shield me from all the complications and dangers that she had endured.

Living in Rowynala had been so much simpler. When we were kids, we completed our studies, learned our trade and played outside, running through the forest and climbing trees. Once we reached adulthood we would go about our day at work and then come home to our families. I missed that. I missed the effortlessness of it all- the routines, the people, the peace. But that was gone now, and I was afraid that I would never get it back.

Finally, I was getting a bath. Pepper gently drizzled a stream of warm water over my head while Mom gently lathered soap in my hair. Once finished, they lovingly washed the rest of me, as I was too weak. I hated being so helpless. Usually I took care of others, not the other way around. I cared deeply for Picel, but after what I had gone through, having a man in the room for too long made me uneasy. I hoped that would go away with time - I didn't want to be afraid forever.

After Mom and Pepper finished cleansing the blood and disgustingness from me, Mom put a pillow behind my head and let me just relax and soak in the warm water. I was almost asleep when there was a light knock on the door. Mom lifted up a tapestry to shield me as Pepper went to see who it was.

"She isn't decent, Sir," Pepper said quietly, not wanting to be rude. I couldn't see who it was.

"Come back later, Picel," my mom called from my side. "I told you she isn't to see visitors right now."

Picel murmured something I couldn't understand, but then obediently turned and walked back out, closing the door softly behind him.

They helped me dress before I got back into bed. It was a slow process as I was so sore, but finally my head rested against my pillow, and I drifted off into a deep sleep, praying the dreams would stay away.

I was back in Rowynala. I was in the pit with Quinlan. He was struggling to breathe; I was laying on the ground trying to reach him, but something was holding me back. I quickly turned, trying to see who or what it was, and screamed. It was Javil. He had a hold of my ankle and was dragging me backward into a wall of flames. He was completely on fire and was

cackling maniacally. I clawed my way forward, trying to reach Quin before he died, but was soon engulfed by the flames.

I screamed and jolted upright in bed.

Mom rushed to my side, and at the same time the door burst open. *Picel. He heard my scream. He never went back to the guest room. Maybe he isn't mad. Or he is, and his care for me is greater than his frustration.* My mom scolded him as he entered, saying she stood by her ruling earlier that he wasn't to see me. I needed space.

Picel started to argue, but thought better of it. He turned to leave but, before he did, he looked into my eyes, searching for my desire for him to stay, but I couldn't give it to him.

Tears flowed down my face as Picel left. I hated that I didn't want him near me. I wanted more than anything to want him to hold me, to comfort me, but after being violated and abused like I had been- I just couldn't. Not only because I was afraid, but because I was still grieving another loss.

"What do you need, Naia?" Mom asked, as she dabbed my sweaty head with a cool wet towel.

I thought for a moment and then looked at her, anguish weighing heavy on my face. I knew what I wanted, who I wanted- and I knew I would never see him again.

"Quin," I whispered. "I need Quin."

69

PICEL

"Your Majesty," Pepper said as she shut the door behind her, leaving Naia and Luria alone. "You need to know something."

I looked at her expectantly, waiting for her to speak her mind but she hesitated. I knew what she was afraid of.

"Pepper, I am not going to hurt you. You are safe, I promise."

She took a breath. "Naia is asking for Quinlan."

I exhaled. "But he's…"

"I know."

"Then what do I do?"

"You be there for her, take care of her, even when she is crying for him. You don't stop loving her. Ever," she said softly, putting her hand on my shoulder.

"Can I see her?" I asked just as Luria walked out.

"She is asking to be alone, Picel," Luria said softly. She doesn't want visitors this evening. Come back in the morning and we will see," she said firmly, but her eyes were soft.

I bowed my head in submission and walked away, knowing that once Luria went to bed, I would be at the door asking Naia for permission to enter. I couldn't stay away from her any longer.

70

NAIA

*P*icel returned in the middle of the night. He knocked first, making sure I was okay with him entering, and then gently walked over and sat down on the edge of the bed, next to my waist. He stared at me for a minute and then spoke.

"Who did this to you?" He demanded to know, but his voice was soft. Comforting.

He reached out to graze my cheek, but I flinched. He sighed, his face twisting in hurt, and pulled back.

"Naia, who hurt you?" He asked again, his voice strangled. He was genuinely worried. Of course he was. He might be frustrated with me, but he still cared. I whimpered again, still not able to speak.

The third time he spoke, he gently put his hand under my chin and left it there, not forcing me to turn or do anything, but letting me get used to his touch. *I knew that touch. It had happened before… after…* I inhaled as he spoke.

"Naia" he said as softly as imaginable. "Naia, who did this? Please. Tell me," he begged.

I wanted to, but no words came.

Even though it was Picel, I couldn't bear to be touched again just yet. Just the thought of having another man's hands on me made me want to throw up. I had never been treated how those men had treated me before, and I didn't want to be again.

It made me feel like a prize, something invaluable that just any-one could put their hands on. It made me feel so dirty, like an animal. All I wanted was to bathe over and over again to try and wash this evil night off me. But I couldn't – I could barely move. I flinched away from his reach, in pain and in fear, and saw him grimace. *I am sorry, Picel.*

"Please talk to me," he pressed softly. "Naia, you can trust me. I want to be here for you. I *am* here for you, and I am not going anywhere."

I took a breath and it caught on my exhale causing me to start coughing and then start to cry.

"Naia?" He lost all functionality. His hands shook, his lips quiv-ered, his fists clenched at his side. He didn't know how to help me. He didn't know what he was allowed and not allowed to do. I was sure he felt useless. My thoughts were confirmed when tears started streaming down his face as he watched me fall into a million pieces.

After a while, I slowly gathered myself and started to talk; shar-ing with him what I had so recently endured through his uncle's hand.

WHEN PRIDE FALLS

As I talked, I showed him the bruises and lashes that covered parts of my body. Picel deserved to know the truth, all of it. Each touch, each hit…. The tenderness in his eyes as he lightly traced some of the bruises was almost too much to take. Almost unbearable. I was so afraid, but never in my life had I had a man look at me the way that he was looking at me. Not even Quin. *Picel won't hurt you Naia. He won't hurt you. You are safe.*

I had to stop a couple times to compose myself, but then I forced myself to start again. When I finished, I looked at him, his eyes and mine were red and tearstained.

I hated that he had to be so careful around me. I knew that he was only trying to take care of me. I could tell that he was fighting himself to not take me into his arms, but because of his respect for me he didn't. His love for me ran deep. So deep he would deprive himself of my touch, when all he wanted to do was comfort me, if it made me feel more safe.

"Picel, I'm sorry," I cried. It took him a moment, but Picel's face sank as he realized what I was apologizing for.

"Naia, no. You have no need to apologize… for *anything*. What you have been through is… no woman… no one at all, should *ever* have to go through what you just did," he said, his voice growing more intense with each word.

He stood and walked over to the wall, punched it without a sound and then, straddling his arms out, hung his head between them. His breathing was so heavy. I could tell he was doing all he could to not lose his composure completely. He didn't want to scare me more than I already was. He was afraid that if I saw his anger then I would never let him near me again. Like Javil. *He isn't Javil.* I had never seen that side of him so intensely. The protective side; not to the level he was at. He walked back over to me as he ran his hands through his short waves.

"I am sorry that I didn't get here sooner. I am sorry that I ever left in the first place - if I had been here... Oh, Naia," He whispered, kneeling down next to me.

"Picel, it isn't your fault. No one could have known...."

"I know but," he said, placing his hand on my arm.

I tensed at his touch. "Picel...."

"It's okay, Naia. Really. Whenever you are ready. I will never rush you," he said as he pulled away again. "But...."

He then asked me a question that at any other time, or any other night, I would have answered with a resounding "no". And even now, I was not sure if I could say "yes".

"Would you mind if I at least stayed here for the rest of the night? I need to make sure you're safe... I couldn't bear it if someone came back and...." The fear behind his eyes consumed me. *This man really loves me. The thought of something else happening to me is almost destroying him.*

I hesitated just the slightest, dragging my eyes to meet his but nodded my head slightly. *I can trust him. He won't hurt me. He won't hurt me.... He won't....*

71

PICEL

"No... No... please... stop!" she cried.

I jumped out of the chaise and grabbed my sword, ready to attack. I winced as my reinjured chest wound throbbed in pain. Seeing no one in the room, I dropped my sword and rushed to Naia's bedside. She was thrashing and moaning, as if trying to escape someone, as if reliving.... No. I had to do something, but I didn't know what. I had learned the hard way from warriors and my brother, to not awaken people from a deep slumber after a traumatic event. Especially if they were actively having a nightmare. But I couldn't stand to see her so frightened.

"Naia, Naia? Hey, it's a dream, it isn't real... not this time," I said gently touching the side of her face. "Naia, wake up– everything is okay. You are safe. Naia, you are safe."

"Please, no, I can't take anymore! Stop!" She cried, getting a little louder, still asleep. "No! AAAHHH!"

She jolted up into a sitting position; her breathing was labored and heavy with sweat beading at her hairline.

"Hey, I'm here. Naia. Naia?" But she couldn't hear me. Her eyes had glazed over and she rocked back and forth on the bed. I gently touched her shoulder–bad idea. She began thrashing and swinging her hands trying to hit me and keep me back- like I was an enemy trying to….

"NO!" She cried. I let her hit me at first, only protecting my face but, after a while I gently but firmly grabbed her wrists and brought them into my chest, and sat down next to her, pulling the rest of her body in with her arms so she was resting against me. My arms wrapped around her back. She fought for a moment, but then took a breath and stilled. "Ssshhh, Sweetheart, you are safe," I whispered as I held her, never wanting to let her go again.

Her arm draped across my chest and rested on my shoulder. She was nuzzled into the crook of my neck and was finally breathing softly again after another nightmare.

I was afraid to move. I didn't want my touch to startle and wake her, causing her another episode of fright. What I wanted to do was hunt down Ahiam and his men and make them pay, but Naia's needs came first.

As she stirred, I began talking softly, letting her know that though she had draped her arm over me during the night, I hadn't touched her. I had kept my promise - she was safe with me.

"Pi," she murmured softly.

"What is it, Naia?" I whispered, resisting the urge to pull her tight next to me again. She still had her arm over my chest, which was amazing, but I wanted to hold her so badly and feel the warmth of her body tightly pressed against mine. I swallowed hard, knowing that until she gave her permission, I couldn't.

"You can hold me, Picel," she said, oh, so softly. There was definite fear in her voice, but her desire to be near me must have outweighed her fear. I froze. Had she really just given me permission?

"Are you sure?"

"I… I don't know," she answered honestly. "But I… can you just…." she whimpered.

I let out a sharp breath and nodded, not wanting to move too quickly. I slid in closer to her and put my arm around her shoulder and lower back, leaning her against my chest. And I held her there. I tried to be as careful as possible, especially after seeing her injuries, I didn't want to make her hurt worse than she already did.

"I missed you," she murmured into my neck after a few minutes. My heart leapt at her words.

"I missed you too, Naia. So much."

There was a knock on the door and Naia jumped and nuzzled herself deeper into my chest.

"Who is it?" I asked.

There was no answer. *Why would someone knock and not answer? Did they come back? Were they expecting me to still be away?*

"I asked, who is there?" I growled. The door cracked open and I gasped. *Luria.*

"Luria, I am so sorry, I didn't know it was you. Please, forgive me. I am a little on edge at the moment, especially when it comes to your daughter's safety."

She didn't answer. I think when she saw Naia in my arms, she didn't quite believe it. Her mouth dropped a little as she breathed out a small puff of air. She gave a small smile, then shut the door again. I was grateful she hadn't made me leave. I couldn't have left Naia anyway. Not after what she had just revealed to me. The fact that she was letting me touch her, or hold her at all was a miracle.

"Picel, I do not want to be queen," Naia said out of nowhere. I had gotten up and was behind the screen getting dressed as she spoke. I peaked my head over the top.

"What are you talking about?" I asked, starting to walk towards her. She was fiddling with something and looking down so didn't realize I had arrived next to her.

"I only took the throne so I would feel safe since you were hurt. You wouldn't have been able to protect me if…" she stopped and her eyes widened as she realized that I stood before her.

"I didn't mean to scare you," I started to say, but she stopped me mid sentence.

"No, umm, your shirt… it isn't buttoned. I…" She blushed and looked away.

"Oh," I smiled, loving the fact that, for as comfortable as we were getting with each other, I could still make her blush.

I started to button my shirt as she resumed talking, glancing every so often as my shirt started to hide my chest.

"...I only hope that you can forgive me..."

"How could I not forgive you?" I interrupted her. "Naia, you mean the world to me. I didn't show that well before I left, and I am so, so sorry, but I would choose you over the throne any day. I promise."

She looked down at the mattress and her lips scrunched together. *She didn't believe me.*

"Naia," I said even softer, taking both her hands in mine. "I would choose you over anything. My own brother...."

She gasped and pulled her hands away.

"No! Don't say that," she exclaimed. "Please, don't go there. Even after everything, I wouldn't ask that of you. I pray that it never comes to that." I didn't tell her, but I hoped it wouldn't either.

I wasn't sure what time of day it was. The sun was still out, but that was all I knew. Naia had been asleep for a while and I sat at my desk catching up on paperwork; requests from villagers, adding up the accounts. *Being King is hard.* I was almost done for the day when there was a knock on the door.

"Come in," I called softly. I didn't want to wake Naia.

The door creaked open and Luria peeked her head through, seeing Naia was asleep she turned to me.

"Picel, is Naia doing okay? I know that I have seen her, but you are with her more. Is she truly doing alright?"

"She is getting better," I said, "little by little.

"Good," she whispered, starting to shut the door again.

"Luria, thank you," I said just before it closed.

"For what?"

"For letting her stay here," I said. "I can't bear to be away from her. Just the thought of something else happening to her…" my voice wavered. "She told me everything, Luria," I said, my voice heavy.

Luria's face softened, and she stepped through the door completely. "Are *you* okay, Picel?" She asked gently.

I wasn't, but I had to be. For Naia.

"Naia," I murmured into her ear. Her hair tickled my nose. We were cuddled up on the balcony watching the sunset. It was the first time I had gotten her to get out of bed for more than an hour since everything had happened two weeks before. She was finally looking more like herself, and was trusting me more each day.

"Yes?" She whispered back.

"I love you," I paused, "and I don't expect you to say it back right now, and I hope that it doesn't scare you, but you need to know. I need you to know."

She took a deep breath and then tilted her head so she could see my eyes. "Why would I be scared of you saying that?" she asked softly.

"Well… because of what happened to you, because of Javil…and Quin… Naia, I… I don't want to do anything that will cause you to be afraid of me. I am terrified that I will do something, or say something that will send you running in another direction- away from me."

"How long have you felt like this Picel?" She asked, turning over so she was sitting in front of me. We had never had this conversation… and it was time.

"Since you breathed life into my lungs when I was on my death-bed. Since I saw your servant's heart to Javil, even after he treated you so horribly. Since I saw your strength after Quin's death," I admitted, though I was worried how she would respond with Quin's death being brought up.

"I wasn't strong then, Picel. I didn't feel strong," She sighed. I knew she hated that.

"It took you a minute, but once I gave you a little push, your strength came through," I encouraged.

"Really?" She asked, taking my hands lightly in hers.

I inhaled.

"Yeah," I said, holding back the desire to lean in and kiss her. Oh how I wanted to kiss her again, but I had to wait. I would go at her pace. *How would I go at her pace?*

"Naia, do you trust me?" I risked asking. I knew that after everything she had endured, I may have been asking the impossible.

"Yes, I do, Picel," she said without hesitation. "Why else would I be up here under the stars with you?" She replied. "Why do you ask?"

"I... I was just making sure."

"Picel, I really treasure your willingness to be patient with me. Truly." *The wait will be worth it. She is worth it.*

"Anything for you Naia. Anything for you." I sighed, and leaned my head forward so it was resting on hers. Realizing what I had done I immediately removed it, but she whispered "it's okay," so I leaned back in and smiled.

A few months later Naia was up and living life. Everything was almost back to normal after her encounter with Ahiam and his men. We were getting closer, and I could see her slowly moving on from Quinlan and letting herself completely fall for me. *Slowly.*

I had been helping her re-learn what it was to be touched in a non-threatening, non-defiling way. The grazing of her cheek with my thumb. A light kiss on her forehead. Holding her hand. A strong hug. I got to reteach her all of it, safely. It was a long process that we were still learning together, but it was completely worth every minute of it. I still hadn't *kissed her* kissed her again, not since after my stabbing. But I knew that she would be ready soon. I just had a feeling.

She was still hesitant around Javil, which was valid, but he had really turned a corner. He took over as the complete Captain of the Army and appointed a new King's Guard. Dolyon was a well-trained warrior that hailed from the farmlands of Joris. He had been with us for a while and Javil recognized his potential. Javil made it his sole responsibility to make sure everyone was equipped for battle should it arise again. This included the servants in the castle as well as the guards. Even Pepper was required to learn basic self-defense. Javil wanted to ensure that every woman could defend herself.

He had completely changed his heart and mindset and that credit went completely to God. My thoughts were interrupted by Naia. *My Beautiful Naia.*

"Picel!" She squealed from across the Oasis. "Pi! Come here!" The fastest way to her was going directly through the water. So I dove in. She screamed playfully as I came at her, and splashed towards me, a smile on her face. I met her just over half-way and lifted her in my arms, spinning her around. She *smiled*. She *laughed*. How I missed her laugh.

NAIA

The emotions came in waves. Some days I was on top of the world. Others I felt like I was drowning.

"Mom, why, why did I have to go through all of that? I don't get it," I cried on one of the drowning days.

"I don't know sweetie, but I do know that God was with you through it all. He never left," she responded.

"It doesn't feel like that sometimes."

"I know," she sighed, "but that doesn't make it any less true," she said simply. "He loves you so much. You might never know why you had to experience all of this, but hold true to the truth. God has a plan and He will carry it on to completion because you love Him, and He loves you. He is using this. Even if you can't see it."

"Yeah," I said. It was hard to believe, but she was right. I had to keep trusting. Keep up my faith. Keep hoping.

Pepper came to ask Mom to help her with something in the kitchen and they left. I was so deep in thought that I didn't hear the door to the lounge open again a few minutes later.

JAVIL

"Aah!" Naia squealed, jumping up quickly from her seat in the lounge.

"Naia, hey, are you okay? I asked, instinctively reaching my hand out towards her. She flinched slightly. *Would she ever not? Would she ever trust me?*

"I... I'm fine." She stuttered. Clearly nervous at my presence. I internally scolded myself for going to see her in the first place.

"I'm sorry, I'll go." I said quickly, not wanting to frighten her any more. I started to walk away when she did something surprising. She called my name.

"Javil," she said, her voice shaky.

"Yeah, Naia?" I said, turning around slowly; afraid of the words that she was about to say.

She paused for a moment, gathering her courage. This was the longest we had been alone since I had found her, before I hurt her. It was understandable; her fear.

She looked into my eyes and, instead of putting me down or scolding me, said the words I had longed to hear since we were in Rowynala.

"I forgive you." Her voice was soft. She meant it.

My heart leapt with joy. At last.

"Thank you, Naia. That means a lot," I said, starting to leave. I didn't want to stay longer than I needed to. For her sake.

"Javil?" She called again.

"Yes?" I said hesitantly.

"I stand by what I did," her voice didn't waiver.

"I know, Naia. You did what you had to. I deserved it."

She didn't reply.

"Naia…"

"Please go," she whispered. "I can't take any more."

I winced, but understood. I bowed and left as I was asked. I prayed that someday we would be able to talk as friends. I prayed that somehow she would start to trust me again, but I knew that it was going to take time and patience. I owed her my patience. After what I did… I owed her everything.

74

PICEL

As the leaves in Rowynala started to change to their deep oranges and reds, I was still deep in my studies of how those scoundrels had snuck into the castle and had attacked Naia. It was almost impossible. They had just shown up out of nowhere. *How did they do it?* I still couldn't figure it out.

Luria was busy preparing the ceremony for my coronation. She and Naia realized that I had never officially been crowned King of Arilos and they thought that, even though I was technically King, we still needed to make it official. I just think that they wanted to throw a ball. Naia had never been to one, and the last one that Luria had attended was when my father was alive and she had her crowning. And even then she told me that she had been worried about the state of my father the entire time so she didn't really get to enjoy it. As long as I didn't have to be a part of the planning, I didn't care, the women could do whatever they wanted.

I was opening an old drawing of the castle's layout when Javil burst into my study shouting way too loudly. "Picel! Picel! I figured it out! You are not going to believe it. I know how they got into the castle!"

"Well spit it out, Javil!" I said, irritated that he wasn't getting to the point.

"Tunnels," He gasped as he tried to catch his breath.

"What?"

"There are tunnels that run under the castle. I was looking around the place where you found Naia. The servants' room…. I don't know how we missed it! By the stairs…*under the bed*, there is a rug."

"Show me," I demanded as I stood and started walking towards the door.

We sprinted down the stairs and made it to the servants' room. Sure enough. There it was–a trap door hidden under the rug. Just like Javil had described. I looked at my brother, who was still in shock.

"How long…?" I began in disbelief.

"I know as much as you, Picel; but we need to see where it goes."

"Now? But Luria and Naia are planning a ball for my coronation."

"Exactly. Why are we planning a ball? Especially if there are enemies lurking about still, who are loyal to Ahiam. We need to find out where the tunnels go, and then barricade the entrances, before others find out about them. Before there is another attack. We forget that there was a great battle headed up by Ahiam and his followers. Picel, it is how Father died. We have been distracted by everything else that has happened. We need to pull ourselves together and protect our people. *You are our King.* You need to protect your people. Protect Naia. If those men know how to get back in, she is still in danger."

He was right of course. We had to discover where these would lead - fast. We needed to protect the inhabitants of the castle. I needed to protect Naia.

75

JAVIL

We stationed a guard outside of the servants' room with strict orders to not allow anyone inside. The servants who resided there would have to share rooms for a while until we had this all cleared up. I was not going to take any more risks.

What I wanted to know was why our father never mentioned anything to us about the tunnels. Maybe he didn't know. Maybe he was trying to protect us. Maybe there was more to the story than what anyone knew. It didn't matter. What did matter was sealing them off and finding any other ones that could allow enemies to break through.

Picel moved the bed while I folded back the corner of the rug and lifted the trap door. We lit a torch and stuck it down the entryway. There was a wooden ladder that dropped about twenty feet.

I looked at Picel and put my foot on the first rung, I made it to the bottom and called up to him that I was safe, and he quickly followed.

We had been walking for an hour or so when we came to a T in the path. We could either go left or right. We looked for some sort of sign of where the paths might lead. After a few minutes Picel spoke up.

"Look here, Javil," he said, gesturing at something on the tunnel wall. I leaned over to see what he was seeing.

On one side of the back wall there was an engraving. It was a mountain with snow. Weird. I searched the other side for something else.

"Picel, I found something else," I said, my voice rising.

"Ssshh," Picel whispered. "We don't know if there is anyone down here. What did you find?"

"It is an engraving of a cow," I said.

"What is going on?" He asked.

I was wondering the same thing. Mountains with snow, and a cow, what could it mean?

"Javil there are faded arrows next to the mountains. Are there some by the cow?" he asked, holding the torch in my direction so I could see better.

"Yeah, there are arrows… how intriguing," I said, running my hand over them.

We lost track of time while searching the walls for clues. I wanted to keep searching, but I knew this wasn't the time. Only Dolyon knew what we were doing and we needed to get back to the castle before people thought we were missing. Naia didn't need to think that she had lost another man that she loved. She had already lost her father, brother, and Quin.

Thankfully, we had no trouble exiting the tunnel. We got back in time to see the dining room being set for dinner. "Your Majesties!" Pepper cried as we appeared.

"Pepper, what is it?" Picel inquired, glancing at me in concern.

"You have to go get changed! The guests will be arriving any minute! Some are already here!"

I chuckled a little bit. Pepper was so sweet and so organized. We had put her in charge of the food, and she also took it upon herself to organize the guests upon arrival. She had grown up since Naia had arrived. I noticed that her hair was pulled back in a bun instead of the pigtails that she normally wore. I wondered if Luria had said something, or if it was something she had decided on her own.

Picel and I did as we were asked and went to our rooms to put on our best. I don't remember ever having been to a castle dance before. Picel remembered one when he was six or seven. He didn't know why there hadn't been any others. If there had been, we had been kept out of them. Regardless, we were both looking forward to the evening ahead.

Some servants came to assist us in dressing, but we kindly declined, asking them to continue assisting with the preparations for the masquerade. That was of more importance than our attire.

Picel threw on a navy top and pants with a gold suit. I dressed similarly, but wore navy pants, a gold shirt, and a navy suit. As King, Picel always wore gold on the outside.

We made it down just in time for the villagers to arrive. The people of Flykra had not been invited. I remained on high alert, ready for an attack at any moment. I was not going to let anything happen to the people I cared about. Not again.

76

PICEL

All I wanted was for the night to go smoothly. I wanted Naia to be able to enjoy this night with me by her side, completely focused on her. But all I could think about were the tunnels that mazed under our Kingdom.

How did they get there? Have they always been there or had they shown up since my father's reign? What was their purpose? It worried me, knowing that the wrong people could have access to Castle Arilos.

I realized that I had zoned out when Naia looped her arm through mine and pulled me into her so we were face-to-face.

"What is wrong Picel?" She whispered so no one would be alarmed at her words.

"Nothing. Everything is fine, Sweetheart," I fibbed.

Naia raised her eyebrows and frowned. She knew better.

"Picel, please don't lie to me. What is going on? You are scaring me!" I knew I had to tell her, but I needed more time to put everything together. I needed... Then it hit me. I'd figured it out. I needed to find Javil.

"My love, I will return. I have an urgent message that I need to get to Javil. Please, let me take you to find your mother or Pepper so you aren't alone. I need to speak to my brother. Then I promise I will not leave your side the rest of the night."

She nodded hesitantly and, once we found her mother, I left to scan the crowd for Javil.

"Picel, what is it?" Javil asked as I dragged him down the hall a few minutes later.

"The markings on the wall," I stated once we were away from earshot, like he should know what I was talking about.

"What about them?" He questioned.

"I think I figured out what they mean," I said, pausing to figure out how to best convey my thoughts.

"Well, out with it then." His voice was tight.

"What have I done, brother?" I inquired. "Why so angry all of a sudden?"

"I was having a pleasant conversation with a girl, and you had to come in and ruin it."

"I am sorry that I am a horrible wingman, but you have to remember that I am King, and I have a job to do."

Javil sighed and nodded. "Okay, Picel. You are right. What do you think they are?"

"I think that the markings on the wall are supposed to point us, or whomever, in the direction of those markings," I stated, and Javil looked at me like I was talking in another language, so I tried again.

"The snowy mountains… What place has snowy mountains?" I asked, hoping he would catch on.

"Flykra," he said.

"Right. And what place has cows, or is known for them and farming?" Javil's eyes sparked. He was starting to understand.

"Joris, yes, exactly. I think that down in that tunnel, if we went to the left, we would eventually arrive in Flykra. If we went to the right, it would lead us to Joris. And in that tunnel there is probably a path to Rowynala as well."

"You are either spot on, or completely crazy," Javil commented. I laughed. He was right. And there was only one way to find out.

The party went late into the night as the people were laughing and dancing and having a good time.

I stood by my promise and returned to Naia, who was not pleased at my long disappearance. But the minute she saw me return, relief flooded her eyes.

She looked radiant. In a deep blue dress she captivated the entire room. *This masquerade should be for her.* She wore gold heels to match my attire and her hair was pulled back in an elegant pinned updo that Luria had done for her.

I loved having her on my arm. As we walked, I let my mind wander to when I might ask for her hand in marriage someday. Then I would be able to introduce her to the villagers as my wife. Their Queen. My Queen.

Pepper had gone above and beyond with the food. She made chocolate cake with chocolate frosting, vanilla cupcakes, candied cactus, a strawberry cream dessert, followed by even more sweet confections. Bread, cheese, pork, and lamb had been brought in from Joris. Pepper was grateful she didn't need to worry about the savory selections for this many people on a regular basis, though she enjoyed it every once in a while. It was the feast of the year.

"I need to be honest with you," I said after Naia and I had reached the balcony that overlooked the oasis. We had departed from the rest of the castle to be alone for a while. I straddled her body with my hands and rested them on the railing on either side of her. My head hung down next to her ear. I felt her whole body tense against me as she took a sharp breath.

"What is it, Picel?"

"There are tunnels. They run under the castle, and Javil and I think that they lead to the villages. We think that is how the men got in from Flykra when they...." I stopped. How was I supposed to tell her?

"You think that the men will come back?" She whimpered. I tightened my arms around her. She pressed into me, searching for the protection she knew I'd provide.

"I don't know, Naia. What I do know is that I need to go check it out. I have to keep Arilos safe. I have to keep you safe."

"You are going down to scope the tunnels out; to see where they lead?" She guessed.

"Yes. I am."

"You're leaving?" Fear laced each word as she processed what my leaving would mean. She would be unprotected.

"I have to, Sweetheart," I whispered, stroking her hair lightly with my fingertips.

"I know," she leaned into me harder, making what gaps that were left between us disappear, and we stood there, wrapped in each other's arms, taking in the last moments that we would have together for the near future.

"Naia," I whispered against her cheek.

"Mmm?"

"May I kiss you… before I go?"

She pulled away from my embrace and looked deeply into my eyes. A small smile started to form on her face and she looked like she was getting ready to answer me. I could hear her reply, *yes*. Her posture straightened and her eyes were fixed on mine. But she didn't get a chance to start her sentence. Shouting rang out from behind us. Battle cries. The castle walls had been breached. Our enemies had returned.

PICEL

"Naia, get to my room and barricade the door. I will station guards outside. *No one* will touch you," Picel demanded and promised. I wanted to believe him, but we both knew that it was a promise that he might not be able to keep.

"Picel I can help-"

"Go!" He growled, as he pulled me into his chest, squeezed me tightly, and then planted a firm kiss on the top of my head, before he raced away to go set the plan of defense with Javil. "I'll come for you when it is safe!" He called as he disappeared down the stairs.

I knew that he had to leave, he was King, he had a castle to protect, but I wished that he could have seen me to safety first. Maybe he thought that no one would be on the second floor yet.

I tried to move my feet, but they wouldn't budge. With Picel gone, my confidence faded. *You can't rely on him to keep you safe every time, Naia.*

My heart was beating seemingly out of my chest, I was having a hard time taking full breaths. The last time Arilos had been attacked Picel had almost been killed, and King Zaxton had been. I couldn't bare to think of losing Picel.

I shouldn't have waited. When he asked to kiss me I should have answered him immediately with that kiss he so deeply desired, but it was too late. I didn't even know if he would come back to me. I had to get to safety for him. I knew he would never forgive himself if something happened to me.

I forced myself to take a deep breath then willed myself to pick up my feet, to run down the hall and trap myself in Picel's room. I wedged the chaise in front of the door, then shoved the end table into the chaise. His room didn't have a balcony, so I was safe unless someone climbed up the wall… or broke through…. *God please keep people away.*

I huddled up against the far wall with one of Picel's tunics for comfort. Against the wall I was shadowed by the dresser if someone broke through. That made me feel a little protected, but I knew I was far from being safe.

I could hear swords clanging and the pounding of fists. They were making their way up the stairs. Soon they would reach Picel's room and I would be killed or worse, captured again. Men were screaming as they fell after being wounded. I could feel the pounding of the battering ram as the enemy tried to breach the gate from the outside, the entrance to our fortress.

I pressed as tightly as I could up against the wall and covered myself in Picel's cloak. The shouting was getting louder. There was a battle going on right outside the door. *Please let us win.*

There was a loud grunt and a thud and then silence.

I bit my cheek to keep from crying out in terror. The door cracked open. There was a moment of nothing, and then someone rammed their way through. They were strong enough to move both the chaise and the end table. I held back a gasp and inched as close to the dresser as I could. Footsteps approached where I was hiding and then I saw a shadow standing in front of me. I had been found.

JAVIL

We had missed something. There had to be another tunnel somewhere in the castle. The tunnel we had discovered was heavily guarded - there was no other explanation. I was thankful that the guests had left by the time the attack happened, but that meant that more of our staff would be wounded.

I was also thankful that I had made the women take some self-defense and weaponry classes. They wouldn't be as strong as the men, but at least they could try to protect themselves. Hopefully that would throw the enemy off-guard a little bit and buy them some time.

I had been talking with Pepper when the battle cries began. I escorted her to a closet and directed her to hide until I came to get her, then locked the door from the outside. I slid the key under the door just in case something happened to me and I wasn't able to let her out.

As I approached the courtyard to round up my warriors I saw a group of enemy men running up the stairs towards our bedrooms. A second later Picel spotted me and called my name.

He was surrounded by four enemy warriors. I started to move in his direction but he cried out again, "Javil... Naia!" Although he only said two words I knew what he was saying. Naia was upstairs in one of the rooms and Picel was otherwise engaged. He couldn't get to her and he needed my help. She needed my help.

My heart sank. It had been at least two minutes since I had seen those men ascend the stairs. I took off at a sprint and as I rounded the corner saw them coming out of my room. Next was Picel's. There were five of them. *How am I going to do this?*

"Hey!" I shouted! "You aren't supposed to be up here!"

"Who are you, the King?" One sneered.

"Close. I am his brother. Now, leave before I kill every one of you," I commanded as I drew my sword.

"Is that a threat, Your "Princeness"?"

"I dare you to find out," I snarled, then lunged.

All five came at me at once. I was expecting that and was trying to figure out a way to turn them on each other. I swept one's feet out from under him causing him to knock over the man on his left. While they were on the ground I swung around and landed my sword in the third's neck. He collapsed instantly. *One down four to go.*

The men on the floor had started to stand again so I thrust my boot into one's chest. He grunted as he flew backwards, colliding with the stone wall. As he fell, the third man had moved in and, when I turned to raise my sword, I was met with a fist colliding into my jaw. My head flew to the side, but I kept my stance - I would not fall - I would not break.

I threw a punch back and immediately drew my dagger. I was about to go in for the kill when there was a piercing pain in my ribcage. I tried to take a breath, but it caught halfway and I stifled a moan. I forced myself to keep hold of my dagger and turned to face my attacker. My eyes widened in shock upon realizing who it was.

"You," I growled, as pain cascaded through my chest. I was fading fast. I wouldn't get to her in time. I had to get to Naia before he did! He would get to her first, and I didn't know what he would do when he found her. After stabbing me, I knew he would be capable of anything. Though I thought I heard him whisper, "*I'm so sorry*" as he left me bleeding out on the ground.

NAIA

The figure knelt down next to me and tenderly stroked my face. I recoiled in fear and hit my head on the wall. Throwing my hands up in defense I started swinging at the man who had touched me so gently.

"Get away!" I screamed. "Don't touch me!"

The figure spoke. His voice was tender and understanding; it was familiar.

"Naia, it is me. I'm going to get you out of here, but we need to leave. Now!" His hands reached behind me and pulled me against him. He positioned me so I was laying across his lap. I couldn't move. I couldn't breathe. I whimpered. He clung to me so tightly. I didn't understand what was going on. *You aren't Picel...*

"Naia! I need to get you to safety. I know you are scared, but you have to trust me." I recognized his voice. It was a voice that had once calmed me. A voice that was there for me in some of my darkest moments. I shook the thought from my mind. I was imagining things. *It can't be.*

"Naia, work with me, please."

He stood, lifting me with him. He held me so I was leaning against his neck, shielding me from the casualties of the battle going on outside. *But it is. It has to be.*

The room was dark, but when we entered the hall I could see the outline of his face. *My Heart.*

"Naia, I… Javil is wounded. The King will be next, then you. I messed up badly and I have to protect you. I swore to protect you!" He growled.

I almost didn't believe it. I had seen him die. He practically died in my arms. But holding me, protecting me, in this moment of terror, was the man I had once loved. The man I thought I would marry one day. The man who had saved my life time and time again. *My Love. My Heart. My Quin.*

When he picked me up I felt a roughness in his hands that hadn't been there before. They had always been calloused from all of the swordwork that he did, but this was a different kind of rough. This was a scarred kind of rough. *Did he try to claw his way out of somewhere?*

"Cover your eyes, Naia, you shouldn't have to see the fallen. None of this should have ever happened to you. You never should have gone to Rowynala with me. I shouldn't have let you. It was too dangerous." He had a scar running over one of his eyes. They didn't sparkle anymore.

I listened at first, but when we got to the courtyard I couldn't help but look. Men were falling around me. I scanned the courtyard for where Picel might be, but couldn't find him. Quin brought me to the throne room. Picel's throne had been ripped from the ground and was laying on its side. On the ground under where the throne had been was a door in the ground. *Is this what Picel had been talking about?*

"How did…?"

I was cut off. "You need to climb down," Quin said, opening the door. "I can't carry you down the ladder safely. Please." I hesitated for just a second, but then looked at Quin's pleading eyes and descended down the ladder into the darkness.

I thought Quin was going to follow me, but as soon as I made it to the bottom Quin called down to me, "go straight till you reach the crossroads, then take a left. At the next crossroads go straight until you reach the end. There will be a ladder that goes up. The door at the top will be open." Then the trap door closed. "Quin?" I called, but there was no answer. I was alone in the darkness. I sank to my knees and curled up into a ball. Not a half a second later, the tears came.

I wept for the potential loss of the King. Picel. The man I had started to fall in love with. I wept for the miraculous return of the man I had loved and lost. I cried and cried and cried.

I knew that I needed to pull myself together, so I gave myself a long moment to grieve before wiping away my tears and rising to my feet. I needed to either climb back to the top, or I needed to follow the tunnels to see where they led. If Picel was dead, then I needed to finish his search. I had to find out where the tunnels led.

Why would Quin leave me down here? How did he know that these tunnels existed? He was dead when Picel and Javil had found them. Unless… no. I wouldn't let myself think about that. There had to be a reason why he knew they existed. Maybe he ran into Javil on his way to me and Javil told him how he could keep me safe. That had to be it.

I stood and started tracing the wall. *Go straight at the cross-roads… then take a right? Wait, was I supposed to go left at some point? Was it the first crossroads or the second. Oh no.*

Breathe Naia. you have to get there first. Maybe there will be a sign or something. I laughed at myself. *A sign in a dark tunnel? I was dreaming.* I put on a brave face and took a right praying that someone would come find me. I didn't want to be down there alone.

The journey was slow. I couldn't see my hand in front of my face so I shuffled my feet the entire way. Every once in a while I would stub my toes on a rock. I hoped they were rocks. I shuddered at the thought that they could be something else. Someone's bones… I walked a few more steps and felt the wall curve. I had made it to the crossroads.

"Hello?" I called, hopeful that someone would answer even a stranger letting me know that I wasn't alone. But there was only a loud silence. I took a deep breath and took another step, pressing further into the darkness.

80

QUINLAN

I dragged the throne back into place and quickly made my way out of the throne room. As I exited I saw the battle was dying down. Picel and his men had chased out most of the enemy and were finishing off the last few. I started to walk towards him, a plan already forming to break it to him that I was back.

"Picel!" I shouted and started to run to where he was finishing off an enemy man. "Your Majesty!"

He jolted at my voice, made sure the man was dead, then looked up at me wide eyed.

"Quin? What are…?" I didn't let him finish.

"Picel, Javil is gravely wounded. He is dying. Hurry!"

I led him up to where I had left Javil on the ground by his room and was shocked to see that he wasn't there. I looked at the ground and saw a trail of blood leading into Picel's room.

"Naia," Picel breathed, and bolted inside.

Upon entering, instead of finding Naia like he had hoped, he found Javil flat on his face, barely breathing.

"No!" He cried. "Javil, wake up!"

Javil stirred, just a little. Then spoke. His words were barely audible.

"Quin is… Naia… mmmhh."

"What about Naia! Javil, where is she?"

"I couldn't get to her… Quin…"

"Did Quin drag you in here? He probably saved your life. Javil, where are you hurt?"

"No…" was all Javil was able to muster out before his eyes rolled behind his head.

"Quin, help me carry him to the infirmary."

I took Javil's feet while Picel took his shoulders. We managed to get him down the stairs and into the infirmary just as Zahir was walking back in.

"What happened!" He gasped rushing to assist us in getting Javil laid down.

"We don't know," Picel said hurriedly. "Please, don't let him die. I need to go find Naia." He started out the door.

"Why don't you let me do that?" I suggested. "You don't want to leave your brother like this."

"No, I…" his eyes darkened.

"Picel, I will find her. Stay with Javil," I said almost as a demand. It was a risky move, but it paid off. Picel nodded and I rushed out the door before he could change his mind.

I knew where Naia was of course, I had sent her there, but Picel didn't need to know that. Not yet.

81

NAIA

Orange light flooded in from the ceiling ahead. I made it! Hope lit in my heart as I began walking just a little faster. I was so tired. I didn't know how long I had been walking, but I knew I needed water fast - and that my legs were throbbing with exhaustion.

As I came to the end of the tunnel my breath caught. It was suddenly so cold. I could see my breath. *Where was I?* As I reached the ladder I paused and listened hard for any kind of sound around me. But there was only an eerie silence. I hoped there was safety at the top of the ladder, but I had a bad feeling that I was walking into a trap.

I needed to make as little noise as possible. If this really was a trap I needed to find a place to hide. I needed to figure out where I was.

As I stepped out of the tunnel I slipped and caught myself from falling the twenty feet I had worked so hard to climb. I steadied myself and looked around. Everything was covered in ice and snow. *Ice and snow… oh no. No, no, no. I can't be here. Anywhere but here. God, please don't make me go through this again!*

There was only one place I could be. Snow, ice, the feeling of complete despair and brokenness. I was in Flykra. And I had been set up by the man I once loved.

82

PICEL

Most of our warriors made it out alive. I had miraculously managed to take down the men that I was fighting before Quin showed up to tell me the bad news. The warriors we lost had been burned or taken back to their families to be buried. The wounded were healing up, and all who were able were preparing to scour Arilos for the men behind the attack. I asked around and no one had seen Ahiam, though he could still be behind it.

It had been days and Quin still hadn't returned with Naia. I was out of my mind with worry, but I knew he wouldn't come back until he found her. I so badly wanted her by my side, but I was also worried that she would decide that she wanted Quin again and leave me. I couldn't bear it if she left me for him. She was my soulmate and I loved her and needed her with every part of my being. I sat by Javil's bedside. He was alive, but had been unconscious since Quinlan and I had brought him in. I wondered if the panic I was feeling in any way mirrored what he felt when he thought he might lose me and need to become king in my place. Looking back, it made sense that he had the temper he did. I was feeling that way, too.

"Majesty," Zahir said as he walked in from his break. "Any changes?"

I sighed and shook my head. "Nothing at all. Will he ever… is he going to…?" I couldn't say it. I couldn't ask if my brother was going to die.

Zahir read my mind. "I don't know, Picel. I wish that I had answers. Even before you found him he'd lost a great deal of blood from the damaged muscle. That alone could cause him to not awaken. At the same time, whoever did this was very careful to not penetrate the muscle any more than they did. I don't think the attacker wanted Javil to die. The question is why."

My fists tightened. I would find whoever did this and they would pay. I didn't care if they went easy on him. He was still on his deathbed. He was still my brother. And I was still king.

"Picel, Picel!" A voice called, getting louder as it got closer to the infirmary. It was Quin. He was back.

"Picel," he rounded the corner and flew into the infirmary completely out of breath. He was alone.

"Picel, I got word that she is imprisoned in Flykra. Ahiam has her. We need to leave now!"

I jumped up and flung my cloak over my shoulders. I loved my brother, but if Naia was in danger, he would want me to leave him and go rescue her.

"I will be back, brother," I promised.

My horse was ready to be mounted. Quin must have stopped at the stables to alert them I would be riding.

I got on and without waiting for Quin, took off at a gallop towards Flykra. Towards my girl.

Quin caught up to me quickly and matched his horse's stride with mine. I needed to talk to him about how in the world he survived, but this was not the time. All of my focus and energy needed to be poured into saving Naia. After she was safe I would interrogate my friend.

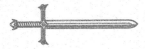

"We need to dismount and leave our horses," Quin said as we approached Flykra's borders.

We had taken the long way into Flykra, deliberately going through the woods from Rowynala instead of cutting across the desert. Hopefully that would protect and hide us longer. The alternative would result in the enemy immediately finding us and taking us down..

I'd debated in my mind for a while as we rode, but decided that I wanted to know how it came to be that Quin was still alive.

"So, what happened?" I asked. It wasn't a very deep question, but I was a little mad that Quin didn't send word sooner that he was still alive. Instead, I had to find out in the middle of a battle. It would have been nice to have him fighting by my side.

"Picel... now isn't the time," Quin warned.

"No, I want to know what happened," I shot back. "You were dead, we all watched you die.

"I know."

"I had to tell your parents. I had to watch as they realized that their only son was never coming back!"

"I know," he said louder. I knew it must be hard for him too, but I was so mad at him for what he put us through. Though I had been blessed with Naia in the process and was so thankful for that gift.

"I had to watch Naia grieve for you!" Quin tensed, but I didn't let up. I needed him to know what he had put Naia through - what he had put me through. "I have had to listen to Naia cry in my arms over losing you while trying to understand her feelings for me! Do you know how hard it is? To see someone you love still be in love with someone else! Do you?" *Thwack.* He punched me. Hard. I hit the ground with a thud.

"What was that for?" I yelled.

"You took my girl!" He said, scrambling to stand, but he was already on the ground pinning me down.

"You left her!"

"I... didn't... have... a...choice!" He snarled and squeezed his hand around my throat.

"QUIN!" I wheezed. "Let go!"

He was going to kill me. I had taken his girl. I was a threat. I was his King. He didn't care.

I was wobbly and lightheaded - struggling to stay conscious when there was rustling in the woods in front of us.

I had been so focused on hating Quin that I had forgotten my mission to rescue the person I had been fighting for. The woman I loved.

"Who goes there?" A voice boomed. "State your business!"

"It's me, Cathan. Calm down," Quin said, raising his hands. "Lower your weapon."

The man lowered his weapon as asked. He was a massive warrior; an intimidating force, but I would never let him know. I tightened my posture and took a step forward, ready to fight.

83

JAVIL

When I woke up Picel was gone. I had heard him talking and praying that I would live, but I was so weak I couldn't respond.

"Zahir," I called, my voice raspy and deep.

"Sire! You are awake!" Zahir gasped excitedly.

"Your brother…"

"Is in danger," I interrupted. "The King is in grave danger," there was a newfound energy in my bones.

Zahir knelt down next to me. Consternation lined his face as he leaned in close, not wanting anyone to overhear what I was about to say.

"Quin," I whispered. "Quin was the one who stabbed me," I said. "I know Picel left with him to go find Naia. He took her. Quin did. I think he has known where she has been this whole time. Something happened. I think Quin betrayed us. I have to go to Flykra."

"No, absolutely not, Sire. I will not have you leaving this place in your state. You have been unconscious for almost a week! You will not leave this bed, and that is an order!"

My blood boiled. How *dare* he command me. *I* was his superior. It took everything in me not to hit him, but I knew that I would pay the price. I didn't want to strain or re-open my wound before I left. *I was still leaving.*

"Sire, please, I know what you are thinking, what you are planning, and I beg you not to do it. I know I can't keep you here without restraining you, and I know that you would have my life for that, or at least my job. But I beg you, please stay in bed. Your brother can take care of himself."

I took a breath. "No, he can't. Not when it comes to Naia's safety. He will lose all rationality when he figures out that she is in danger, especially at Quin's hand."

Zahir's face dropped. He knew I was right. He'd known Picel and I for a long time. He knew how quick we were to protect our loved ones, especially when their lives were on the line.

He sighed deeply, knowing that he had lost the fight.

"Please let me bandage you up tightly before you go. And I ask that you don't go full speed on your horse."

"You know I can't promise that, Zahir," I said solemnly. "But I will definitely let you wrap me up. I can't afford to die on the way to Flykra from blood loss."

I could tell that Zahir wanted to tell me that if I didn't go I wouldn't be at risk of dying at all, but he bit his tongue and went to fetch the binding cloth.

I could barely breathe by the time Zahir was through with me. I assumed he was trying to prove a point, but I was too stubborn to care what that point might be.

I hurried out of the infirmary, saddled my horse and headed for Flykra.

84

QUINLAN

I hated myself. I hated the mess I was in, but I couldn't back out now. Maybe there was a way to save everyone - well, besides Javil. I wasn't sure if he would make it or not. It killed me to do what I did, but I didn't have a choice. I knew Javil was going for Naia, to save her; and I knew that there was no way that he would let me take her, even if I was taking her to safety. So I had to take Javil out.

Picel would never forgive me for any of it. I would never have his trust again. What scared me the most, though, was that Naia might never forgive me.

Cathan stepped out of the trees and motioned to Picel.

"You did well Quinlan, now hand him over," Cathan grunted.

"How could you?" Picel seethed as he turned to me in shock. "You were my most trusted man. You were my friend!"

"Oh come on, Picel. You know what it is like to need to protect your loved ones. You would do the same thing if you were in my position." I retorted.

"And what position is that?" Picel spat. "I would *never* betray my family. *Never!*"

I walked over to him and leaned in so close our foreheads were almost touching. The only thing keeping Picel from tearing me apart was Cathan's iron grip as he had moved in from behind and had seized Picel's wrists. I didn't owe him an explanation, but he was my friend. I needed to explain.

"I didn't have a choice..." I gritted out painfully.

Picel's eyes lit with rage.

"What could be so important that you would betray your *King?* What would make you risk *everything?* I should execute you for treason. In fact, if I ever get out of here, you are dead! Do you hear me, Quinlan? You better hope that I die in there. And I swear if something happens to Naia... I will make you suffer slowly, before I slit your throat!"

"Naia is safe... and Ahiam... He threatened them... my parents... I... he has ruined me... the things I have seen..." I shuddered. I couldn't think about it. Not now. Not ever. "Cathan, take him, now," I growled.

Cathan wrapped his meaty arms around Picel's torso and half carried and half dragged him away. I got back on my horse and took off galloping around them. Off to the fortress.

"You'll pay for this!" Picel cried. I heard it, but I was already long gone. His voice- a whisper in the wind.

"Remember what happens if you double cross me, Boy," Ahiam snarled. "Don't test the waters. It won't end well for you."

I made it back to the fortress and went down to the dungeons where Ahiam had instructed me to meet him once I had taken care of Picel. Ahiam didn't want me interfering with his plan for Picel in any way.

"Right," I muttered and started to turn away.

As I turned, there was a soft whimper and a voice called through the door.

"Quin is that you? What is going on?" *Naia? No! She wasn't supposed to be here. I sent her a different way!*

"Quin? I think I turned the wrong way in the tunnels," she called out, her voice shook.

I took a step towards the door towards her and was met with a sword to my chest.

"Ahem," Ahiam shook his head and gestured for me to leave. *I can't leave her with him. Not again.*

"Please, just let me make sure she is okay; give her my cloak; something," I begged. "She will freeze!"

Ahiam pondered this for a moment and waved his hand at me. "Be quick about it," he commanded and unlocked the door.

I should have been worried that Ahiam let me in so quickly, but I didn't stop to think. I was only concerned about Naia. I rushed into the cell and heard it click shut. I really hoped that I would be let out again; otherwise I would prove to be not only a betrayer, but a completely useless one at that. Maybe Ahiam already thought I already was useless. I didn't care, as long as Naia made it out alive.

"My Heart. Hey, Naia, I am so sorry," I grabbed her face so delicately in my hands. And then quickly took off my cloak and draped it around her shoulders, covering her head with the hood. She was ice cold. *How long has she been here?*

"Quin, why are you here? Why are you doing this? I thought… I thought you loved me," she whispered.

"Naia, you weren't supposed to be involved in any of this. There was a place set up for you. A safe place. I was going to come find you once everything had gone down. Did you turn right instead of left at the crossroads?"

"I must have," she whimpered, a tear forming in the corner of her eye. I brushed it away with my thumb before it could slide down her cheek.

"Naia, I am not going to lie to you. This is all a trap to get Picel here. I have nothing against him, but Ahiam has my parents. Or, he said that he would kill them if I didn't obey. I… there was no other way. You have to understand. You will be free to go once he is locked up and in chains," as I spoke, a look of horror spread across her face. Something wasn't right.

"Naia, I am sorry. I… I didn't have a choice." She didn't respond. "Naia?"

"I love him, Quin," she said, her voice barely audible.

"What?" I replied. I could hear my heart pounding.

"I am in love with Picel. Quin… Please, please don't take him from me. Please don't do this. He is your friend. He is your King. Quin, *I love him*," she said again. She enunciated the last three words. I cringed. *She loves him, too? Naia and Picel?* If she was telling the truth, and why would she lie, then I was about to send the man she loved to his death. My breathing picked up and my chest tightened. The world started spinning around me. *What have I done?*

85

PICEL

Cathan dragged me through the forest and brought me into Ahiam's fortress. I had seen it a few times as my father had started to train me to be the next king of Arilos. It was just as intimidating now as it was then.

Castle Arilos was big, but Ahiam's fortress was built into the mountains. It was massive and was twice the size of the castle. His brother, Ishvi, started building the massive structure years ago, but after his death, Ahiam had taken over.

I wished that things would have been handled differently. I respected my father and his desire to show mercy. But if I had been king when Ishvi and Ahiam were running rampant, I would have seen them both killed. It would have saved a lot of loss and a lot of heartbreak.

Cathan threw me down and hit me with the hilt of his sword, preventing me from fighting back while he secured me to two long thick chains that reached the ceiling. He then went over to a wheel and turned it rapidly. As he did, the chains wrapped around it and tightened, leaving me barely on the tips of my toes. And even then, I was sliding on the ice beneath me. He was going to suffocate me. I was already struggling to breathe, but I refused to cry out. I would not show weakness.

"Where is your master?" I spat with difficulty. "Is he too much of a coward to face me and torture me himself?"

A grin spread across Cathan's face.

"He is not with you, because he is with your lady...." his voice was smooth, apathetic.

"No!" I roared. "Do anything you'd like to me, but please, leave her out of it! She has had nothing to do with this! I beg you! Tell Ahiam to leave her alone! It was *my* father that hurt him. She is innocent!"

"It looks like I have found your weakness," He sneered and shut the door. In the distance I heard a devastating wail. It was a girl's voice.

I writhed against the chains trying to slide my wrists through, but they were too tight, and I didn't have enough leverage. I was more hanging than standing. A mangled cry erupted from the depths of my soul. "NAIA!"

But it was hopeless. I was imprisoned behind a locked door. By the time I could figure out how to escape, if I even could, Naia would most likely be dead.

86

JAVIL

I swung my leg back over the saddle to dismount and reached down to find the ground with my foot. Just that little bit of a stretch sent a shooting pain through my ribs, and I collapsed. I reached down and put my hand over the wound. Blood. That wasn't good.

I stood and staggered a few steps but then collapsed again. Dizziness consumed me. *It can't end like this. I am the protector. I...* *I am...*

87

QUINLAN

The door flung open and Ahiam stepped through. He strode over to Naia and me, then stopped.

"Get up, boy." His sword was at my throat. I let out a low growl, but obeyed, my eyes never leaving Naia's trembling body.

"Get out," Ahiam commanded, pressing his sword into my neck a little more. I felt it nick a sliver of my skin, but still I warned him. "Ahiam if you touch her… if anyone…."

"You mean if I touch her again… and you'll do what? My men will be at your throat in half a second if you try to attack me in any way. You best be on your way now," his eyebrows raised, waiting for me to question him again. I didn't.

"What happened to you? Why won't you fight for me?" Naia sobbed as I turned and left her alone with the man who had let her be destroyed.

As I left, my fist made contact with the icy wall outside the dungeon. I growled as pain shot through my knuckles. I didn't even remember balling up my fist.

As the door closed I heard Ahiam say something to Naia that caused her to let out the most gut-wrenching wail. It wasn't a wail of pain, but of anguish. I pivoted to sprint back to her but was met with spears crossed in front of me. There was no going back.

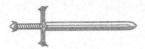

I walked down a hall that was eerily silent. I peeked in each of the doors to see what they held. Torture chambers. I shuddered at the thought of having to be held and tortured in one of those rooms. I hoped I would never have to find out. There was a man in one of the rooms, but it wasn't Picel so I continued on. *Sorry buddy.* I thought as I passed him.

I got to the last door and my breath caught. There, practically hanging before me, was Picel. I could see blood dripping from his wrists that the chains had dug into. He must have been trying to escape at one point. The blood trailed down his white tunic and down his legs to a puddle of red on the floor. His tunic was ripped to shreds. It was barely clinging to him. His abdomen was covered in bruises and cut marks. His breathing was heavily labored. I could see him fighting to take each breath. I grimaced at seeing my friend, my King, in so much pain. And at my hand. I never meant for it to go that far.

I needed to get him out. *He will kill your parents.* I shoved the thought aside and grabbed onto the handle. It was unlocked. I pulled it open and gently closed it, leaving it open a tiny crack, and rushed to where Picel hung.

"Picel, are you alive?" I whispered. His eyes were closed and his stomach had stopped moving in the seconds that I entered and walked over to him. *If I had killed my best friend…*

"Picel?" I asked again, but there was no response.

No.

I scanned the room and quickly realized that his chains were wrapped around a wheel. I ran over and saw that all I had to do was spin the wheel to get him down. *You can't. If you let him down your parents will be killed.*

It hit me, as I had that thought, that there was a good chance my parents were already dead; I was doing all of this, betraying my friends, for nothing. If by some miracle Picel was still alive and I could wake him up enough, maybe we could defeat Ahiam together. Maybe…

I grabbed the wheel and started to turn it. It was hard to not let Picel drop to the ground, but I managed to get him down smoothly without any complications. Once he was on the ground I hurried back and leaned down to see if I could feel his breath against my face. I shook him, and then waited a few seconds. I shook him again and waited a few more. I was about to give up hope when he finally started to stir. He groaned and his eyes fluttered open.

"Picel!"

"No, get out," he grunted, trying to lift his head, but he was unsuccessful. His head thudded back onto the ice beneath him. Blood pooled from the corners of his mouth as he hit the ground.

His breathing was ragged and bubbly. *What had they done to him?* I moved him so he was laying on his side, hoping that would help him breathe easier. I had seen Zahir do that for injured men coming in from battles and thought it was worth a try. He groaned as I rolled him and tried to swat me away, but his arm only got an inch above the ground.

"Picel, let me help you. Please."

"Na-ia," he grunted. His words were gurgled. Something had happened to his throat. "She...screamed...Quin." It was taking every ounce of his strength to speak. I knew he must be in an extraordinary amount of pain.

"I know," I replied, shame coursed through me. "I didn't know she was here; she wasn't supposed to be part of this."

Picel's eyes darted to mine. He tried to say something else, but the words just didn't come.

"Picel, I need to check your injuries. Your voice. Is that from screaming?"

He shook his head.

I moved to examine the outside of his throat. He shook his head again and pointed inside his mouth.

My heart sank. I knew what had happened. Cathan must have used the Pear of Anguish. It was a small torture device that was shoved into someone's mouth or throat and then expanded to the point of suffocation. The one that was used on Picel had little prongs on it that dug into the flesh on the inside of his throat and ripped it as it was forced out. I had seen it lying on the table when I walked by.

"Can you walk?" I inquired, my voice gentle. This was my friend, and I had sent him to slaughter.

He moaned. It was more of a gurgle. "Rack," was all he got out. "What...is...he...doing...to...her?" He asked as he tried to push himself up onto his arms, but dropped back to the ground again. He was too weak. This wasn't going to work.

"I don't know, Pi," I admitted. "It wasn't a scream of pain though, I have heard that from her and this wasn't it. This one was more a scream of despair. Anguish. Mourning."

He nodded. He had heard both before, too.

"Maybe he told her that you were dead," I suggested.

He scrunched his eyebrows asking why.

"Maybe to cause her to lose hope. Maybe to draw you out by hearing her scream."

Picel held up his chains and scowled. He was right. They knew that he couldn't get to her. That wasn't it.

I thought about it for a minute and then it dawned on me.

"Picel…" I hesitated to say more.

"What," he rasped.

"I think I know what he told her."

Picel's eyebrows raised.

"I think he told her that I was there when she, when he…" I sighed. I had no idea how to have this conversation.

"Spit…it…out… Quin," Picel's tone scared me. He was about to blow. I didn't want to be on the other side of his rage; but at this point, without leaving him here, there was no option other than to take what was coming.

"I was there when Ahiam and his men attacked her. Defiled her… I watched it all happen," I admitted. My fists clenched in and out at my sides, shaking with each movement. I hated reliving those moments. I hated seeing her like that, even in my mind.

A low growl rumbled through Picel's throat. His eyes narrowed and his mouth tightened. I was glad that he wasn't in a state to fight me. I would be dead in half a second if he were.

"I didn't want to be," I said hurriedly. "We were going to find you, you were always the target, this was never about Naia…" Picel growled again. I knew that I couldn't win this one, even though I hadn't been given a choice in those circumstances.

"Everything was going to work fine!"

He glared at me.

"You know what I mean… The problem was, you weren't there. So Ahiam took out his rage on watching Naia… well… yeah."

"I… don't… want…to… look… at… you," Picel gritted out. "I… don't… want… to… see… you… *ever*… again!" By the end of the sentence his breathing was even heavier, and he was covered in sweat as well as blood.

I understood that he didn't want to be affiliated with me, I did, but he didn't have a choice. I was his only way out.

"Picel. You don't have to look at me again after this is over, but right now we need to focus on Naia. Please know that I have every intention of doing absolutely everything in my power to get her out of here. She is my number one priority. I promise." Picel nodded in approval. Finally, we agreed on something.

"But," I continued, and he tensed. "I have to also do everything in my power to get you out of here, because if she escapes without you, she will not be able to live with herself and you know it. So I need you to promise me that if there is any danger, you will let me handle it."

"I…can't…trust… you," Picel stated.

"You don't have to, I guess." I sighed, "But you have my word."

NAIA

He loomed over me as I lay shivering on the icy ground. I didn't know what he was going to do. The last time I faced him... I whimpered unintentionally and a big grin spread across his face.

"I see you are remembering our last meeting together," he mused. "That was some night. Did you know that *your Quinlan* was there? Watching. Not stopping my other men from, well, you remember."

My whole body started to shake. I couldn't stop myself. *Quin was there? He knew? He watched?* I raised my head to the ceiling and let out a wail that was so guttural and loud, it ricocheted across the chamber.

Quinlan had been there, at my darkest hour, watching Ahiam's men... watching me... as they... I couldn't bear to think about it. I threw my body onto the floor and sobbed while Ahiam and his men looked on, laughing at my misery.

89

JAVIL

I am strong. *I am the Prince of Arilos. I can beat this. I will survive.* I repeated those words to myself as I finished my trek to the Flykryn fortress. I needed help and fast - time was running out. I prayed that I would run into a friend on my way, someone to help me.

I positioned myself around a corner, strategically placed so I could see others, but they couldn't see me. As I looked on, I saw a frightening sight.

Naia was being brought forth from the fortress. Ahiam was dragging her by her hair. Her clothes were ripped and she was bleeding. *Not again.*

I was filled with rage and the desire to kill. I would see Ahiam's end if it was the last thing I did. It was hard to believe that I had hated Naia at the beginning. I wanted her to leave and I didn't care what happened to her. I abused her, belittled her, and scorned her. I hurt her family. I would have done anything to get her out of my life, but she saved me. She chose my life over hers and it changed me.

Now, seeing her being dragged out having been abused by others time and time again, I just couldn't take it. She was still learning to trust me again, and that would take time; but she was trying. She would have died for me from the start. Now, I would, without hesitation, die for her, too.

He was taking her up the mountain. He was taking her… no. It all hit me at once. He knew that as long as Naia was in his hands he had leverage. He was trying to draw everyone out. If all went according to his plan, he would be king of Arilos by the end of the day.

I had to find a way to get to Naia, but I was still losing blood too quickly.

Since Ahiam and his men were all going up the mountain, I decided to sneak into the fortress to see if I could find Picel and Quin.

I was surprised to see the fortress unguarded, which immediately raised my guard. There was no way that this man, this warrior, would leave his home without protection. But then I remembered that is what we had done. Arilos was currently completely exposed.

90

PICEL

I didn't know how we were going to get me out. I was in such a bad state, there was no way we could go quickly.

We had heard Ahiam gathering his men and later heard the troops walking down the hall laughing and jeering at one another, so we wondered if they had left the fortress all together. If that were the case, this could be our only chance to rescue Naia. Assuming Ahiam hadn't brought her with him.

"Coast is clear," Quin whispered as he motioned for me to walk forward. Thankfully, my legs still worked, but barely. It was my arms that were the big problem. I couldn't defend myself.

"If ...Naia...is...gone?" I grimaced. I hated the sound of my broken voice. I was afraid that Quin wouldn't be able to understand me, but he did. I couldn't bear it if she wasn't there. I would completely lose my mind.

"Don't think like that. Picel. We have to think positively."

"How?" I bit out. I had spoken too loudly and started coughing excessively.

"Picel, keep it down. You will blow our cover. And as for thinking positively, we need to pray. We need to have hope that God will get us through and that He will protect Naia."

He was right. I hadn't prayed in a while. I closed my eyes and stopped for a moment. *God. Please. Help us. Keep my Naia safe. Send us some help.*

As I was finishing up my prayer there was a crash that came from around the next hallway.

"I'll go check it out," Quin stated. He left before I could tell him no. Not that he would've heard me if I had spoken. Every time I talked a little blood pooled in my mouth. I spit it out, and the crimson splattered onto the ice below me.

Cathan left after he chained me, but returned later and tortured me within an inch of my life. Neither the head wound I had sustained in the first battle, nor the bruising on my abdomen, or even the stab wound from my brother compared to the level of pain that I was in now.

On top of the Pear of Anguish, he had hooked me up to the rack and had stretched me - I couldn't believe that my skin hadn't ripped in half, for all I was worth. It took every ounce of strength and concentration I could muster to walk to the door. My entire body shook with each step and when I finally made it to the door, my body finally gave way and I collapsed against the frame waiting for Quinlan to return.

A few minutes went by, then a few minutes more, longer and longer I waited, but there was no sign of him. Knowing I needed a weapon I dragged myself back to the table of knives and shoved one into my belt. I prayed that I wouldn't cut myself in the process as its sharp edge was out and could easily slice me as I scooched back to the door. As I started to make my way back, there was a thud and a grunt.

"Quin!" I called, but there wasn't an answer. "Hello?" I started coughing again. *God give me a break! Please!*

"Picel!" A voice shouted suddenly. "Picel, get out here. I need your help!" It was Quin. *Did he get Naia?*

I struggled to a standing position and staggered towards Quin's voice and stopped dead in my tracks when I saw the scene playing out before me.

Quin had his hands covering someone's rib cage. A guard lay dead a few feet away. Another guard was writhing on the ground and was crying out in pain.

I made my way to Quin and gasped when I saw my brother lying before me, a pool of blood at his side.

"Javil, what…on…earth? You…."

"Did he tell you?" Javil grunted, cutting me off. "Did he tell you that he did this! He was the one who stabbed me!" He turned his attention back to Quin. "Get off, Quin! I told you I don't need your help!"

"It doesn't look that way, Javil." Quin replied. It wasn't a snarky response, but an honest one.

My head was spinning. Quin stabbed my brother, betrayed me, and had Naia locked up in Ahiam's dungeons? Who was he? Definitely not the Quin I had known for so many years. I would never be able to trust him again. I would have to be very careful and maybe rethink Dolyon. Who could I trust? My brother had betrayed me once, now my best friend? Who would be next? Naia?

"… Picel, are you okay?" The voice was muffled. My vision had blurred.

"I…" I hit the ground hard.

The world went dark.

91

JAVIL

I thought that I had lost him. He blacked out and collapsed after he had walked around the corner. I shoved Quinlan off me and rushed over as fast as I could to where my brother had fallen; my arm around my abdomen, trying not to bleed out myself.

"Pi, Pi! Wake up! Please!" I grabbed his body and hauled him into my arms, laying him across my lap.

"Please, I don't want to be King! I will hate you forever if you die on me! Picel!" He didn't move. His breathing was so shallow.

"God! Why? I know I have messed up! I know that I have hurt people, but please! Don't take my brother! Please!" Sobs erupted from me uncontrollably.

"Sire?" A voice called from outside. *Zahir.*

"In here, Zahir! We need help! Quin was…"

As Zahir came around the corner, I realized that Quin had disappeared. *Good riddance.* We were better off without him.

"Sire, let's get you fixed up," Zahir said calmly, noting the blood stain forming on my shirt. "Though I must warn you, I am going to have to cauterize your wound...."

"Zahir? Are you in here?" A female voice called.

"Yes, Luria! We are in here!" Zahir called back and Luria appeared from inside the cave. With her was... *no. impossible.*

"Javil, this is my husband, Gibor." She said quickly. She knew there was no time for pleasantries.

"How?" I stammered. I was terrified to be in the presence of Naia's father... after what I had done... I shuddered.

"Later." Luria said. "Gib," she whispered, "Please be careful. I just got you back." She kissed him goodbye and he raced out of the fortress.

"Where-?"

"To save Naia. Zahir, tell me what to do," Luria basically demanded. She wasn't messing around.

Zahir held out a vial and motioned to Picel.

"See if you can get him to drink anything while I am tending to Javil."

"Of course," she replied, taking the vial and making her way over to Picel.

Zahir turned to me and I grimaced thinking about the pain that Picel must have endured when I stabbed him. I deserved it.

"Let's get it over with then," I muttered. "But hurry. Picel is in dire need of your help too."

Zahir nodded in understanding and lit the fireplace. Once it was hot enough he inserted the tip of his dagger into the blue of the flames. Once the dagger was red, he looked at me and gave a pained look. "It is time," he sighed.

I bit down on a piece of leather and braced for the pain. It was worse than I could have imagined. I already regretted what I did to my brother; but actually feeling his pain made me regret it even more.

As Zahir tended to me, Picel started to stir. Luria tried to talk him down, but his moaning only got louder.

I braced myself again as Zahir bound my ribcage. It needed to stay secure until I got back to Arilos and I didn't know when that would be. I prayed that it would be sooner than later.

"You are all bound, Javil. Please try to restrain yourself from physical activities. Though I know in our current situation that is going to be next to impossible."

I laughed. He was right. If I needed to fight, I was going to fight. No matter the cost.

"Jav," Picel slurred after Luria managed to get some of the vial down his throat. "Jav...where...Naia?" He dropped his head down again... unconscious.

Zahir walked over to where Picel had collapsed and ran his hand through his balding hair. Luria stepped to the side and Zahir bent down and did a quick examination of Picel's condition. When he was finished he turned to face me. His face was downcast. He cleared his throat. "Javil, Sire," he paused. "You need to prepare for Picel to die. He is..." He sighed. "Things don't look good at all."

I didn't know how to respond. I knew that it wasn't Zahir's fault. I knew that if there was something he could do he would, but I was so angry. I knew that I was mostly angry with myself. If I hadn't been so obsessed with Naia, then maybe we would have been more prepared for an attack. Maybe Father would still be alive and my brother wouldn't be dying before my eyes.

I couldn't help that I let out a blood curdling cry. As I did, the room around me began to shake. Icicles broke from the ceiling and shattered all around us.

"Take cover!" Luria yelled.

I had started a cave-in.

NAIA

We were up so high. The wind tore through the fabric of my clothes pulling me to the side as we walked. The only thing keeping me upright was Ahiam's firm grip on my abdomen. I hated that he held me there, but at least I wasn't at the bottom of the mountain sprawled dead on the icy rocks below.

I knew I was going to die. I was alone and there was no one to save me. Quin had betrayed me. Picel was nowhere to be found. And Javil, I didn't know where he was. He could be dead for all I knew.

I held my head high though. I would not give up - I would fight til the end, I would not let him see weakness.

Ahiam moved forward and I heard him wince. He was in pain. I had no idea how he had made it up the mountain with his bad leg. He was stubborn, too.

I peered over the edge of the cliff and inhaled. I had never been afraid of heights, but this was different. I knew that I was going to go over the edge. *God, give me strength.*

"Any last words, Majesty," Ahiam sneered. He knew I wasn't Queen, but he knew that his brother stole the throne from my grandfather.

"I pity you," I said softly.

"What?" He snarled. His spittle flew into my eyes and mouth, but I ignored it. Worse things were happening.

"I feel sorry for you, Ahiam. You could have had a family. You could have had joy, but you chose to be bitter and angry. And now you are going to be alone forever."

"How dare you speak to me that way," He growled and whipped me around so my back was to the cliff. He adjusted his hand to be around my throat and leaned me back so I was one slip of his hand away from falling to my death. *God, if he lets go... please keep me safe.*

"Those are your last words? Shall I relay a message to your King? Shall I tell him that his true love is about to fall to her death at the bottom of the mountain?" A light sparked in his eyes. "Oh, I really wish that he were here for this. I think I would like him to watch..."

I tried to shake my head but his grip was too tight.

"I need two men to go fetch the King from his quarters. Kerrin. Go. Now," he said, turning to a warrior standing next to him.

"Yes, Sir," he bowed and scurried down the path leading down the mountain.

"Now, while we wait..." Ahiam gave the most sinister grin. "While we wait, let's see..." his eyes danced with ideas of torture. It took everything in me to keep from crying.

"Take your hands off my daughter," A voice thundered from across the mountain. "I swear Ahiam. If you so much as move, I will make sure you suffer a long, agonizing death. There will be no mercy."

I gasped at the realization of who it was. *Dad.*

No! Dad! You have to leave! Please, don't put yourself in this danger! I am begging you! I tried to scream, but Ahiam's grip on my throat had tightened even more at my father's arrival. I flashed back to when Javil had pinned me against the wall and Quin had come just in time to save me. My dad must have seen the panic in my eyes, because he spoke to me as if he was reading my thoughts.

"Naia, let me handle this, Sweetheart. You have dealt with enough at his hand." He turned back to Ahiam. "Ahiam, let's finish this once and for all." Dad snarled, and stepped forward. He looked awful. He had a black eye and he looked like he had been starved; he also had a slight limp. There was no way he could win against Ahiam.

Ahiam thought for a moment and then slowly raised me back up. "Fine," he growled. He threw me onto the ground right in front of the drop off. I grunted as I hit the ground and immediately scrambled back a few feet so I wouldn't be looming over the edge any longer.

Father and Ahiam grabbed their weapons and started circling one another as I had seen Quin and Javil do months before. *Please God, keep my Dad alive.*

"Don't go easy on me, Boy," Ahiam spat. "I want a real fight."

"I wasn't planning on it, Old Man," Father retorted. "Zaxton should have killed you when he had the chance."

"How is your wife?" Ahiam hissed as he lunged at my father. "Is she well?"

"I'll kill you!" Father yelled as he deflected the blow. "You will die today!"

"Will I?" Ahiam questioned. "I have made it this far. I am not sure you are correct in saying that."

"You hurt my wife!"

"Your wife? Oh, you don't know? I hurt your daughter too," Ahiam laughed.

Father's eyes darkened.

"We had lots of fun," Ahiam sneered.

"You monster!" Father roared, lunging at Ahiam again. Their swords clashed together. *God, please!*

I was so invested in their fight that I didn't see the man sneaking up from the side. And I didn't notice as he slid his hand around my mouth to keep me from screaming.

As his hand made contact with my mouth I yelped and started to struggle. However, the hand held me tightly and an arm wrapped around my body keeping me from thrashing around.

"Ssshh, Naia. Shh. It's me. It's me." *Quin.* "I am going to let go, but you can't make a sound. Do you understand me?" I nodded.

"Picel?" I mouthed.

"He is in bad shape, Naia. I have to be honest with you about that. Javil is in rough shape, too. I am so sorry. I…I know I don't deserve your forgiveness, but…."

"Quin, do we have to talk about this here?" I interrupted.

"You're right. Yeah, this can wait. Let's get you to safety."

"Quin, my father…" I pointed at Ahiam and my dad who were still circling and jabbing at each other every once in a while. "Your… father?" Quin's face whitened. I realized that they had never met.

"Yes," I said softly.

"Have you talked to him? Does he know who I am?" *That's what he is worried about?*

"No, I just found out my father was alive…"

Quin sighed. "I wish…"

"You can't. He is in the middle of a fight." I knew that Quin wanted to apologize, to try to fix the disaster that he had caused. But it wasn't the time for that.

"Stay here," he instructed.

"Quin, what are you….No!"

He stood up and started striding towards my father and Ahiam. *He is going to get himself killed.*

"Quin!" I screamed.

I threw my hands over my mouth as I realized my mistake. Everyone had been so focused on the fight that Quin's presence hadn't been noticed yet. As I called his name, all eyes turned to me. But to look at me, they had to look at him first. His cover was blown.

QUINLAN

Naia, why did you have to yell my name? I braced as all eyes turned to me, ready to attack if needed.

I moved my hand to my sword and pulled it from its sheath as Ahiam's warriors surrounded me. I wasn't going down without a fight.

I looked back at Naia which was a mistake. Her face was struck with terror. I hated the thought of her watching me die, again, but it might come down to that. I wasn't going to be captured, and I wasn't going to let anything happen to Naia's father. 'Kill or be killed'. That is what King Zaxton had always taught. Unfortunately, a lot of us had failed to heed that advice recently.

"Quin!" She wailed. As she did the earth began to tremble. An avalanche? Everyone stilled, willing the snowy mountain-top to calm. After a few minutes of silence, the warriors began moving again.

I drew my sword ready to fight back. I counted seven men. There were seven men surrounding me. There was no way I was getting out of this alive.

The first man came at me and I deflected his blade with such force that he went flying back into another warrior. I took that opportunity to swing at another. I hit his sword, swooping underneath and catching my tip on my opponent's crossguard sending his sword flying to the ground. As I followed through, I connected with a third sword. I pushed back as hard as I could, but this warrior was freakishly strong. A quick glance at his face revealed the source of that strength - Cathan - of course. This battle might break me. We crossed swords a few times, but I quickly grew weary. Thankfully, he had signaled his men to back off - he wanted to take me down himself.

My breathing was labored. It was taking every ounce of my strength to block his blows. Our swords collided again and he pressed in with all of his strength, driving me downward to the ground. My arms shook with fatigue as I tried to keep his sword off my neck.

"Naia!" I cried out. My voice caught between concentration and tears. "I am sor-"

94

JAVIL

I dove to shield Picel, but Zahir had beaten me to it. Instead I dove over Luria, covering as much of her as I could.

"Javil, you need to take cover," she pleaded. Zahir agreed.

"Sire, you will most likely be king by tonight, unless Ahiam kills us all first, or we're killed by falling ice shards." His words sunk in. He meant that there was a good chance that Picel wouldn't make it even if we survived the cave-in.

"No!" I wouldn't leave her exposed. I owed it to her. I would face the consequences

"Sire, please!" Luria begged. "Javil, please listen!"

"No! This is my fault! "

"Javil, this isn't about you. This started long before you were made part of the Royal Family. This is what happens when pride rises. You are suffering the consequences. But they are not just from your mistakes. They are consequences from your father and Naia's father and myself. They are from Ahiam, Ishvi, and perhaps others even before them. It is now all culminating and about to explode. I beg you. Please don't blame yourself. I know you have made mistakes. You know that, too. But it is time to accept God's grace and mercy and stop beating yourself up. Your sins are forgiven if you ask and believe in Him who forgives. Please take cover!" she wailed again.

Tears formed in my eyes. I made my choice.

"Luria, I am not leaving you exposed, and that is final." I growled. "Don't fight me on this. You won't win."

She shrunk down more, and I checked that all vital parts of her were covered. If something happened, and one of us died, I wanted it to be said that I had done everything I could to protect my people; Protect Naia's mother.

I squeezed my eyes tightly shut and prayed for protection. In the middle of my prayer there was a large crack from above and Zahir shouted, "Sire, look out!" The next thing I knew Luria and I were flying to the side. I hit my head and must have blacked out. When I next looked up I realized a huge block of ice and rock had fallen where my legs had been. Underneath it was Zahir.

Once the rumbling had stopped, I moved to the boulder looking for Picel. He had been sitting right next to it. There was no way it had missed him. The block was so big I couldn't see around it. My heart stopped. *No.* We can't have lost them both. I peeked around the other side of the block and drew in a sharp breath. Picel was there. The ice had missed him by two inches. He was still alive.

I rushed to try and lift the boulder off Zahir's body, but he stopped me. "Check... on... Picel."

"I did. He is alive. I have to get you out of here! Luria, help me!"

"It is too heavy, Javil. You have to leave me," Zahir replie, his voice pained. "You and the King are okay. That is all that matters," He whispered. The ice block was crushing his legs. I could see blood flowing from underneath.

"I can't! You are like family! I can't leave you! What about Pepper? She needs her Uncle!" A sob erupted from Zahir's mouth.

"Tell her I love her. Tell her you did everything you could, but you just couldn't save me."

"But I haven't tried everything!" I argued.

"Javil, you have to get the King to safety."

"The King would want me to go after his girl," I replied.

Luria spoke and gave a small smile. "She is being taken care of." I tilted my head. *Right, Gibor.*

"I will stay with Zahir and then see how I can help Naia. You need to protect your brother, Javil. You need to protect the King," Luria said softly.

My life's mission flew back into my soul. I had said years ago that I would do anything to protect my brother, and I had failed on so many levels. It was my chance to hold to my promise. It was my chance to start repairing the brokenness I had caused. I bent down to see if there was breath coming from his lungs. It was faint and thready, but it was there. I turned to Luria and stood. "Okay. I will get him home."

95

PICEL

I was moving, but the world was dark. *Are my eyes open?* I blinked and saw light. *No, they were closed.* I opened them again and looked around. I was in some kind of hammock attached to a horse, swaying back and forth with the horse's movement.

There was a flask sitting next to me. I wondered what liquid was inside. I took a sip and spit it back out. It was some kind of attempted herbal mixture. Whoever made it didn't know what they were doing. *Or is it poison?*

I tried to call out, but my voice was gone. I hoped that I wasn't in the hands of enemies.

After a while I felt us slow down and come to a stop. I heard footsteps approaching me. I balled my fists ready to swing. Not that I could have done much damage as weak as I was. A friendly face peered over the hammock and called out in glee!

"Oh Picel! You are awake!"

Javil. I was safe…. But where was Naia?

I struggled to sit up and Javil quickly rushed to my aid. He wrapped his arms around my torso and I wrapped mine around his neck as he got me situated. As he pulled away I saw he was covered in blood. I didn't know if it was more his or mine, but I knew he looked like death.

Naia. I mouthed. It still hurt to talk. *Where is my girl?*

Javil pursed his lips and looked at the ground.

My eyes widened as I realized what his look meant. He had left her there. He rescued me but left the girl I loved with the enemy.

Go back. I mouthed, my face filled with rage. *Javil, go back now.* I was starting to panic.

"Picel, Naia is being taken care of. Luria said that there is a plan," Javil said quickly. I didn't care.

It took every ounce of willpower I had, but I slowly got the words out. "Javil…this…is…an…order," I coughed, "from…your…King," I paused to compose myself and took a few breaths. "Go…back…now."

Javil stared hard at me for a minute deciding how to respond and finally nodded. He had no choice - I was commanding him as his King.

He nodded. "Of course, Your Majesty," he said. "But first let's get you on to the other horse. Do you think you can ride?" He questioned.

I knew that I shouldn't, but I nodded. I didn't have a choice. If Naia was in trouble, no matter how close to death I was, I would get there.

96

NAIA

Quin, no. Not again. I curled my hands up to my chest and sank into the ground. He had betrayed us, but I had loved him once. I hated seeing him die before my eyes…again.

Ahiam took Quin's death as an invitation to go after my Father again. He swung, catching him off guard, and sliced my father's calf. He screamed in agony and almost dropped to the ground, but refused to give up. Father held his ground pressing back into Ahiam's strikes and driving him backward. I had never seen him fight before. He was amazing.

"You…shall…not…hurt…my…family…again!" Father cried as he swung with all of his might.

"Dad! Be careful!" I called. They were heading for the edge of the cliff.

My Father swung again and held fast as Ahiam pressed back against him. He was gaining leverage! He let out a scream of triumph and flung Ahiam's sword out of his grasp. In a split second he kicked the sword over to me and I grabbed it so no one else could.

Ahiam's men started to move in.

"Stop!" Ahiam cried. "He is mine to finish."

"Good luck with that," Father snarled, and shoved Ahiam back one step closer to the cliff. Then another, and another until he was just inches away from the edge.

"Goodbye, Ahiam," Father whispered and gave Ahiam one final shove over the edge.

What my father hadn't anticipated was Ahiam latching onto his belt, pulling my father over the edge with him. Father kicked at Ahiam and managed to break free, but he was still going over the edge.

I cried out and lurched forward, frantically grabbing the collar of Father's cloak. "Hold on, Dad!" I wailed, but I wasn't strong enough - it was slipping! He was slipping. "No!" I couldn't lose him. Not now!

I dug my toes into the snow and rock and prayed that I would be strong enough and that the cloak would hold.

Just as I felt my grip loosening, I felt a pressure on top of me. Arms reached over and grabbed onto my father's cloak next to mine.

"I'm here, Naia. I've got him."

Javil and I pulled my father up and got him to solid ground. I wrapped myself around his neck in a bear hug as he lay on the ground recovering from the extreme events that had just occurred. Tears of joy, relief, and disbelief rolled down my cheeks as he cradled me in his arms. I'd missed him so much.

I looked up and realized that Ahiam's men were growing restless. Their leader had gone over the edge of the cliff; they didn't know what to do.

"Javil, please keep an eye on my father," I said, noting his calf injury, and stood to face Ahiam's men. Some of them were the same men that had laid their hands on me earlier. Others looked on unaware of the trials I had endured prior to coming up the mountaintop.

"You best be rethinking your alliance," I warned. "Your leader is gone," I motioned to Javil. "This is your Prince. Your King is gravely wounded. You were part of that. I don't know why you chose the side you did, but you still have a chance to turn back. You will be shown mercy if you decide today; if you decide right now, to follow King Picel."

"And who are you to be making these promises?" A voice called from the crowd. "You are nothing."

"She is not, nothing," Javil stood. "She is everything. She is wise. She is gracious. And she is your future Queen," he said with power. *He would make an amazing King.*

A murmur rang out through the crowd.

"So... standing before us is the current Prince, and the future Queen." Cathan chuckled.

I realized my mistake in the timing of my words. We were still trapped on top of the mountain surrounded by enemies.

Cathan let out the most evil cackle. "Men, end them!"

97

PICEL

had ordered Javil to go on ahead. I would only slow him down with the injuries I had sustained. As I neared the mountain pass I heard shouting coming from the top. I kicked my mare as hard as I could and she sped up a little bit more.

"Picel, what are you going to do?" Naia's voice rang out in my head. *You need to turn back.*

I shook my head trying to dissipate the thoughts of retreat. I hated that my loved ones were in trouble. I hated that I wasn't there to do anything about it. And I hated that I was in so much pain. I let out a mangled roar and immediately regretted it. Searing pain flooded my throat and I had a coughing fit which made it even worse.

Picel you need to stop and gather yourself! You won't be any help at all if you are dead before you get there!

I shook my head again more aggressively. I was not going to stop. Not until Naia was safe in my arms and we were back home at the Castle.

I made it halfway up the mountain. My mare was panting as hard as a horse could. The temperatures were below freezing, but she was covered in sweat. I couldn't ride her anymore. I dismounted and started on foot. One step, then another. I had to stay focused; alert, ready.

I could see the top of the mountain. I was so close to Naia. I took a huge step forward, and was met with a blow to the back of my head. Darkness consumed me again.

98

JAVIL

As the enemy warriors advanced, they pushed us to the edge of the mountainside; right over the dropoff. I grabbed Naia and clung to her with everything I had. If we were going over the edge, I would make sure that I took the brunt of the fall. Gibor stepped behind us. I guess he was thinking the same thing I was: *Protect Naia at all costs.*

"You will pay for this!" I shouted, knowing that it wouldn't do any good. "Picel will come after you!"

"Your brother is coming up the mountain as we speak," Cathan sneered. "He will meet his end as soon as we deal with you."

"He is your King!" Naia wailed.

"Ahiam, was our King!" A warrior spat as he jabbed his spear.

We were on the last bit of solid ground before we would fall through the air. Naia squeezed me as tightly as she could. I reflected at the miracle it was to have the girl that I once tortured look to me for comfort. I despised myself for what I put her through, but I was glad that I could be there for her now. I was glad that she could see her father one more time. *God, I am sorry. Please forgive me for my wrongdoings. And thank you for sending me this amazing woman to show me who you are again.*

They pressed us forward once more and we were onto the point of the cliff. Gibor slipped and fell over the edge. Naia screamed as she watched her father fall. She wouldn't make it if she lost him again. A few seconds later, Naia and I were over the edge too, and plummeting downward. *God, please let there be snow at the bottom.*

AUTHOR'S NOTE

Thank you for taking the time to read *When Pride Falls*! If I am being honest, it was never my aspiration to become an author. This is the second time in my life where I saw someone else doing something and I told myself "I can do that." Whether that is pride, or confidence, I will let you be the judge of that!

The first time was when I started writing music in high school. My friend had written a song and I thought that I could probably write one, so I did.

From there, writing music became a way that I processed the different events I went through in my life. Some of these details were covered in this book.

This book started with a map that I created on a piece of cardboard at my old job. It was a far off idea, one that I never expected to actually happen.

Staying with a task for an extended amount of time is not something I excel at. I have ADHD so I jump from thing to thing. I have tried painting, duct tape projects, sewing, crocheting, and other things that, once I have gotten bored of, I quit and move onto the next thing. But with writing… I have stuck with it.

I wish I would have kept track of how many versions of this book I have written, but it has changed so many times I don't even know where to begin. I am confident that I have written at least 500,000 words in the last year through all of the drafts that I had.

When Pride Falls started off as another fun thing to do in my free time. However, with each version and more developed characters, I realized I wanted it to be a testimony – a way to be a light and tell people about Jesus through my writing.

If you couldn't tell by the title, a big theme is pride. Pride is something I have struggled with my entire life and in different ways each of these characters deals with issues of pride in some kind of way. For me, it is the desire to do everything alone. I am strong enough. I don't want people's help. I don't want their pity, and I don't like to be told what to do… the list goes on.

Writing this book has led to some accountability from my friends. People who know I am writing this book have said to me in different moments when my pride is rising… "so, what is your book called again? Oh, when pride FALLS." Right. Right.

People have asked me who my characters are based on in real life. There are one or two who resemble different people. Ingrid and Edwin, at least in name, represent my parents. But, personality wise, most of the characters are different parts of me and my story.

I wrote Naia to show the side of my life that involved abuse. While my story isn't as intense as Naia's, it is still there. I, along with so many others, have been abused by different men that have been involved in our lives.

For me, the first time was a matter of being young and naive. I wanted to believe the best in someone, and I was used and manipulated in different ways because of my blind trust. There are a few lines in this book that were actually words that were said by my dad and me after an incident I had with a guy in my car.

The second time I was deceived into thinking someone was different than he said he was. Even after going through what I had before, I didn't see it until it was almost too late. He would use scripture, and he would say "I think this is what God is calling us to do." But at the end of the day the question was would I regret going further than my convictions? It wasn't until then that I realized I needed to completely cut things off with him. In both cases the men reached out to me months to years later. Thankfully when they did, I was wiser and turned them away.

Like I said, Naia's story is different from mine. My abuse didn't go as far as hers did, but I wanted to have hers in the book so I could share how much God protected me. On more than one occasion with both of those men I "should have been," taken advantage of more than I was. But God, in his graciousness, spared me of that.

At the end of the book Naia and Javil go over the edge of the cliff together. He takes hold of her, trying to protect her. He is trying to save her from this situation for which he blames himself. Ironically, Javil ends up having no control.

I made Javil's character to have mostly the worst parts of me. The parts that Satan wants me to believe and make my identity. Javil, like myself, is prideful and likes to be in control. He struggles with controlling his anger. He believes that there is in no way, shape, or form that he should ever be forgiven for his past mistakes. He dwells on them and thinks he doesn't deserve anything good because of what he has done.

Even in those dark parts of Javil, he does have some good qualities. He is a protector; he will do anything for those he cares about, even risking his life at times to keep the people he loves safe. He, after seeing that Naia would sacrifice her life for him, decided that he didn't want to be the person he had been. He started making the changes in his life that he had needed to change for so long. I have these qualities as well. Writing these scenes and chapters for Javil have been great reminders for me of how far I have come and what the truth actually is.

God LOVES me even though I have messed up, even though I have turned away from Him and pushed Him away time and time again. Like what Luria told Javil as the cave was collapsing, "Your sins are forgiven if you ask and believe in Him who forgives." Javil doesn't have to carry that burden. I don't, and you don't.

God loves us and wants us to have a relationship with Him, even though we are broken, messed up people. He loves us so much that he sent his Son, Jesus, to die for us.

"For God so loved the world that he gave His one and only Son, that whoever believes in Him shall not perish but have eternal life." (John 3:16 NIV)

We have the chance to spend eternity with our Creator. And we don't have to earn it. It is a gift because of God's love for us, His creation.

"For it is by grace you have been saved, through faith—and this is not from yourselves, it is the gift of God— not by works, so that no one can boast." (Ephesians 2:8-9 NIV)

God uses everything. He actually gave me the idea for this book after giving into a sin I have struggled with my whole life. One that I have been trying to break. I prayed and asked for forgiveness, and then it hit me. I had been praying for a way to use this book, this series as a testimony, as a way to share the Gospel. God used *my brokenness* to show me how to do that. God uses everything. We might not understand why, or how, but if we have a relationship with Him we can trust that He has everything under control, and that He will never stop loving us, (whether we love Him or not).

I say all of this while still trying to remember and believe it all myself. Like I said, I am a lot like Javil and am super hard on myself. I struggle to let go of that control and my pride. I need the daily reminder that God has never left me, and he never will. Through my trials and struggles I want to be an encouragement to others to let people know that they are not alone. You are never alone.

"I have told you these things,

so that in me you may have peace.

In this world you will have trouble.

But take heart! I have overcome the world."

(John 16:33 NIV)

ABOUT THE AUTHOR

Olivia Anne is an aspiring author who never intended to be one! She's also a lyricist, composer, and music producer; that was her focus until starting *When Pride Falls*. She credits that process with beginning her fiction writing journey. She has loved creating stories since she was a little girl and is thrilled to have completed her first published work!

Olivia is from Rockford Michigan, but currently lives in Missouri.